MW01616815

Cover art by Doug Hoppes

DRECK

ALEX GRASS

CHAPTER 1

"**M**erry Christmas," I said as the cops wheeled in a body. The gurney was huge, the kind they used to use for housebound Bundt-cake enthusiasts and professional-grade hotdog gobblers. And the body wasn't bagged. It was too big for that. It was under a tarp. And it looked like antlers were poking out from under it.

No reply.

"Cat got your tongue?"

"W-we-we are s'posed t-ta-to..." The kid at the front of the gurney cleared his throat. "We-we're s'posed t-to..."

Stuttering is one of the symptoms you see a lot after The Long War. It used to be called shell shock. Or PTSD. Now it lodges in the throat.

"The form?" I asked.

He shook his head.

"Police report?"

Shook his head again.

"Kid, I can't help you unless I know what I'm taking in here."

Without a word, he went into silent-stutter mode and, with his arm trembling, simply pointed to the gurney. His larynx throbbed, but not a word escaped.

"Kid, I don't do animals. There's no health department anymore, so you can just dump it in the—"

But then I saw it. The Three-Finger Hand.

The Three-Finger Hand whose digits can grasp
'round infants and necklines and fine ladies' clasps
Appendages strange, both angry and long
In the hour past light the beast sings his foul song

Everyone knew the tune. Mothers whispered it to their naughty children at night. It sent superstitious dock workers scurrying from their jobs during twilight shifts.

It was the song about Dreck.

The other cop—a fat, waddling hump—slapped a clipboard down in front of me. "You and baby-bitch-boy here can be as a-scared as yins want, but I say he's just a kiddie-rapist in a Halloween suit."

The fat cop rattled his throat and spit out a wad of phlegm and tobacco residue onto the ground. His teeth were black around the roots protruding from his withering gums.

"Oh yeah?" I said, pushing my lips out like DeNiro. All DeNiro's films got burned by the censors during The Long War. Why am I the only one who remembers these ancient yokels?

"Then how come yins didn't just de-costume the feller?" I sputtered.

I have a lockjaw memory for the way things were before The Long War, when etymology bit the dust. Sometimes the sword is mightier than the pen. *Yins* is a leftover from the hillbilly contingent that settled in the Land of Quakers, Shakers, and Amish candlestick makers. It's the sort of word that comes from the bubbling brew of linguistic pidgin-talk from yonder West Virginia and the Pennsylvania hillbilly-hills way. They used to say "What's Pennsylvania? Philadelphia and Pittsburgh with Alabama in between."

But we're not in Pennsylvania no more. Not even Pennsyltucky. There is no Pennsylvania. There's just… whatever this is. I guess as things move along, we'll figure out where we are. Hell, if the Balkans sorted it out, so can we. Did they?

The fat man spit tobacco on the floor again. "De-costume? Fancy word, college-boy."

In the old days, spitting on someone's floor was something you didn't do, even if you were an inbred disease-pit. But spitting *is* a thing you do these days—especially when you're a monkey-faced fatty like this festering turd-pile I'm talking to. So, I spit too. Right on fatty's shoe.

"I didn't go to college. I went to a trade school. And I served." I looked at Lardass; there wasn't a scar on him. Probably not even a bone spur. "What's your excuse, fuckhead?"

He jiggled in impotent rage. A coupl'a decades ago, this was the kind of incident that would have ended with me having to shove a draining tube into his eyeball while the gangly kid cried in the corner. But these days, someone like Lardass knows better than to fuck around with a soldier. Even one as old as me. Being forty-seven used to be young, I suppose. (weren't people living into their nineties at one point?)

Lardass looked at the ground and shuffled his feet. Like a dog showing another dog his belly. "Flat feet," he said.

"Mmm-hmm."

With all the dick-measuring between me and the pear-shaped turd, the stuttering runt who'd manned the other end of the gurney had fallen into the background. He'd loosened his grip on the metal handles of the gurney. He sprawled atop the stacked milk crates I had set next to my desk. Sprawled in Fear, in the Cloud of Unknowing, in Holy Terror.

"The Three-Fingered Hand," the skinny kid whispered.

"Hey, junior," I called.

No answer.

"Hey skippy," I yelled. "Hey, *kid!*"

The boy looked up. "Ye—yess—ssir?"

"Don't believe everything you hear. This is just a guy. Just

3

some dude. He's just an old, ugly, diseased fuck."

I smiled at him; we were sharing a laugh, that's what my lying eyes told him. I took a clipboard from Lardass and looked over it —*strange. Since when have I had to fill out the forms?*—while soothing the gangly boy-man. "You ever heard of the elephant man?"

"N—naw," the boy replied. "Wuhh—wassat?"

"Some feller from a place they used to call England. Maybe more than two-hundred years ago, before all the wars, there was this guy in the freakshows…"

"Wuhh-wha—whatsa ff—freakshow?"

"It's a circus where they trot out a bunch of weird people. A bearded lady, a strongman, a lazy fatfuck," I said, looking over to Lardass. That made the kid laugh, a long high-pitched laugh that didn't stutter at all. The poor kid must've weathered some godawful abuse.

"Y-y—yeah?" he piped as he came up for air.

"And there was the elephant man. The elephant man had this disease that made his skin hard and gray. And it was tough and wrinkly, like an elephant's skin. Elephants went extinct decades ago. Before The Long War."

The kid's eyes widened. Got 'im interested, at least.

"Ever seen a picture of an elephant?"

The boy nodded.

"Well, this feller," I went on, pointing at the massive gurney, "is kinda like that guy. He's got some disease."

The kid looked a little relieved, until Lardass cut in with his triple-chin smile.

I hated fat people before the war, and I hate them even more now that half the fucking world is starving. Let me channel Mother Teresa for a moment—jeezy creezy, another ancient reference. A fat guy in a time of famine is surely an exploiter; maybe he's a pimp. At minimum, he's a Tastycakes terrorist, a thief whose specialty is pastries and packaged sweetcakes.

Lardass had clearly been waiting to cut in for payback. He

recited another stanza of the song:

> *"Grown great from the dirt, not a man, but a beast*
> *With blood on his hands and death in his teeth*
> *Horns like the devil's, yoke 'round his neck*
> *Be wary when passing the creature called Dreck"*

The kid started shivering and Lardass gave a smile, as if to say *there's one for the road, cocksucker.* I rolled my eyes and decided I was tired of them both.

"I'll take it from here," I said. "Yins can git."

"What about the gurney?" Lardass asked.

"I'm keepin' it until I move him on the table."

Lardass protested, sputtering, "Yins can't do that! We only got the one that size, and we need it. We pay for that stuff ourself, y'know!"

"You don't look like the type of guy who pays for anything except sex," I shot back.

And just like that, I was back in the lead.

It's a petty game, insult-for-insult, but when I'm loaded— which is quite often—and when the opponent's a lolling scumfuck like Manbooby McPervus, I find playing the game to be irresistible.

I was tired, and curious, so I decided to cap the conversation. "Now get the fuck out of here, or I'll see you out."

Lardass balled his chubby little fists up and stomped off like the jiggly babyman he was. The kid sloped his shoulders and followed meekly behind him. I felt bad—*maybe I was a little harsh?* —but these days, if you let yourself get pushed around, you end up like the kid. And I felt bad for the kid. I knew that I had probably escalated the collateral damage surrounding Lardass, but them's the breaks, man. *Kid... he's just a kid... just a kid.* Yeah, them's the breaks, kid. Stutter on.

I decided I'd look at the paperwork after I had myself a little rest.

CHAPTER 2

onfession time. I went to school to become a mortician. I tried to shyst my way out of the embalming class. I took inspiration from my friend, Alex. A Jew… "Jews don't embalm," he said. So, I tried to convince an administrator that I was aiming to work at a Jewish funeral home. She asked which one I had in mind, and since I didn't have an answer, that was the end of that. I'm a coroner now. I became intimately acquainted with the ins and outs of arterial injection and drainage, and the delaying of decomposition.

I don't know if there are many Jews anymore. I don't know much about the Hebrews. But I think Alex wasn't like most Jews.

What are most Jews like anyway? A beard and four corners worth of twining strings, a lone strand of royal blue left dangling in the middle? Is a Jew just a skein of yarn hanging out of an untucked shirt—reverentially murmuring and dovening: *That shall be your fringe; look at it and recall all the commandments of the Lord and observe them, so that you do not follow your heart and eyes in your lustful urge*?

But Alex wasn't like most Jews. Not that I know any.

He was a powerlifter. Big guy, big personality. We used to go to the little triangle of back alleys across from Baum Boulevard, right across the way from the mortuary school, and we used to drink a lot (I still drink a lot. Putting corpses into an aluminum rolodex for postmortems hasn't helped to change that).

Alex was born in the wrong time, I think. He was the kind meant to draw crowds while he bent pennies and lifted women above his head. He would have been a strongman in the circus if he were born in the Dust Bowl, would have been Apollon if he were born in the French countryside, would have been Marc Henry if he were born a poor black kid in East Texas. But he would have been louder.

Alex loved death metal. When I met him, he was screaming at the bartender to put on the new Cannibal Corpse album he'd just bought—"I know Alex Webster, Alex Webster was a friend of mine, and you sir, are no Alex Webster!" he shouted, telling anyone who'd hear it that he was pen pals with Cannibal Corpse's bassist. Alex had three strawberry-flavored framboises and three shots of whiskeys in front of him. He pounded all six of those. Boom, boom, boom, boom, boom, boom. Right in a row.

This is all to my point: Alex wasn't like most Jews.

(But, again, what are most Jews like anyway?)

Alex—*Big A, A-Train, Big Poppa Push-Press*—made me an alcoholic. He was *too* much fun. The kind of guy who never leaves more than a millisecond between hearing a quip and delivering a better one right back. The kind of guy who would tell a girl at a party *exactly* what was on his mind, and then, amazingly, end up locking her in some sort of trance where his every word was gospel. The kind of guy who, despite his boisterousness and bluster, *listened* to people, and made you feel good about yourself. And that's what happened to me. I wanted to feel good, and Alex made me feel great. He liked to drink, so—so that I could hang around him—I started to drink, and then I started to like to drink, and then I started to like to drink all the time, and finally, I just *needed* to drink.

Alex was the last Jew that I knew. Or the last one that I knew about. If you've been living in a bunker—as you probably do—

you're also probably wondering what happened to them. Well, we'll get around to that.

Alex and I were close. Thick. Buds, even. For about a year, we spent a lot of time together. Us and two other guys: a fifty-year-old diabetic gambling addict named Jimbo, and Alex's power-lifting teammate, Bess, who was about the size of an industrial refrigerator. Jimbo was a funny guy. He had a terrible fear of woodland creatures, specifically deer. Jimbo—and I'm not exaggerating here—thought that deer were perpetrators of a wide-ranging conspiracy being conducted by the Dark Forces of the Forest to eliminate the obnoxious bipeds paving over their habitat and mucking up the starry nights with the sour stink of light and noise. Jimbo really believed this, even with his all-materialist worldview. He was also a compulsive better.

Bess, who Alex called Ol' Bessie, was a quiet fellow. He mostly sat and listened and only seemed to talk to Alex in hushed tones.

One night, we were sitting in Jimbo's apartment. Alex was yelling at Jimbo's television and slapping the side of it—"get a fuckin' signal, you cocksucker!"—while Jimbo was yelling at Alex not to yell at the television. All this while I was cooking venison that I bought from a classmate who killed and cleaned the meat himself (this, of course, pleased Jimbo to no end, since it meant that another deer was "off the streets").

Anyhow, at one point—and it may have been a different night from the one I'm describing; my memory is fuzzy about this shit —Alex pulls out a jug-handle gallon of this sweet-wine called Manoshovits or something. Jimbo smiles real wide. Alex had been promising Jimbo to bring him some of this—well, I'd call it *swill*. He gives Bess a sip, and Bess passes with a quiet murmurous shake of his hand. He gives Jimbo a sip, and Jimbo is *over the moon*. I take a sip and nod in assent—*yes, it's good, real good, plenty good*.

That was only one of two Jewish things I remember about Alex.

Pretty soon after that Manoshovits Midnight Meeting, Alex

had to go home. His brother Sam had been T-boned by a pickup truck some four-hundred miles eastward across the state. That was the last time I saw Alex until he showed up on the slab in front of me. I hadn't heard from him since he left mortuary school, since that last night where we got loaded on sweet wine and laughed like devils every time Jimbo would drunkenly rant about the multifarious misdeeds of the deer out in the Dark Forest.

And then... Alex was in front of me on the slab. Somehow, I'd always believed he'd wiggled his way out of the war.

But he'd been in the war. I could tell by looking at his body: discolorations around the extremities (this from the blue and yellow lights; the ones that made the soldiers sick. No one knew what they were). He'd been in the enemy camps, too: His body was laced and lacerated by some of the symbols of The Long War's more brutal factions. Mounds of closed, once-gashed flesh healed into pink and gray bumps. Two fingertips melted off (this was from the new weapons that soldiers started using toward the end). A missing testicle.

I didn't quite recognize him. I had, of course, thought of what Alex would look like when he finally came in on a slab. We all imagined, when we were in school, what we'd look like dead—it was part of the training. But he didn't look like I'd imagined he would. There was no smile.

To my memory, I'd never seen Alex without a smile, but here he was, cheeks drawn down, face lined with floorward-drooping wrinkles, the kind that show up from exhaustion and sadness, not the crow's feet that show up around the eyes from smiling all the time. And he was *small*. Couldn't have been more than one hundred and fifty pounds, soaking wet. He looked little. Like an old man. I started crying. It was like finding out Santa Claus wasn't real (although Santa wasn't Jewish, despite the beard).

That's when I saw the second thing about Alex that was Jewish. He'd requested a *burial*. And he'd asked for something called the *Chevra Kadisha*. That's what the paperwork said when he came in.

It used to be, back when there were states and one federal government, that you had regulations. You had things you were *required* to do before burial—maybe an autopsy if things smelled fishy, maybe a corpse-quarantine (*quorpsentine*, the professor called it; he also said "expotentially" instead of "exponentially").

You see, doctors were busy after The Long War with real problems like coming up with enough vaccines and treating poorly set breaks; cleaning out exit wounds and badly clipped amputations. But coroners knew death, and they weren't busy with medicine. So, sometimes, people would bring in their dead—they'd bring in their *longdead*—and ask us to assess the state of their loved ones' bodies and souls. A coroner might have a stinking, fetid, three-month-old corpse in front of him. Once, a black-hooded mother wheelbarrowed in a rotted fleshbag filled with only the teeth that hadn't been gold-capped. She asked us questions we just couldn't answer—"How did they die? Did they suffer much?" And worst of all, in the case of disfigurement, "Is this my son?" Ethical coroners wouldn't answer these questions, or they'd say they *just didn't know*. My only response would be to go down to the library —which was reopened by one of the mega-illionaires who'd made out nice after the world started getting itself back together—and find myself a few books on forensics. But everything I learned was still iffy. I didn't feel confident telling a woman how her kid died, and certainly not in giving the confirmation it was her son.

The worst case was when a woman thought she'd found her three babies under the rubble of her home. (At least she *thought* it was her home, but how could she really know? Like every other block in that part of the city, it had been blown to smithereens. How could she even know which charred black patch covered in broken bricks and smoldering wood beams was *her house*?)

She wasn't a very smart woman—who came in with three small skeletons—and I couldn't tell if she was dumb from before or after the war. She had big blotchy patches all over her face, and probably her hands (although I couldn't see her hands under the rain poncho and dirty, holed sweats). She had a big spot on her face, and I thought it was a birthmark, or a skin disorder, or a healed wound.

"Are these my babies?" she pleaded. I solemnly reached my hands out and asked, with my eyes and my brow, if I could examine the bones. She nodded and extended her forearms, with a square-yard cut of felt cloth underneath the bones, and held them in front of me. I carefully took the bones in the cloth and put them on the aluminum table. I knew before I got my face closer than three feet in what the bones were.

"Are these my babies?"

I shook my head. I can't even remember if I said "*no*" at first. I just remember that she started wailing. She started wailing and screaming and belching. Snot was coming out of her nose and sweat was accumulating and squishing against the poncho rubbing against her skin, making some terrible noise that sounded like what chewing cheap motel bedsheets between your teeth must have felt like.

Mary raised a nice boy, and Frankie Attanasio is a good boy, and I thought I believed in goodness enough—goodness in the abstract, perhaps, but goodness nonetheless. I hugged the woman and said something that I thought the defrocked priest who taught thanatology and psychology would have said: "But you've done a good deed. You brought these bones to me. You've rescued their souls."

She stopped crying so and nodded, burying her drip-skin and wet-patch dermis into my shirt. I couldn't stop thinking about her skin coming off her face and smearing, pink and red and infected and green, all over my shirt. But I held her anyway. I held her tight and thought of everything good that she might have done, and how we were just people, or dumb animals, trying to claw our way through the dark after a thousand and one nights without sunlight.

What I didn't have the balls to tell her, which of course I shouldn't have—and didn't—anyway, was the truth. She'd brought in piglet skeletons. Probably from a taxidermist's or a doctor's home office. Or maybe a butcher? Who knows?

That's all a roundabout way of saying that even without my own practice, even in the city's coroner office, I make my own rules. And when someone asks for a religious organization, especially an obscure one associated with a people—the Jews, who might not even exist anymore—to take care of their body, it's usually something I say no to. Who can be bothered?

For Alex, though, I gave it the old college try. I tried and tried, for as long as I could bear the sight of Alex's malnourished and withering body, to get someone, *anyone*, who knew about Jewish burial to help. But, to no avail. So I went down to the library and found an English translation of a Rabbi's study guide for the rabbinical oral exam (something I didn't know about until I went down to the library to find a way to carry out what I suppose was my long-lost friend's last request, the request that is spoken in death itself and not in dying words—and so is the corpse's asking and not that of the living).

You might ask me what this—what *any* of this—has to do with the story I'm about to tell you. On the night I prepped Alex—washed his body, wrapped him in linen, garbled the transliterated Hebrew words that should be said when burying a sheeny—I saw the same thing I see tonight: a hexagram shape in the sky.

No shit.

I also don't remember Alex having blue eyes, but on that night, he had blue eyes. And every new body that's come in tonight has blue eyes, too. Which means one of two things: Something strange is going on, or I need to lay off the sauce. Or both.

Do Jews have blue eyes, anyway?

CHAPTER 3

I thought I'd fallen asleep, but I couldn't have. I was standing in the vestibule that led from the prep room out into my office. The light in the room was the urban glow of orange streetlamps. I couldn't remember there being a streetlamp in front of the mortuary, or that many windows to let the glow in through the hallway.

Pictures hung along the hallway, many of which I didn't recognize. Like the one with the melted face and a smoky purple-blood hand. That hand crashed like a wave as it reached out for a charred object. It was a burnt heart, lying on a pile of glowing green seedlings. Or the picture of a legless owl with violet plumage and a radiant breast. Another picture depicted two anthropomorphic birds: There was a goose in a sleeveless summer accountant's dress shirt and tie, the other a pigeon wearing sneakers. The pigeon had swollen phalluses and machine guns for hands. When did I put these fucking things up?

I heard something groaning—no, it creaked *and* groaned. Whatever it was also emitted some unearthly moans. The floor shifted beneath me. No. That's wrong. The floor sifted as it shimmered. The atoms within the floor swirled until the cement became sand, and the grains pulled miserably at my feet until they were sunken into a scalding morass that transformed the ends of my toes to glass. The sand melted into glass, too.

The wall-mounted pictures morphed out of their gilded frames, and both the owl and the man with the melted face opened their mouths. I pleaded with them for help, but the owl turned his head away and the face melted more.

It went on like this, until the owl's head was spinning like a top, vertebrae crunching, and the face's skin peeled from its anchored bone by a sourceless heat.

My legs absorbed the heat, and they burned. They were on *fire*, and I screamed, but the screaming did nothing to stop my bottom half from melting, hardening to glass. Sand swirled upward and around about my waist until tingling numbness overtook me.

There was a grandfather clock there. And it had been watching everything—the clock is watching us all, and he is old and he is angry. He stands so tall. A big-bellied chime tolled from his innards, and the owl and the face stopped spinning. Stopped melting.

"Thank you," I said to the clock, who smiled at first. Then it laughed. Not a chuckle. Laughter. Hideous shards of laughter that ripped at my ears. The glass of my body shattered as the laughter tore through my muscle and viscera, which was itself shelled inside of the glass—the parts of me that weren't still unmade. The owl and the melted face vomited sand out onto me. Mounds of desert dune drug me down—buried me, smothered me.

I screamed for help again, only to hear (and feel), again, the piercing mockery of the grandfather clock.

I screamed in a child's panic—*Help! Help!*—like a nightmare patois. I'd forgotten the terror-tongue in which I needed to speak.

"Give. Give hand," a voice came from above me, although I was buried up to my eyes, and couldn't see where it was coming from. I only felt the hand, and I wanted to live so badly. I grabbed the hand and gripped as hard as I could—even at first when I could only feel the fingertips. I pinched those fingertips so hard I could have drawn blood.

It was Dreck. It was the monster. And it was alive!

Thank the stars, thank the moon, thank you, you awful creature, you New Merrick freak who kept me alive! Thank you.

As the antlered savior-beast with the three-fingered hands pulled me out and pushed me behind him, he muttered something. Muttered something in guttural grumbles and closed his hand into a fist. It was his right hand, and the little finger was half-missing. The hand glowed in a deep blue. He slammed that cerulean-lighted fist into the sand. The grandfather clock groaned and dissolved into its million constituent parts, each piece shattering as it hit the floor, which was cold now, and it was concrete again. And the face and the owl crumbled to ash. And the sand—those awful, solar-hot mounds of broiling sand—rose in a great, oppositional wave. Like a final crest of sorcerous protest before it crashed to the floor. When the sand hit the concrete, the octobillion scalding-hot granules turned instantaneously to icy flakes. Oh, the sheer beauty of the snowflakes, as geometric patterns of infinite and unique intricacy floated before me. My woods filled up with snow. Woods that were lovely, dark, and deep.

With that, Dreck was done with his magic, or whatever it was, and the nightmare melted away. But I wasn't awake. Was I asleep?

"This can't be real." I blinked hard, several times, shut my eyes with the desperation of a five-year-old hiding from the dark in the closet, and I slapped my face a dozen times.

"This can't be real."

When I opened my eyes, the snowflakes still swirled inside of the mortuary—impossible—and Dreck's hideousness was closer and clearer to me than it had ever been (I reckoned), to any living being.

The dirty nails at the end of Dreck's wildly overlarge hands pointed to his chest.

"Find," he spoke in a tremulous growl. "You," he pointed one of his three fingers at me. "FIND."

"Find what? What am I looking for?"

He growled and waved his hand away.

"FIND!" he roared.

So, under the gaze of those lifeless blue eyes—there was pressure, though, even though the stare was supposed to be dead, there was *pressure*, and I decided just to nod.

CHAPTER 4

I woke up to a phone ringing. It was still snowing in my brain. Foggy too, but *that* was nothing new. Something was new. Something *inside* the fogginess. Something new nestled in the nexus of a many-yeared delirium.

We still have phones these days. They stopped doing the subcutaneous implants when The Long War broke out. Wasn't it Einstein who said the Third World War would be fought with nuclear weapons and the Fourth World War with cavemen's clubs?

I pulled my head off the paper stack where I'd collapsed, and I peered out the small window that provided the mortuary's only glimpse into the world of the half-living. But not before noticing a healthy dollop of drool that had chemically reacted with the ink of some of the papers—thank G-d most of the laws of chemistry are still in force, even after The Long War. I admit, I stared at the resultant brownish-black Rorschach for more than a moment. Maybe it was to get my psychic bearings or just out of fear for what I might glimpse beyond the window.

Courage, I told myself. Conjure up sights for soaring eyes.

When I revved up the guts to look, nothing seemed amiss. There was still that small triangle of intersecting streets in front of the mortuary. But it was snowing—snowing in heavy drifts, slabs of white, godly waves of ice and water from the sky-spring.

I don't remember hearing them call for snow.

Then again, meteorology isn't exactly a flourishing postbellum profession. Besides, when do you remember the weatherman ever accurately predicting what the sky would bring? I remember friends—okay, acquaintances—joking that being a meteorologist was the best job ever: you could always be wrong, and you still got to dress fancy and prancy for the tube. Fans mattered.

The phone still rang.

The brain-fog was too thick; my reflexes were too dull for me to pick it up.

Then the ringing stopped.

In that thunderclap of silence, I felt an adrenaline shock, one of those ass-twitching biochemical boots.

Dreck. Dreck!

Still half in my dream, I ran from my desk through the vestibule, coming to a brief stuttering stop.

Is there sand? No, that was a dream.

Still, I tiptoed through the hallway like a child sneaking into the cupboard after midnight, clutching my wits just in case. Just in case there were any maleficent little birdies or cosmic burn victims looking to work their sandy hoodoo on me again. You never know.

But was it real? If he's on the gurney...

I ran in to the embalming room and saw the great big tarp draped over some huge figure I hadn't yet seen, outside of my nightmare. But the monster was on the slab.

Did I move him over? Did I put him on the table?

I didn't think I did. But then again, anything was possible in the long wee-lit hours of early morning boozing.

FIND!

Once again, that voice resounded from the crypt to my brain, not like a passing thought, but like a pumping pulse. Dreck's voice, so deep that the rumble of his words rocked the furniture and rattled loose screws and tore wooden seams in the walls; a baritone signal whose clear but dumb pronunciation was terrifying in itself.

Find. What do I have to find? I wondered if I was still drunk (not that it mattered so much).

On two-toed eggshells I reconnoitered, I drew closer to the slab, and I touched the very end of the tarp with my hand, which suffered a bout of tremulation. I grasped the tarp so gingerly, with such a tenuous grip I wasn't sure I'd even touched the hem of the huge polyurethane blanket over the big man (*a man; is he a man?*). Adrenalin kicked in full-force and I pulled the tarp off with a swift yank, unconsciously playacting at being the physics teacher (or magician?) who pulls the tablecloth off a set table, leaving the glassware, plates, and cutlery intact.

Voilà!

Oooh, boy. You got an ugly mug, son.

That much was true: Dreck was an ugly sonofabitch. His eyes were so blue. Like a royal tone, deep spiraling into a teensy pinpoint of sky in the middle. And there was no sclera—no white in his eyes—just those huge, outré orbs. His skin looked soft, like it could have had tiny soft bristles of short-hair fur over it; dark-almond-brown fur. But when I touched his skin, it felt hard. Not just hard, but coldly hard. Unfriendly hard—pavement on the ground when you slam your face into it and break your teeth.

I slid my hand against the skin of his face and moved my fingers down to what I thought was a dreadlocked beard. But it wasn't a beard... it was some sort of growth. With a faint glow coming from it.

Well, that's explainable, I guess. Firefly assholes still radiate after the fuckers've been squished.

It looked like the fugazi-facial-hair had a translucent sheath over some array of metallic flagella, which was apparent due to some light source woven within. Of course, there were the antlers, too. Like elks' horns. Gigantic but barren. Not the flush lively headgear of the helmeted elk. More like dead tree branches made of an unbreakable stone.

And there they were, the infamous three-fingered hands.

On the right hand, the little finger—"little" being a relative term—was chopped off halfway down and bandaged up to the nub, which looked like the stump of a tiny tree branch. His feet were wrapped in—linen, cotton, what?—some cloth, in raveled lumps of hundreds of looped wraps. The gigantic feet had been shellacked by a kind of resin, making them appear to have tumorous grafts of yellowing, dead skin laid on them. All this alien anatomy was draped in a cloak—dark green, but so dark it looked black in the lightless air.

Brother, you make Lugosi look like Michelangelo's David.

My awestruck observation was cracked by a shrill, percolating, liquid beep. It shrieked through the watery sliver of half-consciousness that kept me momentarily outside the world.

Shit! Jesus Fuckin' Christ!

My heart skipped then started pumping at a bunny rabbit's rhythm.

Oh, Jesus. Oh Jesus Christ. Fuckin' fuck me, man…

It was the phone.

I picked it up.

"Frankie's Morgue, you kill 'em, we chill 'em." *Nice, dumbass.*

When I was young, I had the habit of saying inappropriate things when I was nervous. Scared. I guess you never really drop those old habits.

"Excuse me?" a voice came through.

"Sorry, bad joke." I didn't even bother to give a nervous laugh. "Frank Attanasio, how may I hurt—er, help you?"

There was a long pause. "Yes, hello Mr. Attanasio. I'm calling from the Reconstruction Corps."

The Reconstruction Corps. New-ish thing. Kind of like a combination between what the FBI and the CIA used to be. After a few years of chaos and cannibalism, the generals from both the winning and losing armies formed the Reconstruction Corps, or

ReCo, to try and reinstitute some order. They don't have a mandate or a charter by any constitutional measure—or any legitimate measure (then again, what is legitimate in government other than the successful exercise of power?)—but you answer when they call you. Real black helicopter/G-man stuff. I'd never had any interactions with ReCo until now.

"How do I know you're not just yankin' my dick?"

A slight sigh then a barrage of recognizable verbiage. "You were in the unsuccessful Semrock raid. You're the only coroner operating in the Seven Points area. You had polyps around your asshole, at least you did during your last military medical exam."

I cleared my throat. "Yeah, alright. How can I help you?"

"ReCo has received information regarding a potential high-impact individual. You were recently delivered the body of the deceased."

"You mean Dreck?"

"Yessir. I am referring to the recently deceased individual popularly known as Dreck."

"He's here. What can I help you with, Agent—"

"Funny you should say 'agent,' we haven't settled on how that official designation will sound out, but either way, you can call me Agent Mattis."

"Agent Mattis, huh?"

"Or you can call me Aggie."

"Is that your real name?" I asked, half-jokingly.

"No," he said, with the utmost seriousness.

"Ah, I see. Well, Aggie, what is it about Dreck that I can help you with?"

"ReCo is going to send a relocation unit—a ReCoRU—to move the recently deceased individual to our base of operations."

"You want to move him to Philadelphia?"

"Yessir."

"Isn't that another country now?" I said, to make conversation. I don't know why. We were having a perfectly good conversation already. These guys rustled my jimmies a bit, if I was being honest.

"No sir, the former City of Brotherly Love is now within the ambit of ReCo's jurisdiction."

"I see. Okay. What next?"

"Mr. Attanasio, would you have any objections to ReCo's relocation of the recently deceased individual to Philadelphia?"

"Me? No, no. I don't give two shits. I mean, I'm—I'm agnostic on the issue, Aggie."

He didn't get the pun.

"Yessir, I understand sir."

"So, are you all going to come pick him up today with your procurement—your uh, uh—"

"ReCoRU team, sir."

"Yeah, those guys."

"No, sir. Not immediately, sir."

"I don't understand."

"Sir, it has to do with the upcoming storm. We're having logistical issues. ReCo is a fairly new agency, and the recently deceased individual's death is within a timeline that puts ReCoRU's acquisition within the projected peak activity of the upcoming winter snowstorm."

Jesus, what gobbledygook.

"Sure, sure. Of course. So, you guys want to pick him up after the big melt?"

"Yessir. That would be ideal, sir, yes."

I didn't have any good reason why, but I said, "Let me look at my calendar." Probably interpreting my delay as a meaningless bureaucratic power-move, Agent Aggie just gave me another "yessir." I pulled out my notebook. All the important stuff goes in a notebook; I had a boss who said that when the world ends, you'll be happy to be the only one who still has what he needs on paper. Well, the world ended, and he was right, though it's debatable whether my remnant of scribbled thoughts would be needed by me or anyone else. I stared at my tabula rasa: every day for the next week, month, year, decade, and century was completely blank. Ugh, that's disheartening. Maybe I should try dating? No, I'm too ol—

A loud, rattling from the gurney jolted me back to the present. Metal against metal? Antlers cracking against the slab? When Agent Aggie cut back in, I could barely hear him.

"I'm going to have to call you back," I said and hung up the phone. I stood up, slid the datebook in my back pocket and drew nearer to the slab where Dreck lay. There was a humming noise. I felt some magnetism, like what Mesmer and his crew once upon a time called an animal magnetism. But different. Not just some unknown psychical force, but an elementally different thing. Some hidden, unseen thing. Some indispensable knot of dark matter that tied cosmic strands together. But I couldn't place it, so I drew closer. I felt a strong, sacramental urge to lay my hands on Dreck's strange, powerful body. Dreck's body that looked as though it had yet to enter the formal phases of decay, at least in the physical dimension. As I lifted the dark pine pallet of clothing draped over him, that magnetic pull intensified with a swelling sound that stirred within my body more than it resounded through my ears.

There was a wound, deep and pulsating, on Dreck's chest. Splintered bone and viscera had broken through what looked like an exit wound, and I reached my trembling hand closer to the meaty opening.

The humming was unbearable. Its foreign bigness made my bowels drop and my lungs deflate so that I couldn't take in air. Couldn't perform the most basic function of the human body. I tried to pull my hand back, but I was unable to. Whatever force was at work was working me, working the insides of me so that my hands were unrecognizable as *mine*. Foreign extremities attached to whatever *I* was, in that moment. I gasped, pushing my shaking fingers into the gaping wound, beyond the flesh and the bone. I touched something—something metallic and cold (strange that Dreck's body felt much colder than the chilled morgue).

I pincered the metallic thing with my thumb and index finger and pulled it in the same way you'd pull a cork from a wine bottle. A corkscrew would've been helpful, but I managed.

The metallic thing turned out to be a coin. Not just a pocket-change coin.

It was the coin I'd seen on that news show from *Vox Oculii*. It was the coin that an "Anonymous Hero" had been leaving throughout the Seven Points areas as a marker of deeds well done for the good of humankind. The twenty-four-hour news cycle had been obsessed with finding out the do-gooder's identity for three years now. These odd coins were the hero's calling card; left at scenes such as kids rescued after falling through ice or families saved from a burning building.

What the hell?

I went back into the corpse and extracted another coin. Then I grabbed my tools. I lifted Dreck's cloak up so it went over his head, so it hung over his antlers. The width and the depth of the wound was sizable enough that I should've been able to see if there were any more coin pieces lodged in Dreck's chest. But I couldn't see. No glints or white/copper reflective indicators of any more coins.

Hmm. Guess that about does it.

But I felt like no, it didn't just about do it, so I reached back inside. Sure enough, I felt another. I looked closely as I removed the coin, but it seemed like the wound has hugging my fingers (or any tool I tried to insert) whenever I tried. I could feel but not see. The coins were like Warner J. Frog. After I pulled out ten more of them, the humming noise ceased. That unknown magnetic power, all the cacophony of the beckoning mystery embedded in Dreck's anatomy had ceased.

The phone rang. I jumped again, cursed again, muttering—a bellowing mutter: "Fuck. Jeeeeeezus Fuck."

I picked up the receiver. "Sorry about that, Agent Aggie, I just—"

"Yessir, no problem at all, sir. I can wrap up right quick and just tell you what I'm meant to tell you, if that's alright with you, sir."

I sighed in relief. "Sure, sure. That's fine."

"Got a look at that calendar?"

"I glanced at it, but to tell you the truth, I don't have much that keeps me busy other than the dead. You're probably the first call from an official regarding a..." I looked over at Dreck's body, "... client in a long time." There was an odd compulsion for me to tell Aggie the truth in that moment, maybe because there was something ominous; a deep foreboding, like death personified—Death with a capital D—right around the corner. It wouldn't look very good to tell a lie as my last living action, even a white one. So, that —what I'd told him—that was the truth. Most of it, anyway. No reason to tell them I'd tampered with their body. *Is it their body?*

"Glad to hear it, sir," Aggie said, eager to brush past anything I said, like he was a bill collector or a reluctant, estranged relative.

"I just want to go over a few logistics about ReCoRU and procurement-extraction of the recently deceased individual."

I wiped my hands on a nearby towel. "Shoot."

CHAPTER 5

G-d's quiet call from yonder mountain
His vein, once struck, pours like a fountain
Truthfully ancient, white and old
The snow blows in now with the cold

I used to write. Sitting in the classroom at IMS—Institute for Mortuary Science—I would scrawl verses here and there, maybe sketch some abstract illustration next to a poem I'd scribbled. When you're young, you think outside of time. You live in fantasy—fantasies so absurd, only the later-acquired social conditioning of early adulthood constrains your public hollering-out-loud about what your future would be like.

"I'm going to be a combination of William Blake and Elvis Presley."

Next day, it's "I'm going to be an astronaut."

Sure, kid. You and two other people. You'll go to MIT for astrophysics right after your tour with the Navy SEALS. After that, it's only a matter of finishing up your PhD at Cambridge and jogging ten miles every day to stay in Spartan shape.

Then, the cold hard hammer of unadulterated reality crashes

into the protective carapace around your brilliant imaginings. Unless you're Peter Pan, you've grown up.

Now you're not dealing with fantasy anymore, but with all the anxiety of obligation. You learn about "income tax," and about "liability." Worst of all, you discover the dark forces aligned against you. The name of one of these dark forces is human resources, whose evil is so great and whose power so all-encompassing, their warped wizardry can bludgeon even the greatest of child-sorcerers.

Then, a few years later, something starts to itch. It's in your shoulders and your neck, and the itch transforms to a dull pain, aching and throbbing. Before you know it, this feeling has spread under your eyes—migraine pain makes your stomach turn, so that it goes right into your colon. You age. You develop defense mechanisms to cope with this unceasing bad feeling. Maybe it's resentment, maybe it's lashing out at others, maybe it's beating your wife or children. (In my case, I turned to the sauce. Rather have a bottle in front of me than a frontal lobotomy.)

Enter the latter stage of disenchantment. It's black and irrevocable. You become frozen in some sort of Terror and realize that it's all going to end. The world, your life. Not only will it end, but it will be forgotten. And you're so small! What a minuscule figure you are in this cosmic ballet; you're not even a dancer—you'd be lucky to be counted as a fiber in a stocking slipped over the ballerina's calf. Worst of all, this stage hits just as human resources and their allied forces of Rationalism and Realism have won in their lifelong effort at propagandizing you. You're disenchanted, the world is going to end, and all you can do is scream. Believe it or not, some people choose to embrace this turn of events and ideologize it. H.P. Lovecraft referred to this taxonomy of desperation and nothingness as Cosmicism. The most militant anti-theists took refuge in an uncompromising materialism (both philosophical and economic). Politicians imputed their salvation from this darkness in the energy drawn from political power and the proper use of little white lies.

It isn't that all politicians are evil. That's all too simple. Many —and maybe at some very special time, a majority—of them might have even been good if moral luck had aligned their fates with the goodness of their time. The price of admission to this Carnival of Canards is one's integrity, or to be less hysterical, one's dignity. But many willingly surrender their dignity. It's not an unreasonable calculus. Dignity matters only for those who put a premium on it. It can't be bought. And politicians are very much in the business of what *can* be bought.

Now, there is a force even deadlier, lower, and blacker than that of human resources. This is the political flunky, the functionaries and pawns of higher political authorities. These deadlier, lower, blacker flunkies often possess titles that obscure the dumb, banal evil of their station; titles such as communications director, public relations director, and worst of all, *campaign manager*.

And it's that last one—the campaign manager—who has come to trouble me in my own office, in the middle of a snowstorm, when I'm wrecked and wracked with anxiety about the Reconstruction Corps wanting to retrieve Dreck's body unmolested.

Here he comes, a suited feller, slick and smiling, knocking on the polycarbonate front door.

How do I know this man's vocation after only a glimpse of him through the graying veil of snow drifts? First, he's dressed in a full suit when everyone's at home waiting out the storm. Second, I saw the guy's face on the tube during the mayoral elections.

The elections were mostly an invention of the present mayor. Maybe he saw them as a nostalgic holdover from the days before The Long War. Maybe he thought the appearance of democracy would somehow sugarcoat things. People mostly just want to be left alone, and the postbellum populace operates with enough agreement and tribal ease that a larger government isn't necessary yet. Demagogues always find a way, even if it's through elections.

Resentment bubbled in my guts. I stood with my ring-loop of keys and unlocked the door from the inside, peering out.

"Can I help you?" I asked, calmly enough considering I wanted to kick his smarmy, slimy face in.

The man jutted his hand out so fast that if I hadn't known who he was, I would have assumed he was trying to attack me. I looked at that extended hand for a moment.

The man must've quickly realized that I was not one to grease his palms, even with the sweat of my own. "Norman Lavalle, sir. From the Mayor's Office. I was wondering if I could speak to you, as a citizen, regarding a matter of incredible importance to our fair city."

I raised an eyebrow. "*Are* we a city?"

"Huey Purgato believes so, sir. You see, Mayor Purgato believes—"

"Spare me," I said. "Just come on in out of the snow and tell me what you want."

Lavalle frowned. He looked upset that I managed to crack his smile—but immediately put his mask back on. "Well, great! Don't mind if I do."

I plopped down in my swivel chair, the one with the ripped and torn cushion's ratty open edges scratching my ass. Late at night, I used to sit buck naked in the chair, but the torn padding started to grate my rump. Now I wear pants, for protection. After all, you only get one ass. O' the many subtle discomforts a man is made to suffer.

With an outstretched hand, I directed Lavalle to perch his ass on a stack of milk crates.

"Oh—uh, a-hmm," he muttered. A man like this was in the business of putting on affectation—whether lowbrow or highbrow—but he let slip his surprise at my meager accommodations. He was young. Very young; maybe even younger than he looked. He couldn't have been in The Long War. Someone who'd been in The Long War would've known better than to stutter at some raggedy seating. Someone who'd been in The Long War wouldn't even think before sitting.

Lavalle did sit, but he sat with an air of offense, and I enjoyed that. I poured a drink into a tin cup and held it up to him. He shook his head no.

"Suit yourself," I said.

"Mr. Attanasio, how do you see yourself in the world we're now living? What do you think your part to play is?"

Young neophytes have a way of unconsciously condescending to everyone, as if every bit of new knowledge they've recently acquired is completely novel, as if they're the only ones who have any of the answers. But that's just youth, so I let it go. Grownups know that most of life—speaking cynically here—is something to trudge through. And there aren't any answers to be had. I decided I'd humor him.

"I think I play the part of the surly mortician. And if Mayor Purgato is Abraham Lincoln, I think I'd cast John Wilkes Booth to play my role in the movie version." *Careful*, I thought to myself. But Lavalle was too young to catch it, though he did pick up on the Lincoln reference.

"Abraham Lincoln. Yes." He was beaming.

Oh boy, he's at the true-believer stage. Nothing worse than a true believer. They're like blinkered horses.

Lavalle started waxing poetic, dripping with pre-adulthood fantasy. "Yes, Mr. Attanasio. "In many ways, Huey Purgato is *just* like President Lincoln. You see, we're putting the pieces back together. Only now has our fair city gotten to the point where we can start rebuilding the great institutions and constitutional machinery that open the doors of opportunity for the average citizen. I might add, Mr. Attanasio, that I don't think of you as just any old average citizen."

Boy, oh boy, he is really laying it on thick. I bet this rap works well with old ladies or gay men (the kid was handsome).

"Uh-huh." I emptied my tin cup in a swig and poured another double's worth.

"And, just like Lincoln, Mayor Purgato believes in the will of the people. He believes in sovereignty. Now, I know a smart man such as yourself knows what sovereignty is."

I felt like punching the kid. In Semrock, all invasion long, we fought an independence movement whose every other word was "sovereignty." The called themselves the Semrock Sovereign Forces. Jesus Christ.

"Yeah, I've got an idea." Two more mottos and one more tagline from this politico's mouthhole and I was going to stuff it full of human shit.

Ah, that's just the drink talking. Give him a break.

"Well, we've got an issue of sovereignty that we're, uh... that we have... that we are..." he fumbled.

"Anticipating?" I offered.

"He beamed again. "Exactly! We are anticipating some problems. And I believe old Honest Abe would have supported—would have been supportive of—our G-d's honest quest for sovereignty."

Instantly, my mind went to the Harry Jaffa books I'd read some time ago, but that I hadn't forgotten. I thought of how it was Stephen A. Douglas, not Abraham Lincoln, who'd touted popular sovereignty against Lincoln's more abolitionist-skewed notion of natural law. But I figured arguing with this kid was not only pointless, it would be meaningless, like a fart in a stiff wind.

"Mr. Lavalle, I'm tired, I'm in the middle of some very important work. If you don't mind, could you tell me how I can help you?"

He almost sighed. I could see it. He wanted to. His body took the form of a man who was going to sigh, but he didn't follow through. Gutless. Finally, it seemed like he might have given up on the business pitch. "Mr. Attanasio, we have reason to believe the Reconstruction Corps wants to requisition Dreck's body. We'd like for you to refuse."

Some ominous facet of my biology pressed a warning button inside my brain. "Ah-huh. I see."

There was a long pause, and I finally said, "Is there anything else I can help you with?"

Lavalle looked mighty irked by my ambiguous answer. "Well, can you promise not to release the body to ReCo?"

I leaned back in my chair, my eyes locked on Lavalle, and I took another drink. I took my time, letting the seconds pass— these seconds must have felt like years to Lavalle—as I refilled my tin cup once more. "No. No, I don't think I can."

The kid's face turned red. This was the sort of scenario he'd been warned about: the Legend of the Intractable Curmudgeon. His gears were clearly spinning; this flunky must've been desperate to spin things any way he could to please his boss. But I was tired, and irritated, and there was a snowstorm outside.

"Mr. Attanasio," Lavalle started up again, "I don't think that that answer is in your best interest."

"Oh?" I said with the best look of indifference I could put on.

"May I ask why you'd refuse this request?"

"I didn't say I'd refuse this request. I answered 'no' when you asked if I would promise not to release him."

"Ah, I see." *A glimmer of hope*, he probably thought. "Well, let me ask you, what can I do to alleviate any concerns you might have?"

Ah, fuck it. Let 'im have it.

"Listen, son. I don't know how you know ReCo wants Dreck's body. I reckon it's safe enough for me to guess that these are the sorts of things someone would know in a mayor's office, even if I don't know by what right that crook Purgato has made himself king in what's shaping up to be his tiny, stupid fiefdom. But I'll tell you what I do know." I took another drink and pointed my cup at the kid. "I know that I don't like a little squirt like yourself coming down here and laying snake-oil tracks all over my place of business. I know that I take my job serious enough that I'm not leasing my services out to whatever tin-pot tyrant is the latest to try to tell everyone what's best for them. We fought a long time just to blow up the world so that shit wouldn't happen anymore. I know for sure that I don't know enough so that I can just tell you 'sure thing son, I'll have him ready for you in the morning.'

Monster or not, hated or not, my job is to take care of the dead in a respectful manner and see to their proper departure."

His eyes, I swear, his eyes bulged like they'd pop. Didn't matter. I was wrapping up anyway. "Now, tell me son, can you alleviate those concerns?"

Lavalle—red necked and bloated face—looked like he might explode. The pathetic flunky stood and put his card on my desk. "You'll be hearing from us," he said as he headed to the door.

I took another long swig and yelled after him, "Don't let the door hit ya where the Good Lord split ya."

CHAPTER 6

I didn't need to take another swig to know that things were getting *veddy interesting*. Who knew that yours truly (or yours white-lie-ly), humble ol' Frankie, would be at the nexus of a postwar power struggle? Humble ol' Frankie.

And these coins...

What to do?

I had two calls to make, I supposed. First I'd get back to Aggie over at ReCo and let him know that I was uncomfortably situated between a municipal rock and a federal hard place. Then, I'd try and sort out the new numismatic angle that addended itself to the larger Dreck issue.

That's doublespeak for what about the friggin' coins?

First, I'd go back and check on my dearly departed friend.

I sat in the wheeled, steel swivel-stool next to the cadaver and looked at Dreck in all his plug-ugly glory. I'd left him semi-naked, with his cloak pulled over his head and antlers, revealing the wound in his chest and the rest of his body. I pulled the cloak back down over him, feeling a secret shame that I'd left him exposed. I looked over to the tray and saw that there were still two handfuls of coins in the surgical pan. I counted them: *one, two, three, four... thirteen.*

Yep, thirteen. Just my luck.

I fondled the coins, taking them from the pan, one at a time, and felt the ridges and the weight of each one. They were thick and odd, like they'd been made through a prehistoric press before coin making became a precise art. None of them were the exact same size or weight. But there was an artfulness to them that didn't exist in any of the coined money I'd seen. Maybe it was an optical illusion, or some kind of trick, but the lines that linked the tiny glowing jewels set in the coins seemed to waver. I stared long at the animal symbol printed on the front. Something told me that if I kept looking, it would move. I dared to put one of the coins in my mouth and bite it. It was soft. *Gold.* I bit again—hard—and looked at the marks I'd left. I could've sworn that the metal pushed the bite mark back out, making it disappear.

I scooped the coins up from the pan and searched for one of my ancient Crown Royal bags—one of the many that held other little purple bags that my father had collected.

So, my father collected little purple sacks. I collected bigger purple bags—Crown Royal bags, inside which I kept my father's collection of purple bags. That he'd left behind. They didn't make Crown anymore; hadn't even made it in the few decades before the war. I loved these little bags. There was something mystical about them. While I searched, I put the coins in the pocket of my lab coat. Funny how they made no sound, no clinking or metal echoes, as they tumbled against one another. I sat at my desk chair and started sifting through my drawers.

I know they're around here somewhere.

I started digging, pulling up files and rifling through all the junk I'd accumulated in the seven years since I'd come back. There were trinkets I'd bought from the Blue Isles, where we were stationed before launching the invasion—knick-knacks made of wood, like tiki-men but uglier and meaner. I remember the crazed black native who sold them, because I saw him—even waved to him, said hello to him—more than a dozen times while I was stationed there, but he never seemed to remember who I was.

One day, we were all lined up to invade Semrock, and the man looked at me from about a hundred yards away. He held up a sign from where he stood, and I could read that sign, and it said DON'T LET THEM.

Don't let them what?

In those days, there were plenty of "them"—more of them than us, and even more things that should not have been. But the look in his eyes was stern and sober, and he was looking directly at *me*. I knew he was. And I was stone-cold sober, too. I didn't drink as much back then, and certainly not in the heat of the Blue Isles. There's something uncomfortable—that special *nasty* uncomfortable that smacks of raw crotch-rot—about getting boozy in hundred-plus weather.

DON'T LET THEM.

My whole life, I have tried to figure that out. Or at least whenever it pops up in my memory. So, every time I rummage through the bottoms of my desk drawers.

I sat the funky knick-knack evil tiki man down on the table and laughed at my own stupid sentimentality. A crazy wino, nothing more. That's all he was. Don't let them take my tiki-men —that's probably what he meant.

A crazy wino? Then what am I? An alcoholic in a profession; there's a difference.

Memory is a cruelly comic faculty, though. And mine always comes up rip-roaring from the barren, cobwebbed cracks of my brain. I remember sitting passively after we'd invaded Semrock and seeing a broad get gang-raped by one of the grunt units when they were sweeping homes. She was terribly young. I think she killed herself later. Or maybe that was just a rumor.

Jesus, I sure know how to ruin a reminiscence.

I couldn't have saved her. I only saw her through the scope on my rifle. I couldn't leave the sniper's nest. Obeying orders, like any good germane man. Then, just at the moment I was thinking that I could at least *try* to do something, I caught an insurgent moving on the patio leading into our target's home, trailing the team I was tasked to protect. He was about to get the drop on one of the teenage boys trailing in the back of the formation. I put one through the back of the insurgent's head. It came out his eyeball, and down he went.

I looked back at the woman's apartment and saw that the soldiers had finished their business. The last of the rapists must have finished just as I blew out the insurgent's brains. So, you tell me, why should I feel guilty? Listen to my justification: I saved the kid and let the woman get raped. Should I have shot the man raping her at that moment? They would have just killed her and then finished anyway. I told myself that a million times over, and it's probably true. I was two-hundred meters out, at least, and six stories up.

DON'T LET THEM!!

A lifetime of self-doubt remembered in a flash, all because of some wino with a penchant for dark prophecy. A dark prophet's dark prophecy.

Still rummaging through my drawers, I pulled out a single Crown Royal bag that had another dozen bags packed inside of it. It was musty and moth-bitten, but when I pulled the others out they were clean and as freshly purple as I remembered them.

Like royalty.

Those are the only words I remember my old man saying. I can't remember his face, and hell if I know where he ended up. Can't remember how he sounded when he said those words.

Purple like royalty.

Well, there's no royalty anymore. Nobility is usually one of the first casualties of insurrection, monarchy the enemy of revolution, etcetera, etcetera. There's no royalty anymore. Only royal asses.

I picked the bag I thought was most likely to have been used by my old man. I had no way of discerning—hell, I knew it was stupid to try—but I had this strange feeling that I'd picked the right little satchel.

I laid all thirteen coins and the purple bag on my desk. Then I found my bottle and my tin cup and poured myself another drink.

There was still something that told me that if I was *pouring* a drink and not drinking straight from the devil's mouth, I had a chance at remaining "functional."

DON'T LET THEM. FIND.

Find who? Dreck and the wino? Lines of admonition and perdition. Ominous times, these.

I contemplated the nature of these coins, only intellectualizing for a moment—*maybe the chest wound was an illusion; delirium tremens*—before becoming lost in the snowdrifts of fantasy; child-like, trance-like. Trapped in the drifts, I cast an unwavering gaze over the new divinatory implements I'd so recently acquired.

The phone rang again.

Merry fucking Christ on fuck-legged Christmas crutches! I gotta lay off the sauce, I'm getting jumpy.

I picked up the receiver.

"Agent Aggie?" I spoke into the phone. I just *knew* it was him.

"Yessir. Good to speak to you, Mr. Attanasio, sir."

"Likewise. I just had a little—"

"We know, sir. Yessir, we're well aware of the mayor's move to acquire the recently deceased individual's body."

A long pause.

DON'T LET THEM!!

But who? Which? ReCo or the mayor? The boy, or the girl getting raped?

"Well, what should I oughta do about it?" Diglossia kicking in —I was talking in corn-fed Pennsylvania Deitsch pidgin.

"Sir, we're asking that you hold him until we can get down there."

"Until... when?"

"Well, sir, we have orders to not deploy the ReCoRU team until the blizzard is through."

"I see. Well, I have to tell you, it seems like Purgato's boy was mighty eager to get his claws on Dreck's body. Might be best if you could come on down here right away, snow or not. I know you can—I mean, the New State boys used to land the hoverers in the middle of the—"

"It's not logistics, Mr. Attanasio, sir. We have the functional capability. It's just we think it's best not to deploy the ReCoRU team until after the blizzard is through."

"And if things get hairy?" I thought of the fugazi-facial-hair pulsating under the translucent sheath. And the metallic flagella that lay within.

A long pause.

"If things get hairy, we'll reassess our options, strategically—tactically—speaking. We won't leave you in the lurch, sir."

I slowly spun in my chair and looked down the dark hallway that led toward the cold room. "Can I ask why you don't want to pick him up during the storm when you are capable of doing so?"

Another, much longer pause.

"Yessir, Mr. Attanasio, you can ask. I just can't answer."

I gave a bitter laugh. "Well, can I do anything else for you? Wash your car, perhaps?"

"I understand the situation isn't ideal, sir. But we're working with the information we have, and I'll tell you honest: it's a good idea not to pick Dreck up during the storm."

Something about that struck me. It was the first time Aggie had used his name. Dreck. I decided to buck up.

"Well, I suppose as long as you call and sing me a lullaby once in a while, I can hold down the fort."

Agent Aggie didn't laugh, but I could hear him smiling on his end. "I'll do my best, sir."

"Anything else I can do for you?"

"No sir, Mr. Attanasio. We are very grateful for your cooperation."

"Don't worry about it."

"There is one more thing, Mr. Attanasio, sir."

"Yeah?"

"Merry Christmas, sir."

I looked outside at the snowfall. It was coming down in a way

I hadn't seen since I was a child. Brought back memories—maybe not memories, but emotions. Memories of emotions, maybe, and ones that weren't total shit. Looking at the whiteness enveloping the world brought me happiness. Genuine, honest-to-G-d happiness. I replied in my best treetop-glisten-children-listen voice.

"Merry Christmas, Aggie."

CHAPTER 7

I went into the janitor's closet and pulled out the old tee-vee I had stowed away. Amazing how long these vacuum-tube versions held up. Yes, I said vacuum-tube. As in rabbit ears and Howdy Doody time. They say the radiation released during The Long War settled into the old tubes and brought them back to life. Like Video Viagra.

I was a wreck. I didn't know what time it was. Last I looked at the sky, it was a deep blue complexion, starless, rubbed through with spirals of ghost-white flakes.

Apparition.

A sky filled with snow, like the old tee-vee screen. Timeless. A phantom trapped in galaxy clusters.

I didn't keep a clock in the mortuary. Nobody bothered to stay on schedule. What schedules were there to keep? Where did I have to be? People brought in their dead. People left their dead. The dead remained—still and without obligation. The dead can stand to be late. As a matter of fact, they *are* late, as in "the late Dreck."

I plugged in the ol' tee-vee, but it didn't work.

I went back to my desk and reluctantly opened my computer, dusty and unused as it was. It was military issue (we needed them for weapon calibrations when the newer rifles were issued). Half of me hoped it wouldn't work, though I couldn't say why. But it booted up. I ran the telephone line into it and managed to pull up *Vox Oculii*. There was a flapping-head show on. A woman with a lopsided blonde helmet-cut was talking about Dreck.

"Hello, and welcome to Darcy Gantz, the only word in facts and prosecution and the prosecution of facts. I'm Darcy Gantz, and today, we're talking about Dreck.

"Yes, ladies and gentlemen, we have recently received word from an anonymous source in the Seven Points Mayor's Office that the evil death-monster known as Dreck has died. Joining us for analysis is Wendy Morphy, resident expert in sexual deviance and evilness, and Justin Cooke, researcher for the postbellum reconstruction census.

"But before we get to our panel, let's have a brief look at the life of Dreck, that terrific—oops, I mean terrible—sexual predator and genocidal terror-maniac, Dreck."

[Darcy Gantz narrating:] "Dreck: monster, molesterer, and most evil guy with weird shoes. Let's have a look at the life and times of the buck-horned badboy from beyond the black lagoon… or wherever.
"Our sources say that Dreck was born here, in Seven Points, in what used to be called Braddock, in what used to be Pennsylvania, sometime around the new millennium. His mother was an excommunicated Quaker, and his father was a plumber who was known to leave plungers in toilets at his place of employment, the Home for the Blind.
"On Dreck's fifth birthday, he began to leave Upper Deckers in the commodes of every home that he visited."
[Dr. Pepper Peelerman:] "An Upper Decker is where a person defecates in the top bowl of a toilet, so that when a person flushes, instead of water coming into the basin, a never-ending flow of human poopy washes into the bowl instead. It is, perhaps, the most evil thing a person can do."

[Darcy Gantz:] "Then again, Dreck was not a person. As Dreck grew up, he announced to anyone who would listen that he was going to kill every old lady's dog and then commit mass shootings all over the nation."

[Poorly dubbed voice with a picture of Dreck:] "I'm going to kill every old lady's dog and shoot everyone. I love fuckin' people's shit up."

[Darcy Gantz:] "Terrifying. Truly terrifying. But Dreck truly unleashed his evil on the world when he destroyed Washington D.C." [Footage of a mushroom cloud over the capitol.] "Since then, even though we have no video footage and only scarce eyewitness accounts, Dreck has been linked to the mass genocides in Africa, most of the atrocities during the war in the Seven Points area, and is believed to be the reason why people can only find one sock out of a full pair when they are late and rushing to get out of the house."

[Darcy Gantz:] "Wow, just wow. Very powerful stuff."

[Wendy Morphy:] "Very powerful stuff, indeed."

[Justin Cooke:] "Uh, well… I'm not sure—I don't know how accurate some of the information in that piece was."

[Darcy Gantz:] "Wow, Justin, wow. I had no idea we had a child molesterer in the television studio tonight."

[Justin Cooke:] "Excuse me?"

Jesus Christ, man. There's got to be somebody out there who's interested in where he really comes from.

I shut off the feed and closed the computer.

There was too much *bad* building up in these rooms. I had to get out. I had bottles—cases—worth of booze saved up in the janitor's closet. But I needed people. I needed to be around people. Just to hear them, see them—even smell them.

All this was too much to bear alone. *I'll go out.* But where? There was a hellacious white ice-fire snowstorm outside. I'd never gone to any of the *chichi* bars in the neighborhood, in the center of Seven Points, where all the rent-seekers and capos scrambled for their piece of the postbellum pie. But it didn't matter. I had to get out.

First I'll check on Dreck, then I'll get the coins. Then I lock up and go out, just for a few hours. Just to get out of my head.

I still didn't know what time it was.

CHAPTER 8

"**M**r. Lavalle, my most loyal aide-de-cramp. Come on in, boy."

Huey Purgato smiled. It was a smile that curled so far into his cheeks that his grin looked like a Glasgow smile, like a devil's sneer. Purgato was a squat man, a shade under average height, and stocky. Stocky like a farmer whose back, shoulders, and legs looked like bundled layers of stony sinew, but whose paunch had accumulated from shine and overindulgence in the off-season. He had a wild mane of wavy red hair and deep green eyes.

Huey Purgato spoke as loudly as he dressed. He sported a bow tie, almost always a green-and-purple paisley one and a bright blue oxford shirt, almost always with the sleeves rolled up. Purgato preferred monkstrap shoes, in a burgundy red. He'd somehow acquired "braces," to align his jagged teeth and he donned the same suspenders day in and day out.

"Mayor Purgato."

"Huey, son," he said as he sat in his large-backed leather chair and lifted his feet to rest them upon his grandiose wooden desk. "You call me Huey, son."

Lavalle looked pained. He didn't want to call him *Huey*.

Lavalle was the kind of fellow who called people by their titles, even while feigning familiarity. Huey Purgato stuffed a handkerchief over his bowtie into his shirt collar, bit into a sandwich, and chewed loudly.

"Huey," Lavalle began, "we had a bit of a problem with the, uh—the—this Attanasio fellow."

Purgato looked up and spoke through the huge-gobbed ball of chewed-up chicken salad in his mouth, "Whorrmph?" Purgato pointed at one of the chairs in front of his desk, signaling Lavalle to have a seat. Lavalle obliged. Huey wiped his mouth with the handkerchief and raised his eyebrows. "Give me the good news, son."

"Well, Mayor Pur—uhhh... Huey. There really isn't good news. Attanasio said he wasn't giving up the body."

A dark cast set over the mayor's face. He yanked the handkerchief from his shirt collar and leaned back in his chair. "Ah. I see. So what do we do?"

"Hmm. Well, I'm not sure. We could..."

Purgato removed a letter opener from the top drawer. The opener's gilded handle shimmered beneath the banker's light that sat atop the right side of his desk. He put his reading glasses on and reached into the bottom drawer, which held a stack of dusty parcels bound by a twine knot.

"Mr. Mayor? Are you upset, sir?"

Huey Purgato looked perplexed, yet irate. But that Glasgow smile still creased his cheeks, and he hummed in a ragtime rhythm. "Upset? Why no, sir," he said as he rapidly looked through the parcels, turned each one over to inspect it, then neatly piled them to the left of the banker's light.

"No, na-no, na-no, na-no, son," he smiled. "We don't get mad. We get even."

He finally found what he was looking for. It was a ratty red thing—it looked like papyrus—and slid the gilt letter opener through the top.

"Here, son, take this." Purgato pulled out a piece of paper with an odd symbol on it—a butterfly with pointed wings and red eyes. "Take this down to Pop's," he ordered.

Boiling acid churned Lavalle's guts. The mayor had bought the establishment, Pop's, first thing after he'd returned from the war. Whores and gangsters infested that brothel. Lavalle must have dropped Mayor Purgato off there more than a hundred times.

"Sure, I know it," Lavalle replied. He fought the urge to further examine the paper. "Who should I give this to?"

Huey Purgato resumed eating his sandwich, looking like he didn't have a care in the world, chomping away while he gave Lavalle his marching orders.

"Givf isht to…" he swallowed the chicken salad lump in his mouth, "Cotton Lenny."

"Mr. Mayor—"

"*Huey*, boy. I said call me Huey."

"Yes, Huey. I'm not incredibly comfortable going down to Pop's to find Ms. Lenny."

The mayor chuckled at that, muttering to himself in humored disbelief. "Ms. Lenny? Goodness."

"Huey, we worked very hard on putting all the pieces together, on setting things up just right so we could put you in office. I worked for you, and very hard on your campaign, sir, because I *believe* you're the man for the job."

Purgato sat back in his chair and crisscrossed his fingers, interlocking them over his belly as he faced Lavalle with purposeful concentration. This hyper-charisma looked well-practiced. A look that said *I am indeed listening to ya, suh. Yessah, yessah.*

Emboldened by the mayor's look of seeming openness, Lavalle went on. "And, sir—Huey—I have to tell you, I think it's really bad for you to be associated with th-the… the, um, the pimps and whores down at Pop's."

Huey raised his eyebrows and let out a gum-flapping guffaw.

"A-are—are you laughing at me?" Lavalle asked.

Purgato popped up from behind his desk. He approached Lavalle, and placed an arm around his shoulders.

"Aw, come on now, son. Laughing at you? Goodness no! Shit, I'm proud of you, boy." Huey gripped Lavalle's shoulder with a firmer grasp and shook it toward himself. "Shit, that's why I knew you were the man for the job. The only man. Can't nobody say I'd make it here by my lonesome, without my four-star general to strategize."

Purgato continued, arm still slung around Lavalle's shoulder. He leaned in to closely talk into the young man's ear. "Right? *Campaign* manager. You're my trusted second. You get me?"

Lavalle smiled and nodded. Huey released his grip and walked the whole length of the gigantic room toward an armoire.

"Good. That's real good son. Now you go ahead and run down to Pop's, and deliver that to Ms. Lenny, as you would call her."

Purgato arrived at the armoire and squatted in a catcher's stance, feeling around underneath it.

For a moment, Lavalle didn't move. He'd just been had. "But-but… but Mr. Mayor—"

"Huey."

"But Huey—"

"No buts about it, son. You head on down there. Go ahead, scoot. We'll talk about it when you get back."

Lavalle's shoulders slumped, but he left the office at the same brisk business-like pace he always did, defeated or not.

ONCE MAYOR PURGATO was sure that Lavalle had left, he reached under the armoire again and felt around for a small box. It was the kind that realtors used, once upon a time, when they wanted to let clients into unoccupied homes for a showing. He popped in the code—L O V E—and pulled out a key: a copper rod with an array of gears, teeth, and arms at one end.

Purgato took the key with him over to a candelabra. He ran his fingers along one of the candelabra's arms until he felt a seam, and popped open the candelabra arm. Huey gingerly inserted the copper key into the opening of the candelabra. Gears whirred and metallic *clicks* sounded. Metal shutters descended, covering the floor-to-ceiling windows, and at the same moment, every entrance and exit to the great room clicked. One could neither enter nor exit.

The south wall shifted, moved, receded into a corner seam of the triangular building.

Purgato descended into a dark alcove.

CHAPTER 9

W hen I came back some thirteen years ago, I kept in touch with a lot of my military buddies. After the War, the guys were optimistic: some were even what you might call *sunshiny*. You'd think they'd be terrified. The world had ended (more or less) and the economics of it painted a piss-poor picture of a future with any prospects. Despite that, they acted like a huge weight had lifted off them.

Here's my take on it. For thousands of years, there have been all sorts of folks—Incan priests and messiahs from the Middle East, Slavic seers and millenarian misers—who warned about the End Times. The End Times, surely, were just around the corner. In 5000 B.C., in 1 A.D., then 30 A.D.; one thousand and two thousand years later, the End Times were still just around the corner.

When The Long War took off, it *was* the End Times. Anyone could see things they'd never seen before. There were machines that could melt you down to an atom and pop you out of space-time's asshole onto the other side of Earth. There were freaks whose footsteps shook the ground like the Nephilim (Alex referred to them as fallen angels). There was a man—some say he was our savior—whose organs appeared on the outside of his body, and a beam of light shone from his mouth when he spoke.

We'd never seen this shit before. And more importantly—
excepting my (maybe hallucinatory) experience with Dreck—we
haven't seen shit like it since.

The apocalypticism of the past had war, tragedy, and warn-
ings, but our generation hit the mother-of-all-shitstorms-jackpot.
We had tangible evidence for the End Times. It's why people
believed we were really living through some Book-of-Revelation-
type shit. People were jubilant at the end of the War because *we*
were the ones who'd lived through it. We saw it. Prior generations
hadn't. The *anxiety* concerning the End Times faded from our
collective consciousness. We were no longer terrified. The End
Times came and went and we felt pretty damn good.

Christmas was *huge*, even if you had no idea who it was
named after. If you were a guy walking through the street on
Christmas Eve, people called out from their homes, yelling at you
to come in because *ain't you got a place to go to? Come on in!* We'd
made it through the shit, and the world-left-after was our reward
before the world-to-come. People figured this shared feeling of
euphoria was what Redemption was.

My memories of Christmas are of wood and lights—multi-
colored radiance dancing on wire-peaks inside glass bulbs,
spilling out onto the bodies of my brethren; dim light set darkly
against the faces of family, shadows accentuating their smiles and
laughter.

I remember having Christmas with my friend Janosek. I didn't
have anywhere to go (which I didn't mind), but Janosek thought it
was a dirty shame for me to be alone on the first Christmas after
the End Times.

Janosek's father—also named Frank—was a rabbit farmer.
He'd built a hutch and a rabbit run out in the back of the shanty
he'd come to occupy after the War. My first impression of Frank
was that he was a stupid guy. He didn't speak English, he was a
drunk (a judgment that, given my own circumstances, I regret
having made), and he made his own moonshine.

It never struck me, at the time, that successfully raising rabbits and making his own distillery out of junk-yard crap probably meant that Frank wasn't as stupid as I thought. Thinking back, my assessment of the man was likely based on his illiteracy. I should've known better too; I'd been in enough places during The Long War where I'd had to communicate with non-English-speakers through an intermediary or by pantomime.

I also thought a smart guy wouldn't *choose* to raise rabbits. Now I know better. The warm and fuzzy wood and lights feeling came back when I went with Janosek to his father's home. We got drunk on that brown sugarshine, ate ham and baklava, and when we were exhausted from drinking, we sat outside on the log-benches Frank had carved up, looking up to the stars. Janosek laughed and poked fun at his father for speaking to his rabbits.

Distinct memories. Definitive memories. I thought I'd lost them for good.

A train set. Memories are passengers, fleeing from commuter trains, disembarking on a hundred-stop line until only the empty train remains.

The empty train had strangely, impossibly, returned to the station. *All aboard!* The paradox of the mnemonic puzzle box: when you wanted to forget, you remembered; when you wanted to remember, you'd forget.

Christmas Eve in the mortuary differed a bit from my first Christmas with my friend and his father. I decided that it was time to lock up the old cadaver coop, venture out into the snow, and find myself some place to go. I took my key ring and went room by room, door by door, before working backwards—first toward my office as I sealed the mortuary like the thing it was, a hermetic tomb.

After closing up shop, I went back to the desk where I'd left the satchel and the thirteen coins. *Idiot, you shouldn't leave those out.* Dammit, I must be fraying around my cognitive edges (does cognition have an edge? I suppose so, if an incisive thinker is referred to as *sharp*). I whipped around to gather the coins into the purple pouch and was struck full in the face by a physical (and metaphysical) improbability.

The coins levitated, arrayed in the air in the pattern of a floating pyramid. Ten of them floated in the shape of a pyramidal tetractys: four on the bottom level, three above those, two above the three, and one at the very top. The remaining three coins orbited around the larger structure in inconsistent patterns.

I stumbled backwards, startled by the radiating hum the floating coins made. I'd heard that noise before, in that desert horror-show of a nightmare. I heard, as if coming from a distant room, the clanging of bells, high-pitched but sweet and celestial. I felt a million different urges—some good, some bad. *Kill the Mayor. Feed the poor. Adopt a needy child. Fuck a whore.* The strongest urge was to touch the coins. But at the same time, there was something in me—or outside of me—telling me not to.

I stretched my fingers out as long as they'd reach. My sense of touch seemed stilted, dead. As my cold unfeeling hand moved closer to touching them, the three orbiting coins shot into my hand, embedding themselves a quarter-inch deep.

It was like getting ambushed by a swarm of wasps. *"Fuck! Motherfucker!"* I tried to pull them out, but the harder I struggled, the farther they sank. They bled an iridescent light-marigold liquid into me, and a glowing ooze pulsed through my veins. My hand was no longer my own—and I'd quit fighting, since it just meant the coins would push deeper. Maybe burst an artery.

I watched in horror and fascination as my now-alien appendage held out its palm, into which the other ten coins piled in a perfect vertical stack. My hand dumped the coins into the purple satchel, and the three coins that had sunk into my hand expelled themselves from my limb at a disorienting speed and hovered over my wrist. My hand still moved, but with the three remaining coins hovering above, the hand looked like a marionette, directed by some invisible puppeteer. Some of my own blood, along with the viscous marigold, dripped on top of the ten coins inside the bag. Finally, *finally*, the three body-snatcher money-pieces relented and followed their gilt cousins back into the bag.

I pulled back, yanking my hand too hard, not realizing I had full control of it again. I stumbled, tripped, and fell backwards over my chair, feet flying. I landed on my back, which knocked the wind out of me and puckered my asshole. *Figures. Oh, my fuckin' back.* I dragged myself to my feet and picked up the satchel now filled with coins (and my blood).

Thought of all the inexplicable and impossible shit I'd seen through the War and after it. This was odd. This was odd, indeed.

Calmly, like any sane person, I tried to reason with the coins. "Alrighty, fellas. You don't give me no more trouble and I don't give you none. That a deal?"

No answer. "Okay, we're square."

I walked out the front door and took out my key ring, locking all three bolts.

I deserve a drink.

CHAPTER 10

Amazework of subterranean tunnels reveals a disparate nation of folks ill-suited to life in the world above. They are ugly, they are odd, and some of them are... ugly oddballs.

Geoffrey Hammond Bimmelberger was one such oddball, though he possessed none of the mutations that would meet the prerequisite for "an ugly oddball." Geoffrey Hammond Bimmelberger did not go by his birth name, favoring instead the somewhat unique abbreviation of GHB (aka The Grand Hubba-Bubba, aka Geoffie Jeffs Jefferson, aka Pappa Burgerbiter). GHB dwelt in the underground tunnels. He wore socks over his ears while lecturing other undermenschly creatures on the details of his plan for world domination, which existed in the limbo of planning stages and had never quite come to fruition.

GHB had a penchant for oratorical flourishes as well as a morbid eloquence. He could have been a politician before The Long War. Or a reality-show host. Or a revival tent preacher.

"Brothers and sisters, I ask you, why demand cheese when the cheese of the earth flows ever beneath us? Why seek to suck in the air of the aboveground when the sweet stew of sewer pipe scent wafts through our every nostril? And, I should add, to all three nostrils, for those of us who have three. I'm looking at you, Jeffonia! These tattered rags we wear, they aren't the rags of exile; they aren't the vestments of a poor underclass. They are a symbol of our freedom—we are too good to shower; I say to you! What does the well-heeled *heel* of a man know about the good life? Look at me, friends. I found a tuna fish sandwich in an overflow drain a couple days ago. And the Lord spoke unto me: *Retrieve, Son of Man, the tuna sandwich from amongst the tatty toilet paper and the mucky muck of The Deep Brown Below. And yea, did I retrieve that tuna sandwich.* And now, brothers and sisters, I will eat this tuna-fish sandwich before you, though it be old tuna, and possibly bad tuna, and even though this tuna surely walked through the valley of the stank of the doodoo canals through which it came to be laid before me." GHB sat down on an old, broken, fallen refrigerator. "Now, I will field questions."

A dirty woman sat among the crowd of revelers and acolytes. Her nose curved so far to the left that its point rested directly below her left eye. She raised her hand. It had three fingers.

GHB pointed to her. "Yes, the young lady in the back."

"*Grrrrmph urgl blargarful intur?*"

"Tremendous question. Simply a tremendous question. Did everyone hear Jeffina? Jeffina asked if a man can catch a venereal disease by looking at a woman. Jeffina, for this question, I will have to refer to the Book of What's Written and What is Yet to Be."

GHB opened the refrigerator door under his legs and fished out a huge three-ring binder, torn and taped magazine pages oozing out of its sides like foam from a rabid mutt's maw. He flipped through until he landed on a picture of a man and a woman each seated in Adirondack chairs. The happy couple held hands while staring out at a sunset. To many *oohs* and *aahs*, he held up the picture for all to see. GHB held the binder higher with both hands, in the pose of Moses at Mount Sinai, thrusting the binder and its pages in the air as though they were the Tablets of the Law. GHB was close enough to read the fine print, which indicated that the picture was for something called "erectile dysfunction medication," but the others could not see it. And GHB, in his vast expanse of ostentatious language, did not know the meaning of those words in their current juxtaposition.

"See and be witness! I will impart to you the wisdom of the Maxim. As it is written: *A man who wipes his hiney with his left hand —he may eat with that hand, for the wiping of the hiney is like the sowing of the field. And so, a man may wipe in the summer or in the rainy season, during weekdays and most weekends, and may keep the remains of his wiping. But a woman who does not eat of the sown field is like a bird. She has skinny legs and may possibly fly off to Canadia and never return, unless she has brought a worm for her children. That worm is the seed of sin.* So, short answer, *yes*, you can contract a venereal disease from only looking at a woman. Unless it is a woman like Jeffina, who is too ugly to be desired by a man. Other questions?"

A giant of a man—around seven and a half feet tall, weighing approximately five-hundred pounds—raised his hand. He was sitting on a pink bicycle with training wheels and streamers on the handles.

"Yes, Mr. Jeffo."

"Kerml et kerml et kerml?"

"No, Mr. Jeffo, we're not addressing the issue of game night."

"Et kerml monfrof?"

"Well, there's a process for these grievances. This is why we have the community board, Mr. Jeffo."

GHB scanned the crowd and addressed them. "This is why we have the community board, everyone! Did everyone hear Mr. Jeffo's complaint? He's upset because people have been skipping ahead of him to use the good shitting hole. We have a system in place for the good shitting hole, everyone. Okay? Can we just put our names on the board under the 'Good Shitting Hole' heading and try to follow the rules? Thank you."

A four-foot-tall old man near the back of the crowd jumped up and down, frantically waving his hands. GHB prepared to take someone else's question when he noticed the midget's pudgy, wrinkly hands, pumping up and down behind the horizon of heads in front of him. "Yes, all the way in the back." But the tiny old man didn't speak, he just ran up to the front of the miasmic amphitheater, huffing and puffing. By the time he reached the front row, he handed GHB a waste-covered slip of paper with a black circle drawn on it. GHB took it, folded it up, and tucked it into the pantyhose he was wearing.

"The lecture is over for now, everyone. Let's take an hour break and reconvene in two hours for song-writing night. As a model we'll be looking at *Gimme Shelter* by The Rolling Stones and *Meat Hook Sodomy* by Cannibal Corpse. See you tonight, brothers and sisters!"

GHB rushed from his refrigerator perch to follow the tiny old man. The man had run toward the infinite blackness of one of the underground pathways lined with stone and brick and slime and rust. GHB caught up with the tiny man and walked alongside him. The tunnel supplied scant lighting. It was almost solid darkness, but they had been living under the tunnels so long that their eyesight had adjusted, and lightlessness was not a hindrance.

"Well, what's the trouble?" GHB asked.

The tiny man hurried along, hobbling as he went. His feet angled toward one another, and he had six toes on his left foot. "The signs. They're there. I saw one of them, clear as day."

GHB laughed. "It couldn't be. Then, that would mean..." He stopped walking.

"Yes," the tiny hobbler whispered. "He is dead."

GHB let out a disappointed whistle. "The others mustn't know. Not before we've had a chance to act. Sadly, I'll admit to you that I never planned in great detail for contingencies such as this. I always figured—"

"—that he'd live forever," the tiny hobbler finished GHB's sentence.

"Yes."

They continued walking together, strolling through the effluent labyrinth with purpose and reservation, perhaps because of their anxieties, perhaps in mourning. They reached a convergence where flowing streams of shit and gray water met to form a frothy river.

GHB held his hand out. "Age before beauty, Jeffersaint."

The tiny man-creature rolled his eyes and muttered, then dove, disappearing into the center of the axial point of the streams. GHB awaited the man's resurgence. He sat on a ledge where one of the first transit systems had been built and abandoned. He looked to see if anyone had followed them before reaching into the billowy sleeve of his dirty robe-like clothing and—with a flourish— removed a candy bar from inside. He bit into it and slowly chewed, savoring it. "Oh, my Dear Satan. So motherflipping good." And then he began to sing.

> *"Oh my sweet candy I love your sugary taste*
> *Your ingredients promise me a world beyond this*
> *   brownish waste*
> *But our love is forbidden, and so only I can know*
> *That nightly I eat your body in the sewers below"*

The song evinced a melancholy country twang.

GHB sucked his fingertips and wiped his hands on his dirt-robe. No one would find out he'd eaten chocolate. The stains would simply look like fresh shit.

A plastic cube emerged from the depths of the confluence of sewer streams. Heaps of refuse and contaminated water rained from the edges of the cube, which opened for a ladder to descend from it. The old man's weathered face hovered as if disembodied behind the ladder. "Come on up," the tiny old hobbler yelled down. GHB crossed the shit-river and climbed the ladder.

Once aboard, GHB and the tiny old man descended into the earth until they reached their stop-off point. The cube opened to an underground cave where the tiny old man kept all his trinkets and toys. Most importantly, though, it housed the *Kromee-Ohm*.

The *Kromee-Ohm* sounded formidable, though its original name had been considerably more innocuous: *A Register for*

Consulting. GHB changed the name to the *Kromee-Ohm* because it had come to him in a fit of prophecy—or so he'd claimed. This was the awesome name he gave to a journal that had been kept by the oldest man in the world for some three-thousand years. At least, that is what the author claimed. Then again, its predictions were so prescient that the *Kromee-Ohm*'s track record on prognostication was somewhere around 99.99% spot on. The only passages out of the *Kromee-Ohm*'s thousands that had proved wrong, were those that were written in what GHB referred to as an *altered state*.

The tiny old hobbling man, whose real name was Truculento—but whose cult-name (or *prophetic* name, as GHB called it) was Jeffersaint—had an alternative explanation for the exceedingly rare passages in the *Kromee-Ohm* where the author had been wrong: "He went senile."

There were two predictions near the end of the great book which GHB and Jeffersaint had frequently discussed in order to determine who was right. One of the predictions had proven to be correct, and one had proven to be incorrect.

Prediction #1:
Under the clocktower's gleaming eye
Where nobles wrest and crowns have passed
Treachery lurks, a traitorous seed
A nation torn by one man's greed

Prediction #2:
I once met a maid named Mary
Whose pussy was awfully hairy
I boffed her doff
Behind that coif
Then found she had a husband named Larry

The book had been passed down to Truculento-Jeffersaint as a gift from one of his father's friends. Inside the *Kromee-Ohm* were beautifully illustrated plates, many of which seemed to emit some faint sound and whose figures and sketched backgrounds appeared to morph.

Truculento-Jeffersaint opened the book somewhere past the middle and showed GHB one of the illustrated plates, which didn't merely creep a little or hum an inaudible aural shadow. The picture transformed itself in a full-bore rotation. First, a picture of Dreck lying dead on a slab in a mortuary. Then, a picture of the coins flying in front of a man's face—three of the coins piercing his hands. And lastly, a picture of a neon sign that read *Cocktails & Dreams*.

GHB stared in awe. "What the Lord's fuck is this?"

"My best guess is that Dreck is dead, that the coins have been recovered, and that this is a bar sign for a location that has some significance in the unfolding of all pertinent, current, and future events."

"I see," replied GHB, tapping his finger against his forehead. He quickly removed it to press his fingertip on the illustrated scene. The image rippled and with a fluid response when GHB touched it. "Find this place."

CHAPTER 11

I palmed the coin bag in my pocket as I kicked through the snow.

I usually don't carry valuables on my person—Seven Points is rife with muggers. I avoid carrying any pre-war items like money—we're barely past the point where people use IOU slips and the barter-and-trade system—and I don't have "valuables" as defined by the prewar system. Stuff like jewelry, cellphones, leatherbound classics. You'd think I'd be safe, but you'd be wrong. Street kids are always after shoes. Thing is, I got me some flat feet and sensitive ankles—no bone spurs, though—and when I found these *Marmot* loafers, I knew it'd be another twenty years before I could find another pair that'd suit me. So, whether I was mugged, whether I fought back (I always did), I made sure *nobody* took my shoes.

Shoes are among eternal actualities, like truth and justice. You see, your average Long War veteran has a sizable advantage over the average street kid: When a veteran fights, he mauls like an animal. *Like an animal.* I bet you've heard that a lot. But 'like an animal' doesn't mean out of control or rude or dirty. It means digging deep down into your bowels and heart and bashing the machinery until the governor flies off, until there are no words, no social conditioning, and especially, no memory of the rules and limits that belong to the civilized world. The world as it was before The Long War, with real ruthlessness held in check by the better angels of our nature. No, *'like an animal'* means fighting for life or death, but more often, fighting for death and death, fighting to kill your enemy even if you or they are already dead. Consequently, fighting *like an animal* involves all the stuff you'd never dream of doing in your most desperate hour: biting a man's dick off, for instance. So, the last time some punk kid tried to take my *Marmot*s, I did that. I left his nuts intact to show that I'm a gentleman at heart. Call me Dickophage.

I could see some lights through the white and gray veil; figures moving in and out of a building. Hopefully it was my destination. That whipping wind was making my nose run.

I've always been a quiet guy. Not shy. I say what needs to be said when I need to say it. But I don't speak without cause. The only problem with that is, when you spend most of your time around people who don't talk back, you don't find yourself in a garrulous way. Once, I saw a movie where the coroner character talked to her corpses. I decided I'd try it out. But I felt ridiculous. I had a harder time talking to the dead than I did to women back when I went on dates.

I'm quiet. So what? Is that a crime? I ain't hurting no one.

No one but myself.

I entered the bar, passing a neon sign—*Cocktails & Dreams*. I laughed at the sign as a well-heeled man in a suit shot me a peculiar look.

Cocktails and dreams? The dreams don't go down easily, and the cocktails go down *too* easily.

The inside was all refurbished—wood shellacked, poles greased, brass shining—and the scent of perfume and cologne and wine and brandy was preferable to my familiars, bleach and formaldehyde and vomit. I thought of Christmases past: multicolored radiance dancing on wire-peaks inside glass bulbs, spilling out onto the bodies of my brethren.

This wasn't exactly a place that could become my regular joint.

Vox Oculii channel was on in the background with the sound turned down. There were subtitles. When I first came home, there wasn't even television. Now they have enough people putting enough pieces back together to caption shows.

Shall wonders never cease?

I sat at the end of the bar and pulled out a pocket notebook and a draftsman's pencil I'd taken off a dead guy in Semrock (they had a lot of engineers on that tiny island). Usually, when I went to a bar, which wasn't often, I'd get a solid forty-five minutes of thinking in before my mind turned to shit. I wrote out a list. Resources for finding out about the coin:

- University?
- Translator from the service?

Somewhere between sweeping away the cobwebs and dusting off the shelves of my memory bank, I was on the verge of knocking something useful loose when I noticed a woman staring at me. She was tall, probably an inch taller than me. Blonde. Blue eyes. Not quite blue, though, when I got a good look. More like blue-green, and when she looked down or over, they transitioned into a copper-like hue. An unusual, if not impossible, color for someone's eyes. There was a certain poise there, something between a child's lack of self-consciousness and a doctor's high self-regard, or a combination thereof. A straight-backed confidence. She wore all black clothing; a peculiar choice, since that fashion had, for some time, been almost taboo. Black was for mourning, only for mourning. Not for hipsters longing for late-twentieth-century New York angst. Then again, maybe times were changing.

Sign of the times.

I signaled the bartender and pointed to the tin cup I'd brought in. Bringing one's own cup for filling had become a custom for veterans of the War, and though most of the old farts no longer observed that custom, it had become a habit of mine. If you brought in your own cup, you were supposed to get your first drink for free. I hadn't done it in a while—hell, I hadn't been in a bar for a while. But the blonde in her all-black outfit didn't elicit a response. I figured if no one noticed that, they wouldn't give a shit about my cup, either.

The bartender poured me a drink. I smiled and nodded. Sign of the times. But all black.

I tipped my head down and tried to peripherally view the blonde in all black with the iridescent blue-green orb eyes. She was closer, and she was staring right at me. I tried to ignore it, but something about the way she was looking at me made me want to get away, made me feel some sort of shame. By rights, I should've welcomed that sort of attention, unusual as it was. But I felt— *ugly? Horny? Angry?* —loud. I didn't like feeling loud. I don't talk much.

Like the priests of old who put a linen pall over the Grail, I set a napkin on my tin cup and decided I'd go to the bathroom for either a piss or a pretend-piss.

CHAPTER 12

As Truculento trudged through the deep terrarium of hidden mutations, he worked with patience and care as best he could, given the urgency of the moment. The underground universe was a honeycomb of rancid nectar where stairwells gave way to viaducts, which in turn gave way to sundry scenes of rusted and forgotten industrial monsters, lurking like tarnished automata in the darkness. After each ascent from one level to the next, Truculento took care to seal off the places he left behind. He had spent fifty years constructing an apparatus that ensured the secrecy of his rancid residence.

He stopped, pulled out an old map, and traced a blue line with his finger.

"Fuckin' shit. This is a bastard of a bitch. A bitch of a bastard. Lots of effort."

Truculento continued muttering as he spun a circular crank that unsealed a gigantic iron door. "Lots of bastard effort, for fuck's sake," he repeated, as he pulled at the wrought-iron door. It was large and heavy enough that the average person would not be able to create a visible crack between the door and its seal.

He closed the great iron door. It automatically resealed itself, audibly locking behind him. *Well, there's that.* The mixed feeling of pride and burden rose whenever he came up to the surface; he had to walk all the way around the city to come back down—the door would not open from this side.

Truculento walked along the abandoned waterway lined with old shacks on stilts—once populated by the offspring of fishermen who lived there. He arrived at an abandoned half-wrecked boat along the shore. The water had pulled it far enough out that he couldn't retrieve his things. *Shit. Bitch's shit.* He continued on to the next boat and smiled when he saw it was in the same place it had been when he'd last hidden his stash.

He limped aboard the ruin, clambered up the deck-ladder, then descended into the hull. A bench down there concealed a storage area beneath its cushioned top. He pushed aside the cushion and reached farther down, then knocked, blindly feeling for where he'd hidden his stash. Truculento fished out a water-proof bag—his above-ground kit—from which he removed a set of children's clothing. He also found old ration vouchers that were likely useless and a wallet pouch of genuine silver dollars. Currency changed, but people still traded silver.

He changed into the children's clothing, pocketed the pouch and the vouchers, and headed toward his destination.

CHAPTER 13

L avalle hated the idea of going into Pop's—the townie watering hole. Pop's was the kind of place where he had found himself derided by the patrons because of his fancy clothes and his buttoned-up demeanor. Lavalle had worked *extremely* hard at a political ascent that demonstrated an inhuman work ethic and an inexhaustible reserve of intellectual resources that had given him the upper hand.

Being with Huey Purgato meant having the upper hand. Being on the ground floor (the very designer, in fact) of the reincorporation of a great city, was having the upper hand. The most powerful man in Seven Points had allotted him this assignation, which to Lavalle, was the very definition of having the upper hand. But places like Pop's were filled with folks who didn't trade in this currency. Drunks, gangsters, and whores didn't *really* care what kind of clothes you wore or how much of a big shot you thought you were, even if the whores play-acted at giving a shit.

One of Huey's gangsters—a multiple-tour-terror who'd been at every front of The Long War—served as Lavalle's chauffeur. The chauffeur went by a strange name: 86. If that name was a reference to something, Lavalle certainly didn't get it. 86 was tall, taciturn, and intimidating. 86 had driven Lavalle to Pop's in one of the remnant Crushers—an armored transport vehicle that resembled a small tank. The blizzard posed only a slight obstacle for the Crusher, but Lavalle's stomach had reacted to the ride and by the time they reached the bar, his face dripped with sweat, and he had a bit of trouble standing inside the vehicle without wobbling. *Well, I'll fit right in,* he thought.

Lavalle struggled to exit the Crusher, stumbling on his way out (he had to climb through the rear porthole, which opened to a four-foot drop). He turned to face 86, "I guess I'll just let you know when—"

86 closed the door without letting Lavalle finish.

"Yep. Good enough," the youthful politico said to himself. The Crusher's diesel engine roared as it kicked up snow and ice, disappearing into the blizzard.

When he approached the entrance, Lavalle expected the place to be packed. It didn't really matter whether the weather was fair or foul—there would always be pimps, whores, and Purgato pawns lying around getting wasted and picking fights with each other. But when he reached the door to the place—with the wind and icy flurries of the impossibly strong storm stinging his cheeks —Lavalle heard nothing.

Absolutely nothing.

Lavalle knocked at the door, but nobody answered. So, he walked in. The bouncer—a beefier but dirtier version of Mr. Clean —wore sweatpants and a black tank-top, and sat on a stool just inside the door. Mr. Dirty didn't bother to look up. He was engrossed in the book he was reading. The bouncer flicked his eyes up toward Lavalle to inspect him before looking back down his nose through his pince-nez. The bouncer pointed to a pair of red curtains from which a cold, black slit of otherness peeked through.

"She's through there. Been expecting you."

Without a word, Lavalle nodded and slid through the curtains into the other room.

Cotton Lenny sat at a table, and her legs stretched out to the side as though she were riding a horse side-saddle. She was sketching on a piece of paper. Without looking up, she waved Lavalle over and pointed to the seat across from her. She was an older woman—somewhere in her fifties, Lavalle thought—but wiry and tough. Long white-gray streaks flowed through her hair. She wore a very sharp houndstooth jacket (with a paisley purple-red-and-royal-blue kerchief pushing out of the front pocket) and crimson-blood-colored pants. Her wrists were adorned with scars, and she was missing the top half of one of her ears.

He sat across from her, and though she still hadn't looked at him, her eyes were more than noticeable.

The irises and pupils both looked like they'd had a dull knife dragged across them—there were zigzags of red and traumatized off-white tissue cutting through the sclera. But she wasn't blind, or at least she didn't appear to be. Cotton Lenny's feet were bare, and Lavalle noticed that they were pedicured; unlike the rest of her body, her feet were perfectly clean. Even beautiful. Beautiful feet. Lavalle loved feet. But no one could ever know about that. No, never. Feet could really trip up a man and be his downfall. Feet could undo a good campaign.

She smiled. Her teeth were all gold. "You have something for me?"

A burning curiosity, so powerful that it momentarily seemed irrepressible, came over Lavalle—he wanted to ask her if her teeth were capped, or if they were gilded dentures. But his animal brain was overtaken at the last second by a deep-seated urge to keep himself alive.

"Yes, Ms. Cotton Lenny, I do." Lavalle reached into his peacoat, gripping the manila folder Purgato had tasked him to deliver. His hands shook, only a little, as he recalled the ominous butterfly stamped onto the paper inside.

"Calm down, Mr. Lavalle. You ain't gon' get hurt."

She looked at the piece of paper and chuckled to herself. "Call me Lenny, Mr. Lavalle. I don't know that I've ever been a Miss. Sure as shit, I've never been a *Missus*."

"Yes, Lenny."

Cotton Lenny traced her finger along the outline of the macabre entomology print she held in her hand. "Do you know what this is?" she asked him.

Lavalle stared at the red eyes of the butterfly. Its sharp wings. "No."

She set the paper down on the table and looked at him. "Do you want to know?"

Her scarred eyes unsettled him; they'd fixed on his eyes—they made Lavalle fearful and nauseated all at once.

He didn't hesitate before answering. "No," he squeaked.

"Probably for the best." Cotton Lenny sighed, tucked the paper inside her jacket, then patted the pocket concealing the paper. Lavalle noticed that her fingers were abnormally long, and the nails were cut down to the quick.

"Alright, Mr. Lavalle. Why don't you head upstairs, get your reward?"

"Sorry?" Lavalle ran his hand through his hair. The room temperature resembled that of a boiler, even though it was the dead of winter and—judging by the puffs of condensation coming from Cotton Lenny's mouth—the heat was turned off.

"I said go on. Git. Git upstairs and take your reward, you slick little monkey-man," Lenny said, licking her lips.

"Oh, no, I-I couldn't," Lavalle answered, fully convinced that he meant it. "I'm not really that type of—"

"Not a man? You're not a man? Huey done closed the whole joint so yins could get wet, monkey-man."

Cotton Lenny smiled and kicked her feet up on the table. Her bare feet looked incredible. She pulled out a sugar cube and licked it, then pinched off a bit of sucrose and wiped it on her big toe. "You want some sugar?" She laughed.

Something about the wrongness of it excited him. He had stayed buttoned up for so long. *Who would know?* The sight of that foot was too much. He leaned over, his tongue waggling, involuntarily pushing in and out in stutters, salivating, reaching to lick her big toe. But Lenny briskly kicked the sugar cube off the table and laughed.

"You're a sick little puppy, ain't'cha?"

"So, s-so there's no reward?"

"No, there is. Just not from me. Just wanted to see if the monkey would bite. Go ahead, monkey-man. Yins'a bitey little fuckey monkey."

Lavalle encountered the bouncer, who was waiting with a welcoming smile. He waved Lavalle over to the back stairwell, now seeming much more congenial. Lavalle *was* a customer, even if he was being comped, and even if this proved to be a one-off. First impressions, especially in fleshly enterprises, were *very* important.

COTTON LENNY TOOK the paper from her pocket and unfolded it. She balled it up, opened her mouth, and swallowed it down. Her feet shifted to their original texture and appearance: swollen masses of decaying flesh. The compact mirror she carried in her purse came in handy during such times. She enjoyed viewing her transformations. There were flecks gathering around the scarred ridges in her eyes; morphed into a deep, glowing red. And in the pall cast over her, the gold teeth came to long needling sharp points, like the thin razors of a deep-sea predator.

CHAPTER 14

I found myself in Cocktails and Dreams' surprisingly swank bathroom. "Well, fuck me, *chichi*."

How did people have enough money stashed to open a joint like this? I suppose things were changing. For a while, people just moved into whatever structures still stood and took ownership of what was left. Years later, it now seemed like there was enough to go around. Enough of the younger generation had resources at their disposal, so that commerce and trade—the invisible hand, etcetera, etcetera—had become a thing again. Which meant things like black mirrors, shimmering marble, and copper fixtures were back in vogue.

Who was that crapper who wrote that a civilization is measured by its indoor plumbing? I smiled to myself briefly. *Well, we're making things again. How about that?*

The attendant in this highfalutin bathroom looked sharp, too, in his button-up shirt. Despite looking like he would be in his sixties, he was a burly feller with a ponytail and a bushy beard that looked like it was tucked and pinned up under his chin.

He smiled as he handed me a full bar of soap. "I ain't sure if I's s'posed to lather yins hands for ye." He looked embarrassed.

"I ain't sure neither," I said.

I took the bar of soap and washed my own hands.

I dropped the affect I'd adopted from the man. "That's a pretty big mane you got growin'. Any chance you were one of the Hill Boys?" I asked.

His face lit up. "Yessir. Final Wave. I's there when we took them north sentinels, then grabbed them towers back for're *damn* selves. How'ju know?" He handed me a towel to dry my hands with.

I lifted my shirt and showed the bullseye that had been carved into my ribs.

"Hot damn! Yins'a sniper?"

"No more," I said, embarrassed.

He grinned and came to a salute. "Ignus Hardesty. Pleasure, sir."

I saluted back. "At ease, Hardesty. Frank Attanasio, pleased to meet you. So, what's a pack-walloping Hillboy doin' in a penguin-suit shindig like this here?" I asked.

"Kin owns it," he replied, grinning wide to reveal a half-empty bottom row of teeth. "M'boy, if ya believe it."

"Anything's possible now."

Something glimmered in his eye. "That's what I say! Always done so. Always said it. Said it to m'boy his whole damn life. He owns it, this gin-joint. Put his old man in here. Me. Gave me an employment, what to keep me busy. He listened, see? Boy listened good, and here we is! Brung me here to work for'm. Yins cain't make up a story like that, can yins?"

"No, sir," I replied, handing him back the towel. "Well, Ignus, I'ma get out there and get my drink on."

"Yessir! Go on hav'n for me?"

"Shit, I'll have two for you."

He cackled at that. As I turned to walk out, he stopped me for a second. "Say, Frank. You brought a boy in here, wait on yins outside de bar?"

I'm sure I looked more confused than I felt. "No. No, I think I'd remember that. Ain't got no kin to myself, sir."

"Ah," he said. "Strange thing. Boy outside. I saw'm. Thought maybe could'a been yins kin. Maybe I go out and check on the boy."

I had a funny feeling. "You know what, Ignus? Why don't you hold down the fort? I was about to get some fresh air. I'll take a look."

"Good man. Nice meet'n yins."

"Likewise, Ignus. Don't let these youngins run you down, now."

"Nossir! Not me sir! Not so long as we got the longshot legends like yins comin' in."

I waved my hand behind me in as friendly a gesture as I could manage while walking away.

Back at the bar top, I collected my notebook and cup, put on my coat, and walked through the back to find the service exit. Outside, next to a great big pile of trash and broken bottles, I detected a barely visible figure hiding in the shadows, obscured by the now-manic snowfall.

I cupped my hands around my mouth. Make sure the little guy heard me through all the white noise. "Hey kid. Kid, you okay?"

The tiny figure was hobbling. I felt uneasy.

"Kid, you hurt or something?"

The kid came closer, their face obscured under a hooded sweatshirt. They hobbled in an odd asymmetrical shuffle, drawing nearer. I got a strange sense that they wanted to speak, but for some reason was reluctant to do so.

"Kid, it's alright," I said, showing my palms in the universal gesture of means-no-harm.

A glint of light, just a sliver that had miraculously peeked down through the snowy darkness, cut across his face. *Does he have a disease?* He was the same size as a large seven or eight-year-old, but his face was weathered—wrinkled, even—and it looked like he was in the habit of shaving. I felt uneasy again, and moved onto the back of my heels.

"Do you have the coins?" the kid asked.

No. No, he's no kid.

I reached into my pocket and gripped my tin cup. Between ReCo and the mayor, it seemed like a lot of folks were interested in Dreck, and now, maybe even interested in what he was carrying on his person—*was he a person?*—when he was gurneyed into the mortuary.

"You need change, kid?" I forced a collected, confident tone.

"No change," the figure said as he hobbled closer.

I noticed scars and knotted hands. Not a kid.

"I want the coins, you bastard bitch. You bitch bastard."

I gripped the tin cup tight in my hand. "I guess you're gonna have to come and get them, ya wee little fuck."

CHAPTER 15

Purgato's secret lab was dark as absence, where completeness was realized in the full sealing off of any light. The large room was dark in the sense of infinity, where comprehension of meaning is necessarily incomplete. The room was dark in the way of the mortal soul's forever night.

And then light. Brilliant, terrible light. Wide, looping arcs and orbits of neon red shining over the eyes and the Glasgow smile of Huey Purgato, making his teeth look larger and more curved than they were, blood-dripping from their very tips. Wide, looping arcs that turned his blue shirt a brilliant purple while glistening against his silk bowtie; looping arcs and orbits that turned fast. Purgato's disfigurations remained hidden, or at the least, barely discernible. Hematomas covered the mayor's body. The scales on his hands and neck were another almost-visible thing, along with slits of broken skin oozing fat and viscera between hair follicles.

Purgato held his hands out, and his wide calloused fingers appeared to stretch out—out into the air, sparking with brilliant red electricity, drawing his digits closer into the core of the orbiting energy that had coalesced into a sphere. An ooze—darker, shimmering, and more iridescent than blood—pushed out from the center of Purgato's skull and crept over his eyes, leaking from within.

The now-less-than-absolute darkness was sufficient to reveal a semi-spherical device of sorts that operated the electricity through an accelerator. The accelerator was open, of course, and the relentless energy pushed through—and pushed something *from*—Huey Purgato.

The electric fire oscillated, changing shades in a brisk overturn of red and violet. Purgato's skin hardened, his body lengthened so that his racked limbs stretched out beyond the cuffs of his shirt and the hemmed bottoms of his pants until he morphed into a dandyish version of an Appalachian hillbilly kid in too-short, hand-me-down bib-alls. The scales grew and his skin hardened. He transmuted further into a macabre porcelain doll.

The metamorphosis was quick and unflattering.

Vaporous streams of Purgato's person chipped and broke away from him. The sculpted texture of his new skin flaked off and flew into the nucleus of red electricity, combusting in a burst of flame.

Purgato's red eyes vaporized, and the porcelain flakes were sucked into the storm of electrical energy. Crimson blood leaked from his eyes and spiraled out in ruddy streams, spun around the pieces of him that broke away and disappeared into the igniting and reigniting core. Like a bone-chilling Cheshire cat at the end of his ninety-ninth life, that Glasgow's smile disappeared; and Purgato screamed in terror as a thousand-fold hastening of the process drew the rest of his transformed body into the sphere of red electricity.

CHAPTER 16

Back at Pop's, Lavalle was also in turmoil. His heart pounded so hard he was sure the pulsations were audible, even among the din of the barroom. A heartbeat that came in bursting echoes, with rhythms that ached his body and made his eyes warm and blurry. The burly bald bouncer who wore sweats and a wife-beater handed him a short glass with a straight no-rocks double-finger of bourbon.

"Go ahead, pal, drink." The big man smiled at him, probably thinking *poor guy's nervous*. "You'll be alright, buddy. This is supposed to be a good time. No reason to have a heart attack, am I right?"

Lavalle took the drink, with hands that trembled and teetered violently. Heart still pounding, he swirled the liquid, letting the bourbon play around in the lighted rim of the lens-glaring glass. The big man placed his hand at the bottom of Lavalle's beverage and gently pushed it up with his palm, the way a mother might reposition a formula bottle into the mouth of an infant whose motor skills weren't developed enough to grip the bottle itself.

As if to also lend a hand, the madam emerged. She parted opaque strands of beaded glass that resembled a starry curtain stretching from one wall to another. Lavalle drank deeply and sank back into a yellow-cushioned armchair. The madam had a well-practiced smile, a professional demeanor. And her name was Amie Lynn. Smiling Amie Lynn.

"Sweetheart, are you okay? You look a mess." Dressed in black and an off-white blouse, she looked more like an accountant, which she was. In a manner of speaking.

"I-I-I'm a little nervous," replied Lavalle in a choking voice.

Amie Lynn sat on the armrest of the overlarge cushioned chair Lavalle occupied. The bouncer, now smiling almost perpetually, also came in closer, but with an open, unassuming stance.

"Sweetheart, there is *no* reason for you to be nervous," Smiling Amie Lynn said.

"That's right," the bouncer added, "we're a friendly, non-judg-mental, have-it-your-way kind of place."

"Billy's right," Amie Lynn added.

Lavalle thought to himself, *Billy the Bouncer—well, that's kind of funny.*

Amie Lynn went on, "The worst-case scenario is that you ask for something and we say no. And let me tell you something, sugar: I've trained all these ladies myself. They are sensitive, they are caring, and they like their job. And if you don't like what you get, we gon' fix that, too."

Lavalle turned to Billy and asked, "Is that true?"

"Cross my heart," he said, drawing an X across his chest with his index finger.

"What does that mean?"

Amie Lynn and Billy started laughing. Amie Lynn said, "Boy, you *are* young. That's just something we used to say before the War, baby. Now…" she signaled Billy to go to the bar top and get the bottle to refill Lavalle's cup. "I think it's about time for you to stop sitting in the corner here like a Nervous Nelly, and time for you to take a look at some of the ladies."

Billy came over and poured Lavalle three fingers, then gently pushed the glass up to Lavalle's mouth in that same odd, maternal gesture. "Go ahead, buddy."

Lavalle downed the whole glass, nearly gagging. But his unmatched self-control in all things related to not losing face kicked in, and he kept the booze down. A warm wash came over him, and Lavalle managed not to slosh out his sick; he was able to experience the immensely satisfying—*relieving*—booze timebomb.

A procession of women sauntered out and stood in front of Lavalle. Twelve of them; three unnaturally, almost *perfectly* pretty —some in the nude, some wearing exotic lingerie, some wearing easily shed clothes.

Amie Lynn gave Lavalle the lowdown: "Now, you can pick whoever you want, but if you let me know what you like, we can go ahead and narrow it down for you. Choice is yours."

Lavalle looked to Amie Lynn, then at the line of preening girls, letting his gaze drop to the floor. It was not a nod of inebriation, but one of liquid resolve. He blurted out louder than he intended:

"Feet."

CHAPTER 17

"**Y**ou bastard bitch. Bitch of a bastard!"

"You dirty little fuck!" I responded.

The guy was strong. He may have looked like a toddler-aged gimp, but when he got ahold of me, I felt his strength in the steely stone-like quality of his arms when they locked painfully against my shoulder and collarbone—uncomfortably close to my neck. If he'd had even the slightest inkling of martial knowledge, I would have been wrapped up, choked out, and maybe had my head caved in. As it was, I barely managed to keep him in a guard position.

It was the oddest thing—the wee little fuck wouldn't hit me. There was something about him, too, showing some reluctance, as though he were operating through some outside agency and not on account of his own desire. Such as the situation was, I returned the favor and neglected to bash the grubby little imposter. *Pretending to be a child? Is there no end to the lowness of low-stature people?* My tin cup hung from my thumb.

Then, with a sudden viciousness, the little fucker got a grip around my whole left arm and crossed his legs over it. The legs went over my torso, pressing down to anchor him onto my chest and stomach—then he ripped backwards in a single fluid, unstoppable motion. The bones in my left arm splintered—I could hear them—and he leapt off. I screamed. The little fucker fucking got me.

He headed to my other arm. *Well, one good turn deserves another.* I finally permitted myself the luxury of fighting dirty—*like an animal*—and I kicked him as hard as I could right in the nose. He staggered back, still hobbling, then wobbling like a whirling top. When he was far back on his heels, I speared him—shoulders forward, head tucked down, neck stiffened—and tried to grip his nuts with my right hand. To no avail. *The little fucker didn't have any nuts.*

Nevertheless, he was reeling.

Once he was on the ground, I trudged through the thick blanket of snow and bit him on the forehead, tearing off a chunk of flesh, leaving him bleeding and panicking. I flipped my tin cup from my thumb into the full grip of my palm, and with my cupped hand, I brought it down as hard as I could, edge-first, right into the bite wound on his head. This pain was clearly unfamiliar to him. He was so bewildered by it, that he seemed to go full possum. I stood and looked around to see if anyone had witnessed our tussle.

Snow, gentle and ruthless snow. The pure white drifts were disrupted with heavy footprints and smatterings of red and pink. Standing over the unmoving body of the deformed midget, I had the unfortunate problem of looking like an adult who'd just murdered a kid.

I stood there, almost hyperventilating.

The cold air heaving in and out of my warm, wet lungs was sharp and painful, and after so many minutes of this, there was a gnawing ache in my chest. I don't know how long I stood there, but as the adrenaline wound down, I realized my arm hurt like a motherfucker; it wasn't quite hanging, but it was a compound fracture. There weren't exactly hospitals set up yet—a funny thing, since I never had any trouble finding a decent medic in the field. One of the benefits of a total war executed on a global scale is that even the physicians fight at your side.

"Fuck. Fuckin' *fuck*," I muttered to myself, wondering what the hell to do next.

With all the mercy I could summon from my frozen frame, I settled on a course of action just a notch above abandoning the little fucker. Going into Samaritan mode, I drew his hoodie over his head, picked him up—*unbelievable, he's so light. How was he so strong?*—and carried him hitched to my hip, with his head leaned against my shoulder, and my arm around him like I was carrying a sleeping toddler.

CHAPTER 18

Still lugging my fugazi youngin' at my hip, I managed to walk through the alleyway and back to the triangle out in front of the mortuary. When I got closer to the entrance, I ran into a small group of kids (well, they were much younger than me. Teenagers, young adults, what-have-you—but to me they were kids) waiting outside.

"Good morning!" one of them called out.

The kid was wearing a winter jacket and had a bone through his nose. He had tattooed eyelids, tattooed lips, tattooed ears. He looked like one of those old out-of-date maps that the military issued to us when we were in the middle of urban warfare. But the maps were more reliable; any computer database showing city routes was either hacked or just as wrong. Funny how old-fashioned cartography made a comeback that way.

"Morning?" I said weakly. *What the fuck time is it anyway?*

I looked up into the sky. The snow was still coming down furiously. We were standing in it up to our knees.

"Yes indeed-a-lee-doo. It's the morning. Sir, may I ask you, do you happen to be the proprietor of this here death establishment?"

"This here—what?" I shuffled my hip to rebalance myself and secure the little fuck's position on my body.

"Oh, what a cutie!" a woman with two small twigs stuck through her eyebrows yelled out. She had brandmarks all over her body and tattoos on the melted, smudged skin. "How old's your little guy?"

"What the fuck are you talking about?" I asked. *You're carrying a "child," remember? Oh yeah.* "Oh, him. Yeah, he's pooped," I added. "We're just coming back from—" *Don't explain yourself. Lies are the holes that dig themselves. Just get inside.* "Can I help you with something?"

"Absotively posilutely!" the bone-nose cut back in.

About a dozen other freakshow faces stood behind Bone-Nose and Bark-Brows. They didn't look as friendly as their two frontmen.

Bone-Nose continued, "Anyhow, we heard that you might be the guy who's taking care of Dreck's body. We're not going to beat around the bush... we'd really like to see his body. To pay him our proper respects."

My arm was throbbing. Every red rhythmic beat of my heart sent a shocking, unbearable pain through my left arm. It was like my nerves were being stabbed with pieces of broken glass coated in acid.

"Listen, guys," I said, "this really isn't the best time. I've really got to get the... uh, little guy to bed."

"Oh, of *course!*" Bark-Brows enthusiastically responded. "Why don't you go ahead and get settled in with your baby boy, and we'll just knock on the door when you've had a little rest?"

She reached for his hood; I was worried—rightly, I thought—that she'd pull it back.

"How old is the little feller?"

I pulled back in a jump. "Uh... he's, uh—he's seven?" *What the fuck do I know? I never had kids. I don't know how big they are at what age. I'm not some kid-stat-tracking perv who gets my rocks off knowing how tall a kindergartner is.*

"Wow. He sure is big for a seven-year-old!" Bone-Nose chimed in.

"Yeah, I guess so." I pulled my key-loop from my pocket and opened the door. "Well, I'll let yins know when, you know... whatever."

I went inside and tried to pull the door shut in an awkward clutching motion, attempting to extend my fingers and shut the door without having the little fuck blocking it. It was hard enough to even open the door with the snow acting as ballast against it. When I'd finally managed to get the door almost closed, Bark-Brows stuck her foot in and blocked it from fully closing.

She said, "I was just wondering, Mr. Mortuary; when should we give you a holler?"

There was no way I could hold off more than two, maybe three of the freaks. I decided some prevarication was in order. "I'll just get some sleep and then probably open in the early evening. Strange hours, you know? Being the business I'm in."

She smiled. But this smile was more like a malevolent, snotty little smirk. "Well, can we give you some literature?"

Oh fuck, here it comes. "Uh, sure."

She held up a pamphlet with boldface type across the top: *THE CHILDREN OF DRECK AND THE PROPHECY OF GOOD TIMES.*

"Thanks, miss," I said.

She looked like she was plotting. Maybe she wanted to bum-rush me right there—who would've stopped her, and who would've come to my rescue, the snowstorm being what it was? Then a tiny falsetto voice cut through the quiet and the rolling clouds of storm.

"Daddy, I'm tired, can I go to bed?"

That little fuck.

Bark-Brows took her foot out of the door and gave what seemed like a mocking salute. "Have a good evening, Mr. Mortuary. We'll see you later. Good night."

"I thought it was morning?" I muttered.

As the door closed, her muffled voice sounded through the

glass. "It is the morning. But we're at the beginning of The Long Night."

CHAPTER 19

We were both sitting—me on my swivel chair and the little fuck on the milk crates next to my desk. He looked comical with his legs swinging above the ground. I'd given him a bag of ice to put on his head—the dumb-fuck tried to eat the ice before I told him it was better to press it against his forehead. We'd been sharing a bottle of shine between us, sitting in hostile silence.

"You know, you're a bitch bastard. You—you *fuck*."

We looked at one another and busted up laughing.

"Oh, Jesus, my arm," I howled like a fool, a mixture of delight and unbearable pain.

"You should fix that."

"How? It's a snowstorm. The biggest one I've ever seen."

He cocked an eyebrow and looked up at me from under the icepack. "It's not a snowstorm."

I drank deeply again and gestured to the door with my good arm. "Oh, no? Then how comes it's snowin'?"

"It's snowing, yeah. But it's not a snowstorm. Have you ever seen a snowstorm like this?"

"No," I answered.

"Think of it like this. Is an ocean wave the same as a tsunami?"

"No. No, I s'pose they're different."

"Right. And are they caused by the same thing?"

I thought on it for a moment; I vaguely recalled that my child-self had learned these things in school, but I couldn't bring up the actual facts. "I don't think so."

The little fuck was a genius nerd, too.

"The ocean waves are drawn along by the gravitational pull of the moon. A tsunami comes from a rift in the ocean floor. Two different things."

"Okay."

"Yeah, so what's going on outside isn't caused by the same thing that brings snow, or even a great blizzard. Two different causes, two different things. That isn't a snowstorm outside."

If it were any other time, I would have argued back, but given the strange circumstances of the last few days—*were they days?*—I believed him.

"What's the cause, then?"

He looked at my arm. "We ought to fix that."

"How? Ain't no hospital open. Ain't no hospitals nowhere."

Diglossia. Sign of the times.

"Show me the coins."

I laughed then looked at my flappity arm, attempting to lift it. "Fuck no, you little fuck."

"My name isn't *Little Fuck*!"

"Fine, what's your name?"

He sighed. "It's… you're going to just absolutely love this. It's Truculento-Jeffersaint."

I had an incredible urge to start laughing, but I stifled it. "It's a fine name." I held out my right hand. "Frank Attanasio. You can call me Frankie."

"I can?" he asked.

"Sure. I'm not a big fan of Frank. I prefer Frankie."

I sensed movement in the cognitive gears rolling behind the little man's eyes—a tiny idea birthed. His crinkled forehead read *eureka.*

"Well, then you can call me... Truckie. Yeah. Truckie. That's better."

I smiled. "Truckie—I like that."

Truckie smiled back. Somehow, I got the sense that he didn't have many moments like these, *nice* moments.

"Frankie, I'm old and I'm tired. I don't lie. I just don't lie, because lying is for bitch bastards and bastard bitches. You show me those coins, and I'll fix your arm so it ain't looking broken like it's looking right now."

I poured myself another drink and tilted the bottle toward him. He nodded and I poured him another glass too. We brought our cups together in a tinny *clink* and drank down another round.

"Fuck it," I said. "I don't know what I'm fightin' for anyhow. But you're going to have to fill in some of the blanks. I need—or I guess I want—to know what's going on."

"I accept your terms, Frankie."

"Good to hear it, Truckie."

We both smiled. I reached for the bag in my coat pocket.

But the coins were gone.

INTERLUDE

The last battle of The Long War occurred generations after the newest millennium, in the Levant, very close to what used to be Turkey. The site rested atop ruins from before antiquity, a place where the rock face was carved up into disfigurement by untold centuries of fire, ordnance, and munitions. Pillars and natural rock formations—like blocky stones teetering on stilts—surrounded the ruins. It had been a Necropolis before, and during the final battle, it became a Necropolis again.

Frankie was feeling dizzy—not the light-headed kind you feel when you stand up quickly, but the amorphous gut-fluttering feeling you get when you feel truly disoriented, mythless, unable to find your place on the cosmic timeline. He was never much of a historian, but he craved grounding at that moment, hoping to grasp at some shards of fact that would anchor him in the moment. He stumbled around the mortuary, trying to find any old records that would help jog his memory—hell, create his memory. At the bottom of one of the file drawers he found a transcript. It was, apparently, the inaugural address of one of the first leaders who tried to glue together the shattered debris of history right after the end of the War. It was ominously titled, "A Foundational Manifesto After Blood and Warfare." He read.

Mathematical plotting — logistics, coor-
dination, census-taking, and ration-
dispensing — was the sort of orderly
process that always followed blood and
warfare. Its disjunction with the irra-
tional animal orgy that preceded these
calculations caused a dissonance in the
soldier's mind. The higher-ups decided
that the party was over; now it was *time
to clean up the mess*. A foul mood—resentment at the check-listing done in the
wake of victory came over the men. An
opaque darkness descended, one whose
reactive counterpoints lay dormant in the
hearts of all sons of men, waiting until
that time where their ire should be made
to ignite.

Despite the animus, tranquility had — for
the most part — taken hold. The men were
nourishing their aches with their
morphine drips and healing their hunger
with crème eggs. There had been a serene,
nearly inaudible noise radiating
throughout the littered sands of the
ancient Necropolis newly replenished —
with blood.

Then the tranquility was broken.

That calming transmission was undone by
the last gasp of devilry that had desperately clawed its way back into the world.
Crying for apocalypse, crying for the

shattered bones and flayed corpses of
warfare.

Man is a damn fool. He looks to the stars
to find G-d. Foregoing a glance inward.
He sees no Devil. Man sees no Devil in
his heart because he does not see G-d
there. There is a circuitry of soul that
runs its wiring and hums a melody of
microscopic complication. The darkness is
there, too. And for those lucky few, G-d
is there. Waiting to be found. What those
men saw — and, preceding what they saw,
the mood that descended upon them — was
catalyst enough for hatred, for permanent
hatred.

Then came the Apparition of the Door, a
tear in the cosmic fabric that shook the
surviving troops to the core.

The men were lazing about, some reclining
on chairs, others perched on flat-topped
stones, others still on their backs with
their necks on their rucksacks. And there
it was. A door.

The door appeared in the open space
between where the dead — thousands and
thousands — were gathered before burial
even as the officers debated the appro-
priateness of mass graves.

The darkness grew in pitch.

In a bizarre reenactment of the Sword in the Stone, one soldier after the other tried to open the door. But none could breach the apparitional gateway.

The first offender, a young marine — handsome, wiry, flush of fortitude — watched as necrosis took over his entire being. His skin burst, and the young marine fell to the ground, lifeless and ruptured. A dim halo of blue-green electricity lapped outward from the door, encircling the dead marine.

The other six who had participated in what they thought to be a feat of strength — attempting to pry open the impossible handle — now looked to each other for answers. Not just answers as to what had happened to their comrade, but their own fates as well. They watched with wide eyes as the fast routing cancerous, rotting veins pierced their now paper-thin skin. Before the whites of their eyes could return to their natural position, each soldier fell. Bodies thudded against the ground in the same order in which they had pulled on the door. The question of their fate was answered only to those living on the sidelines, watching the seven men fall to oblivion.

The darkness grew in pitch.

When the last man fell, the blue-green
electricity had extended its outer rim
beyond the bodies of the seven fallen
soldiers. In desperation, the officers
decided to deploy a bomb-squad robot.
After a few yards' trek, the robot
imploded. The implosion built into a
globular, fiery reaction, suspended in
the air like a small planet. The fiery
globe burst, spreading its energy into
the outer rim of the killing fields where
lay the thousands and thousands of dead
soldiers.

The darkness had found its pitch.

Over the next few days a convective anger
was palpable, one that cooked the sullen
hearts of the survivors. The men seethed
because they could no longer collect the
bodies of their comrades, could no longer
gather even a scrap of burnt flesh for
their memorials.

It was then that the door opened.

It was then that Dreck walked through.

In all his otherworldly anatomy, antlered
with his strange skin and his stranger
face, with his piercing, fiery blue orbit
eyes beneath a sunken brow, stepped out
into the world. Dreck walked through in
all his armageddonic glory. He stopped
and looked around for a moment. He turned

around and walked right back through the
door.

It was at that moment of utter silence
and suspended animation and wild surmise
that most, if not all, of humankind
decided that they hated Dreck, this odd,
monstrous, unknowable Dreck.

Instead of returning the inaugural address to the archival security of his filing cabinet, Frankie methodically tore up the yellowing papers, fully aware that he was destroying one of his last lifelines to the timeline of history.

CHAPTER 20

Insanity filled the air surrounding Seven Points. The unprecedented storm had bathed the district in the permanent gloom of a winter twilight—and the blizzard was just the backdrop. What was more insane was that those concerned with Dreck's demise, those who stood—in all their exposure to the elements—entirely ignored the atmosphere.

Another night of insanity meant that a clattering gathering of kooks and soapbox preachers, screechers and freaky creatures, had assembled outside the mortuary. Many had set up tents, the walls of which were already sunken into several feet of the drifts, their zip-open flaps allowing snow to tumble in every time someone entered or left.

The throng was a medieval jumble of sages and fools. Bone-Nose and Bark-Brows (and their assembled adherents) sat under a tarp on stilts, which they'd nailed into the ground far below the snow. Nearby sat the Assembled Chorus of Glory: a Mormonesque sect of Manicheans who followed Zoroaster but modified their lore of the battle between light and dark to accommodate the latter-day sanctification of Joseph Smith. The ACG had put up a blue-and-white striped carnival tent, full of knicks and knacks and salty snacks—even a functional grill. Then there was a circle of small, armored transports—the Crushers, the sort 86 had used to drive Lavalle to Pop's. In these vehicles, Mayor Huey Purgato's men sat in silence, occasionally checking their radios. Some of his friendlier goons would even walk over and chat up the bone-nosed freaks or beg for food from the Assembled Chorus of Glory.

Finally, there were the True Hebrews.

The True Hebrews hailed from what used to be New York, where once upon a time their forebears had started a neo-Israelite movement out of Harlem, claiming that they were the true heirs; they opposed the antiquated "wrongheaded rabbinic tradition." The take-no-shelter True Hebrews looked surreal amid the storm: huge curly beards dusted with snowflakes, brightly colored gowns, and cassocks stained at the bottoms with street slush.

Then there were the loons and the loudmouths who commandeered the three soapboxes set up in another circle near the Crushers. Bone-Nose stood on one, shaking his group's pamphlet. A young man in a winter coat, wearing starched slacks and galoshes underneath, stood on another soapbox, waving the Holy Book for the Assembled Chorus of Glory, titled "Eight Things You Should Know About the Battle Between the Good Forces of Light and the Unholy Assholes of Darkness." Next to him, the shortest of the True Hebrews stood on a crate waving a gold-tinfoil-wrapped scepter with a few pieces of colored glass (from broken bottles) glued to the end.

And the True Hebrews loudly demanded their pound of flesh, in the form of Dreck.

Their tiny spokesperson called out through the sheets of snowflakes and howling winds "Brothers and sisters, we, the True Hebrews, the Israelites of the Not-Fake Davidic Lineage, call upon the proprietor of this House of Death to grant us the body of the one called Dreck! Our Chevra Kachonga—the holiest burial society—will ensure that his corpse is treated according to the laws of our people. We will take his antlers, and we will coat them in beeswax, according to the laws of our people. We will clip his toenails and polish them with butter or some other buttery stuff, according to the laws of our people. And we will put on him a pair of really neat sunglasses—I mean, the ones I got in mind are pretty cool—according to the laws of our people."

Without a beat, the clean-cut guy from the Assembled Chorus of Glory cut in, screeching, "Those laws are false! Those laws are the false laws of charlatans and hoodwinkers!"

"Man, you better watch who you callin' a hoodwinker," the True Hebrew responded.

"I'm calling *you* a hoodwinker, you hoodwinker."

"Oh, *I'm* the hoodwinker? Man, you out here talkin' your ACG nonsense, about how Joseph Smith is wielding the light plate to destroy the plate of darkness. What the hell do dinnerware have to do with the apocalypse?"

The Mormon-Manichean gasped in an overdramatic manner, placing his hand over his heart. "Blasphemy!"

"Well, what kind of dinnerware are we talkin' about?" interrupted one of the handsomer goons from Purgato's crew; holding a Styrofoam plate groaning with starches and an overcooked piece of poultry.

"Uh, well," the young Mormon-Manichean responded, "plates that have gold around the edge."

"Really?" the handsome goon replied. "What kind of gold?"

"Why, the finest gold. Like, the kind of gold you've never seen before. Have you ever seen the gold chains that professional basketball players used to wear when there was still sports?"

"Sure," the goon responded. "That's some pretty nice gold."

"Well, Joseph Smith's gold was even nicer than that. And it was *future* gold."

"Future gold?" the goon asked.

By now, the Mormon-Manichean had relaxed his posture. "Well, it's like, you know, like gold where you can see into the future. See, the details of what happens in the future is, like, you know, etched into the plate. But not permanently. But only our High Priest can see the future writing."

The goon looked interested. "Wow. That's actually pretty cool. You got any literature?"

The young clean-cut proselytizer handed the goon a copy of their Holy Book while shooting the tiny True Hebrew a mocking glance.

"That's bullshit," the tiny True Hebrew interjected. His mouth puckered into the firm shape of a butthole, and he crossed his arms over his chest.

"Ignore him," the clean-cut man said to the goon. "You just go ahead and read that book and have all the food you want. We're happy to have you."

"Hey, pretty cool," the goon said, walking away.

"That's bullshit," the tiny and persistent True Hebrew yelled. "Golden calf bullshit."

"Hey Jimmy," the goon yelled to another henchman, who was smoking a cigarette outside one of the Crushers, "I got a free book and some chicken." Then he whispered to himself, "I think I might be into this Joseph Smith guy."

The tiny True Hebrew turned to the larger co-religionist next to him and held out a hand proclaiming; "Urethreus, my Flask of Truth." The giant True Hebrew handed a flask to his smaller counterpart who, with much ceremony, drank it down.

"What's that?" one of the pagans asked.

"It's my Flask of Truth," the tiny True Hebrew replied.

"It smells like Schnapps—"

"Well, it's not," interrupted the bigger one.

"But it smells like—"

"It's not Schnapps!" the massive, True Hebrew repeated.

The young clean-cut Mormon-Manichean cut back in with a censorious, "We don't allow our followers to drink alcohol. It's just one of the many tools of the Followers of Darkness, meant to dull the senses and pervert the soul."

"Yeah, well one of our illustrious Rabbis once said: 'Alcohol gives you infinite patience for stupidity.' And now, my Mormon friend, I feel I have a little more patience for you," The tiny True Hebrew said.

"Pfft," the young Mormon-Manichean replied.

"Hey, which Rabbi said that?" a random voice called out. It came from the small crowd that had lined up for handouts from the Assembled Chorus of Glory tent.

The tiny True Hebrew's eyes lit up. Turning his hands upward and looking to the sky, he proclaimed, "Why, that's a saying by one of our wisest, sharpest, most incisive theological Israelite minds. 'Tis the wisdom of Rabbi Samuel Davis Jr."

"Cool," the random voice answered. "Who was he?"

"Come close, and I will tell you his story—the story of Rabbi Samuel Davis Jr."

The fifteen-year-old (to whom the inquiring voice belonged) huddled in with two of his friends. They passed a joint between them as the tiny True Hebrew muttered to his larger counterpart, "Urethreus, go forth to the Storage Shed of Sanctity and retrieve several thrones."

"Thrones?" the big man replied.

The tiny one whispered back, "Bring out a couple of folding chairs."

"Yep. You got it, boss."

"Now, where was I?" the tiny one continued. "Ah, yes! The story of the Great and Wise Rabbi Samuel Davis Junior. Rav Shmeuli Davis was born in the Land of Har-Lem. He had a voice as sweet as honey, as pleasant as the summer wind, and as precious as gold."

"Gold?" the handsome goon called out from the circle of attack vehicles.

"Yes, my friend, *gold.*"

"Jimmy, hold my plate," the handsome goon said as he passed off his dinner to another henchman. "I'm gonna go listen to this."

"The golden-voiced boy from the Land of Har-Lem came upon another man. And that man's name was Sin of Atra."

"Was he called Sin because he was a sinner?" An elderly

woman asked. She was calling down from her open window, only a floor above. The tiny True Hebrew looked up to her and continued. "No. *Sin*, in Sin of Atra's language, meant something else."

"What did it mean?" the woman asked.

"Frank."

"Well, why don't you just say Frank?"

"Are you telling the story, or am I?"

"I'm just sayin'. It'd be easier to follow if you called him Frank of Atra."

"Fine. Fine. Rav Shmeuli Davis came upon Frank of Atra, and Frank said to him, 'Alcohol may be man's worst enemy, but the Bible says love your enemy.' And so Shmeuli Davis knew then that Frank of Atra was a wise man. And so, Shmeuli Davis followed Frank of Atra to the Land of Nev-Ada. Nev-Ada was a land of great lights and greater monuments. You could walk into any building and get a free drink, as long as you put a coin inside of a machine."

"Were the coins expensive?" one of the fifteen-year-olds asked.

"No! That's the funny thing. The coins were cheap, and once you put them in the machines, beautiful women in shimmering beads and colorful feathers brought you as many drinks as you wanted, as long as you kept putting the coins in the machine."

"Wow!"

"Yes, my son. Truly, Nev-Ada was a holy place. And Shmeuli Davis didst follow his brother in faith, Frank of Atra, as they wandered out to the desert land of Nev-Ada. And together, along with their good friend Brother Martin of Dean, they formed the Packrats."

"Why were they called that?" someone else asked.

The tiny True Hebrew smiled. "They were called that because even though they lived in Nev-Ada, a land of plenty, the land of beaded gowns and happy clowns, they still valued everything they received. So, they always kept more than they lost, even at the machines. And so, they were called the Packrats."

The big True Hebrew trundled back from the Storage Shed of

Sanctity, his huge legs pushing through snow masses with some effort. He set down about a dozen folding chairs, pushing them one by one into the drifts—they sunk in so deep that only the seats and seat backs were visible. The big True Hebrew went to each spectator and handed them a few pieces of candy as the tiny one explained, "What Brother Urethreus is doing right now is a very old Jewish tradition. One of our synagogue members hands out candy during the Rabbi's sermon."

"What happened?" one of the kids asked. "What happened with Rabbi Davis?"

"Ah, yes, of course. Well, you see, The Packrats had become the rulers over the Land of Nev-Ada. And they were kind and benevolent rulers. Their laws, truly, were gifted to them from the Lord Himself. And the wisdom of the law, carried out in a melody sung by Rabbi Shmeuli, and Frank of Atra, and Brother Martin of Dean, was a sweet song that kept their great kingdom in order."

"Tell us!" one boy cried out. Another added, "Yeah, sing it out."

"Verily, I say unto thee: 'May I say with pride where I reside.' Meaning that you should always be proud of where you're from. Verily, I say unto thee: 'I've gotta be me, I've gotta be me. What else can I be but what I am?' Meaning that you should always be proud of who you are. Verily, I say unto thee: 'A lady doesn't wander all over the room. And blow on some other guy's dice.' The meaning of this has been obscured through the ages. Only our greatest rabbinic scholars can decipher its meaning."

"Yeah, well, we've got some good singers too," the clean-cut Mormon-Manichean said.

"Funny you should mention that, because Brother Martin of Dean anticipated it in a prophecy, saying about his fellow Packrats: 'They make the Mormon Tabernacle sound like a trio.'" The tiny True Hebrew smiled.

"Blasphemy!" said the red-faced Mormon-Manichean, as the tiny Israelite went on.

"But as is the case with so many of the Lord's greatest

Prophets—Jeremiah, Ezekiel, Chaka Khan—tragedy befell Rav Shmeuli Davis Jr."

Murmurs arose from the crowd. A whimper of *no* seemed to come from the group of teenagers.

"Yes, it's true. One day, Rav Shmeuli Davis Jr. was driving in his chariot, and the wheel of the chariot had a stick cast in its spokes by some loathsome malefactor."

"Was he okay?" the old woman shouted down from the window. Even the handsome goon whispered to himself, "Please say he was okay."

The tiny True Hebrew allowed for a pregnant pause, then continued. "But the Lord, finding that Rabbi Samuel Davis Jr.'s ways were pleasant, that his songs were true, and that he was a light unto his people, granted Shmeuli his life. He survived the wrecking of his chariot, and he and the Packrats let the people of Nev-Ada into a Golden Age of bliss and true worship. And that, my friends, is the story of Rabbi Samuel Davis Jr."

The tiny True Hebrew stepped down from his soapbox, then added a postscript. "But now, my friends, I have grown weary from transmitting the oral tradition. I must go home and see my baby-mama, where she will transmit her very own oral tradition unto me."

The fifteen-year-old moved away from his friends and shook his head. He approached a soap box and spoke; "It's all wrong. All of you, are here to take this body, right? And you're all fighting over it. Maybe we could all work together for a solution?"

The crowd groaned in disapproval, until Bone-Nose stood high on his own soapbox and yelled out, "Who wants to hear the story of the Grave Digger and the Valley of the Voodoo Dolls?"

A cheer of approval rang through the air, and the next round of tale-bearing began.

CHAPTER 21

W e had been mucking through the sewers for a while now, despite my initial hesitation about following Truckie down the rabbit hole—and who could blame me? Though my arm was in a makeshift sling, I still followed the little guy down into the sewers.

Truckie was clearly a resourceful little feller. We'd been trekking under Seven Points for an hour—maybe longer, I was losing track of time—until we made it to an exit that opened up into a harbor next to an abandoned bridge. For a minute, I thought it was a trap; that is, until Truckie opened a dimly lit mineshaft that looked as if it had been abandoned eons ago. I asked him, "Is it dangerous in here?" And he'd responded, "Oh yes, very dangerous. This tunnel is a bastard of a bitch—bitch of a bastard. Could explode, could cave in."

Not reassuring. But at least he was honest.

In the next couple of hours, I saw some pretty neat things. I imagine Truckie had no idea of his own genius. He had constructed a maze of private municipal mansion-works beneath Seven Points, and most of the caverns and crevices we wended through were sophisticated and interesting enough to belong in a museum.

"It belongs in a museum!" The old half-priest at the mortuary school used to shout that out and then laugh. I think it was a line from a movie he liked.

For starters, there was a room filled with perpetual motion machines. Truckie said, "This is where I develop." To him, *develop* meant something like *exercise*. When we were in that room, he opened an exit door that must have weighed a few tons—I couldn't even get the thing to budge. Not even a little bit. Then there was the "inspection room" that housed all kinds of microscopes—even an atomic one.

The coolest place, though, was something like an amphitheater with Tesla coils arrayed all around it—a great, big, brass cage with electro-magnetic anchoring points that housed wild arms of frenzied electricity thrashing between the great machines. He wanted to rush through, apparently unaware of how remarkable—shit, even *beautiful*—his handiworks were. "Wow. What the fuck is this?" I asked.

"Oh, that? That's just the power plant. Means we're getting close."

My cautious side kept reminding me that I should hate this little freak. But everything I saw and felt made me admire the hell out of him.

We stopped in a giant cavern with intersecting sewer sluices. Here, Truckie turned toward me.

"Okay, Frankie. You're about to come into our home. There's a couple rules you ought to know."

I looked around and thought to myself about the million-billion little paramecia that were probably crawling, shit-stained and infectious, into my broken arm. *Fuck it. No reason to stop now.* "You got it. Shoot, Truckie."

"Okay. Okay..." he said, his eyes roaming like he was trying to spot his thoughts littered on the ground, planning a way to gather them all up.

"Okay. Rule number one: Any garbage you find that seems valuable has to go through sorting. Some people need some garbage more than others, and so we give out garbage on a need-to-use basis."

The concept of valuable garbage seemed counterintuitive, but I went along with the whole thing. "Uh-huh. I see."

"Yeah, that's right. Share the garbage. And have it *cleared* before you claim it. Let me hear you say that—good way to remember rule number one."

"Umm... share the garbage?"

Truckie shook his head. "No, not that. The last part," he said patiently, like a mother teaching a child their ABCs.

"I don't remember."

"For bitch-bastard's sake, Frankie! Clear it before you claim it."

"Clear it before you claim it. Got it."

"Good, good," he said, nervously rubbing his arms and, disconcertingly, picking at the wound on his forehead.

"Rule number two: if you feel the need to practice grappling, you are encouraged to invite a friend."

"What do you mean 'practice grappling'? Like jiu-jitsu?"

"No, no. Well, no, I don't think so. It's like... hmm."

Truckie looked around until he found a piece of PVC pipe. He held the pipe in front of his groin and started moving his other hand up and down over it.

"Gross! Absolutely not. I'm not jerking off with anybody."

"Alright, alright. Fair enough. That one's more discretionary than it is mandatory. Okay, let me see... other important rules? Oh, yes, of course. Rule number three: all outsiders must sit at the Tribunal of Praxis Inquiry once during their visit—twice is preferable, though."

"What's the—what'd you call it?"

"The Tribunal of Praxis Inquiry."

"Yeah, that. What's that?"

"The Tribunal of Praxis Inquiry is a forum for discovery and explanation of the facets of the land-cities that are misunderstood by, or unknown to, the denizens of the city below. The seated Master of Tribunal is asked to speak frankly, openly, and most importantly, *honestly*, regarding matters of inquiry put to shim."

"Shim?"

"Him or her."

"Ah. Gotcha." It sounded like Truckie had that spiel memorized. He looked at me nervously—must have been anticipating another *negatory*. "Yeah, sure. That's fine."

"Great! Great, that's so great. Anyhow, the other rules are sort of play-it-as-it-lays. Okay, you ready?"

"I guess so."

"Here we go," he said as he spun a huge wheel on another massive door. "Welcome to Ulala."

As I was contemplating the vast expanse of Ulala, I sank into a state of wild surmise. *Where did I hear that before? Aha, Keats. "On First Looking into Chapman's Homer." Geez, sometimes you never forget your high school literature.*

Even in that wild surmise I could make out voices in the void. It was Truckie talking to GHB—the first Ulalandian Truckie had introduced me to—over the ether. I was surprised you could still beam voices down in the underworld. It sounded like those two—Truckie and GHB—were in charge down here.

I felt like an eavesdropper, so I kinda wandered around, trying to make sure that if I found valuable garbage, it made its way to the sorting department.

The blonde woman had gotten her hands on the coins. She had watched Frank Attanasio at the hoity-toity bar where he'd gone over to drink. She surveyed him intently as he wrestled with the small childlike man out in the alleyway, then she surreptitiously picked up the purple velvet bag Frank dropped and slipped the coins inside the pocket of her black winter coat.

She followed them on their return to the mortuary. After they left, she found her way inside, using tools that she had at her disposal.

Once inside, the blonde woman ran her long, slender fingers over the desk and the objects on the desk: a little trifling thing here and a dusty old file there. When she finally located the false compartment where Frank Attanasio hid things, she placed the coins back where she assumed they belonged. Then she picked another lock and crossed to the other side of the barrier separating the cold room from the rest of the mortuary. She sat beside the slab and grasped Dreck's lifeless hand. She held his hands in her own and pressed her face against them. Her sadness was quiet at first, but her weeping slowly grew louder until she was sobbing, her shoulders shaking, her stomach flexing.

She stayed there, weeping loudly, for several minutes. Then she left. The coins remained hidden inside Frank Attanasio's desk, in the secret compartment.

CHAPTER 22

GHB stroked his unkempt facial hair. "You lost them? What do you mean you *lost* them?"

"I didn't know I wouldn't be able to take him. He's more able than he appears to be," Truckie replied.

"Well, I certainly hope it was *you* who gave him the broken arm. It wouldn't speak much to your abilities if he had that break and still beat you."

Truckie rolled his eyes. "Yes, I broke his arm. His arm wasn't broken beforehand."

"Good, good. That's important. As I have often said, it is better to break an arm than to have one broken."

I don't think I've ever heard him say that, Truckie thought to himself. "So, what should we do?"

GHB didn't answer Truckie's question. Some time ago, shortly after GHB was born, Truckie took care of their now-leader and reared him. But now Truckie felt tired, worn. His nursemaid days were over.

GHB wasn't like the other waifs Truckie had rescued. He had spent years finding abandoned children and bringing them home. Most of them had been born to unwed mothers out in the wilds of

Pennsylvania and West Virginia. GHB, though, Truckie found him in a field.

By appearances GHB was neither deformed nor especially gifted in some physical manner, like the others were. He was a sexagenarian and looked it. All the other children (as Truckie had dubbed them) appeared ageless. Not that they were *immortal*, as such; but slow to age, in a way that would have been unfathomable before The Long War. It was impossible to tell exactly how old many of them were, short of carbon-dating them. Maybe that's why they all listened to GHB: Because he *looked* older. Or maybe it was because he looked *normal*. Not that the children even knew what normal looked like, really. But they'd seen enough in trashed books, albums, and magazines to understand that the people who lived above ground had a slightly more pleasing personal aesthetic.

The ultimate goal was for the *children* to find *the father*. And they were on the cusp. Now was no time to go fiddling with the hierarchy. *You didn't scrap the playbook at the very end of the game,* Truckie mused. Truckie had never seen a professional sports game. The only athletic enterprise he'd participated in was that brute show of functionalism: strongman. But that was a long time ago. Such a long time that he wasn't certain it had happened, despite his vast store of memory.

It was all related to the mnemonics that started taking hold after The Long War. But also, to Truckie's prowess: in the old days they would have said he had a photographic memory. Thus, in that mnemonic edifice that towered over the rest of Truckie's mental architecture, he was endowed with a filmic catalogue that maintained the clarity of images and the archiving of knowledge without losing an iota of detail. He was different from the other children: shorter, smarter, angrier, more loving, self-loathing, and deliriously happy. These qualities manifested in a dosage that put him solidly out of emotional tune with his kin.

There were some memories he was sure were his; yet there

were other, older ones that he thought must have come from some other poor soul. Some indigenous cultures used to believe that people shared memories, even dreams.

The memory Truckie had of meeting Louis Uni seemed so distant, a lifetime ago. Or within a different life.

ABOUT TWO CENTURIES AGO, he'd met Louis. Louis Uni. Truculento had been living in what was then Alsace-Lorraine, working at night in a fishery; after a while migrated into France-proper, hiding his face, moving through rural carriageways and even the forest. He'd ventured northwest, through the *Forêt d'Éperlecques*, closer to the Strait of Dover. Somehow, he'd gotten lost and came out into a clearing—some sort of field, though the soil looked clean and untilled, healthy and virginal. A cowl obscured Truculento's face. Then, so long ago, his skin was still smooth and unscarred, and he was younger, more curious. He saw Louis in the orange and purple bath of dusk twilight—a huge man, broad and built like an ox; tall and imposing.

Louis must have thought Truculento was a child.

"Boy! Boy! What are you doing out there?"

Truculento didn't answer; he simply kept his head tilted downward so the big man wouldn't see his face.

"Boy, come here."

Truculento knew better than to get close to too many people. Better to be discerning; better to reconnoiter and plan out interactions; better, still, not to get too close at all. But the big man looked friendly, and his voice called out in that way that signaled warm welcoming. So Truculento came closer.

"Boy, it is late afternoon. Oughtn't you to be at your home?"

Truculento shook his head.

Louis followed up, "Why not?"

The segment of Truculento's brain that was profaned by the

sometimes-rational, often-animal world warned him not to speak. But, with the seedling of spirit that sprouts the sacred within, it begged for connection.

Truculento spoke with the barest of phonemes: "No home."

"Ah. I understand." And then, "Fucking Germans. They make you an orphan, boy?"

Truculento nodded. It wasn't completely untrue. He *was* an orphan, and had been in Bavaria, Hanover, and all over Prussia. Louis looked around—making a big show of it, holding his hand up to his brow and squinting one eye like he was closely scrutinizing the horizon through a telescope.

"Well, boy, I don't see my farmhand around. What say you help me? I'll give you some food for your troubles."

Truculento nodded eagerly.

"Pull up that hood so I can see you?"

Truculento shook his head vehemently.

Louis laughed. "Fair enough, boy. Well, this is what we're going to do. I will lift this above my head," Louis said as he pointed to a railcar axle with the wheels still on it—it must have weighed almost two hundred kilos. "I want you to make sure my arms lock out; that I have it all the way above my head. And if I don't, you yell 'push!' Can you do that?"

Truculento smiled and nodded again.

"Wonderful."

"Louis! Louis!" a brunette woman called from the edge of the field, waving a handkerchief at him. She had a picnic basket buoyed over her two folded arms.

"Just a moment," Louis said to Truculento.

The strongman ran over to the woman, and Truculento watched them. It looked like she was frowning while Louis was shaking his head. Truculento looked down at the railcar axle inquisitively, wondering why Louis wanted to lift it so badly. *Well, maybe he needs help—I'll lift it for him*, he thought, reasoning that a useful stranger was more helpful to Louis than a useless one. In one fell swoop, Truculento snatched the axle and held it over his head.

"*Mon dieu!*" the woman cried out.

Louis spun around as Truculento held the railcar axle above his head. He smiled at Louis, shifted the weight of the axle to one hand, and waved. Louis' jaw dropped.

"Louis," the woman asked, "who is that?"

"I don't know," Louis replied, "but I am certainly going to find out."

THAT WAS one of the happy memories. Truckie didn't have too many of those. Finding GHB was a pleasant memory, at first. But Truckie had grown much older. GHB, too, was an old man—a youngish old man, but an old man, nonetheless. And Truckie had grown tired of his foolishness. But with the weariness and jaded worldview of the nearly immortal comes complacency. So nowadays Truckie just followed what GHB said. He had settled into obeisance, a dog whose cunning human master had suppressed his ferocity and primal violence.

"Jeffersaint. Jeffersaint! Are you listening to me?" GHB bellowed.

"I heard everything you said. 'Take the upstairs-man to the outside city and use him to find the coins. Take the book with me, the *Kromee-Ohm,* and when it's close enough to picture the location, cut him loose.' Driftwood, you said? Very poetic." Truckie smirked.

Of course, GHB had said none of that. But it was easy enough to guess what he wanted. Easier still to guess at what GHB would approve of. And the easiest? To flatter the man.

GHB smiled. "Yes, I suppose it is poetic. Very poetic. We'll have to have a slam. Actually, maybe that's why my lolling melodiousness emanated from my thoughts. Behold!" He shoved a magazine at Truckie's face. "The *Maxim* has documented such things!"

"That sounds very good," Truckie answered.

"Now, where is that friend of yours?"

"I believe he's settling in with the children."

CHAPTER 23

"Mmmmrf ingurg lapurt?"

I listened intently, trying to decipher the question
—at least I assumed it was a question; there was a
noticeable upward inflection at the end. I had been sitting on a
large chair made of piled-up auto parts stuck together with elastic
straps and tar for the—what did Truckie call it?—Tribunal of
Inquiry. That was after my arm had been put in a splint by a
strange half-man-thing (to be honest, every creature down here
was a half-man-thing). I was reluctant to let the monstrous
looking nursemaid-man touch me, but the elephantine he/she/it
—adorned in dirty linen bandages and wearing a bright red cap
with an *ouroboros* symbol—rubbed some strange nostrum on my
arm. Surprisingly, it already felt better.

"Mmmmrf *ingurg lapurt?*" another one of the creature-children
asked.

"I'm sorry, I just don't understand what that means," I said,
waving my hands and miming 'empty' and 'no' as best I could.

"He's asking what you do upstairs. In the upstairs city,"
Truckie translated. I didn't even hear the little fucker approach,
but I sure was glad for the assist.

I leaned back to reply to Truckie, "Oh, well you know what I do. Can't you just—"

"They understand you, Frankie. They just can't enunciate. What they speak has all the syntax and grammar of English. It just comes out differently. You tell them." Truckie nudged me in a friendly manner. "I'll help if I need to."

I gave Truckie a thumbs-up, then addressed the children. "I'm a mortician. Or a coroner. That part's a little more complicated— the world up there," I pointed above, "has changed. So 'coroner' isn't as official as it used to be. But my job... well, my job is to receive dead bodies, to determine the cause of death, and to clean and prepare them for burial."

A woman with a striking resemblance to a fleshy giraffe raised one of her four arms, saying, "Yourt yourt. Turt yourt iffn der braucheri im thanas?" Many of the creatures applauded.

"What did she say?" I asked Truckie.

"She said that you must be very important or a holy man. It's a great honor to do what you do."

I laughed at that. "Not in my world. It used to be seen as sort of a scummy job."

"Scurmersh?" the gangly giant asked.

Truckie murmured something back to her in a garbled dialect and then said, "Scummy." They all nodded with many *oohs* and *aahs*, and then some polite applause.

A very small, very young-looking girl who appeared to be missing her neck, but was otherwise thin and somewhat healthy in appearance—she had very large, very blue eyes—looked up at me from near the front of the group. Her mannerisms were those of a child. She fidgeted in her seat, but those big blue eyes stared at me. There was a question in there. I nudged Truckie and pointed her out.

"Jefforsnessia, you have a question?" Truckie asked, looking at the small child.

She reached up and tried to twirl her hair, but her fingers were rather stumpy, so that didn't pan out well for her. She looked scared to be acknowledged.

"Jeffornessia? Come on, it's okay. Ask him," Truckie encouraged.

"Murmsquat fratver latempft fremgroften?" she nearly whispered.

Not taking my eyes off the little girl I asked Truckie what she'd said.

"Ah. She wants to know what makes you happy. About living up there. Very good question, Jeffornessia," Truckie said. Those big blue eyes stared at me, pleading. She really, really wanted to know.

And I had no idea what the hell to say. Happy. What made me genuinely, honest-to-G-d happy? "Uh… well… you know, there's a lot of… it's not…" I fumbled for a moment before recalling the season, the time of year. "I guess I would say that the thing that truly makes me happy is Christmas," I replied.

The girl's face lit up and she clapped her hands. "Ermghef fragtentament," she said.

"You're welcome," I replied, guessing by her shy and polite demeanor that she'd said some variation of "thanks."

A voice squealed from the back, "Hurmeny wurmeny urfeny?"

I looked to my translator for guidance.

"He wants to know how many women you've slept with," Truckie responded.

I laughed again and yelled towards the back, "That's kind of a personal question."

"Burdurferen yourt inguk, guk, guk, outi bano kleptakker, tak takker imguk hernery fern?"

"What did he say?" I asked.

"He said 'So what?'" Truckie replied.

"That's it?"

"That's it."

"Fair enough." I looked to crowd. They were quite eager.

"Well, I'd say there are two types of women that you can count, and that's the first part of the tally."

Suddenly, many of the creatures pulled out rags or scraps of refuse and improvised writing implements. *Jesus, are they taking notes?* I chuckled but continued, "First, there're the pros. Prostitutes, hookers, and the like. Those don't count."

"Erm da prozzy? Erm da hurk?"

"For money," Truckie answered. "To create children. Barter and trade."

"Aaaahhhhh," they all intoned. Then another one spoke.

"She wants to know why they don't count. Are they not like you? Not human?" Truckie translated.

I looked at the questioner and said, "No, no, not at all. They are very much human beings. It's just that when a person—like me—goes to a prostitute, that person has to pay the prostitute money. So, I don't include that in my personal count because they wouldn't have done it if I didn't pay them."

The inquirer responded and Truckie translated again: "But why do you want to have children with someone you have to pay?"

"No, no. You don't have children with them. You just perform… the act."

"The act?" Truckie translated the follow-up question.

"Uh…" I went back to the universal language. I pointed my right index finger and made a loop with my left index finger and thumb, then pushed the right index finger in and out of the loop.

"Aaaaahhhh," was their response.

"So, anyhow, you don't count them because you did 'the act,'" Truckie used finger-quotes to emphasize, "after paying them."

"Hrm glrt un prozzy erm da? Nyik tie?" asked the giraffish woman. Truckie laughed.

"What did she say?"

Truckie smiled and said, "She asked if it's very tiring to have to sleep with every person you barter with. She wants to know what if you just want a sandwich but don't want to do 'the act'?"

I laughed again. Was it innocence, or were our worlds that different? They looked at me strangely, but then joined in on the laughter, like children at the dinner table who don't understand a joke their parent told but laugh along anyway.

I had to clear the air on that one. "You can pay people without doing the act. It's called matrimony. It's just that if you do the act with a prostitute, then you have to pay. It doesn't mean that it's the same rule the other way around. You don't have to do the act every time you pay someone *else* for something not related to sex."

"Ooooooh," they all responded.

"Anyway, my answer is four, minus the pros." I thought, anyway. I remembered four. Or three and a half—just go ahead and round up, I guess.

"And what if you count the prostitutes and hookers?" Truckie translated another query.

I had to guess. I didn't remember all of them. I threw out whatever I thought they would like to hear. "Probably closer to four-hundred."

There was a silent pause, and then everyone started laughing —uproarious, raucous, noisy laughter. My face warmed and I smiled. Truckie was yucking it up, too.

"Alright, alright. Who else has questions?"

Every single hand went up. Because down here, they raised all their hands instead of just one. I felt it didn't have anything to do with kowtowing; they just wanted to better understand my alien existence.

THE SMELL down here isn't so pleasant. It's pretty fuckin' awful, to be honest. But the creatures—or the *children* as Truckie calls them —are all incredibly nice. There's a naivete to these foul-smelling cretins, some kind of innocence. I think this is because they're mostly half-retarded. And that's not an insult. That's just the truth, I think, the technical truth: they're half-retarded. I'm saying this based on what Truckie told me about them. He's a hell of a guy. He built this place for them, Truckie did. He taught almost all of them something useful about crafts from the ancient world—plumbing, electrical work, carpentry. Some of the older ones can even do engineering. My guess is that this is because of their long memories.

Photographic memories. Truckie told me that all the children, including himself, remember absolutely everything that's ever happened to them. *Everything.* I can't imagine what that must be like. I'd want to off myself if I had even half my life constantly running through my head, with every detail remembered clear as day. The point is, the older ones remember more, so they can learn more complicated things. But gathering the rudiments together—math, physics—is almost impossible. Somehow, they retain all the information, they can recite it, but actual comprehension is different.

After the Tribunal thing, we all sat down and had something of a grand feast. I tried to be polite, but most of what they served I couldn't eat. Afterwards, Truckie was nice enough to sneak a bottle of milk and a pouch of jerky to my room. Oh yeah, I have my own room. All the others, though, sleep together in the same communal hall where we had the feast. Just like in *Beowulf.*

My arm is feeling much better. I have no idea what the elephant-man-nurse did to it, but the pain is nearly all gone. Truckie says tomorrow we'll head back up to the surface. I like him. I admire him. For now, though, I can't think anymore. I'm too tired. I just need to close my eyes—just for a little bit.

CHAPTER 24

I found myself in a weird state of half-sleep-half-wakefulness. *What is this place?*

A long dark hallway extended as far as I could see, and my feet treaded forward, even though my mind was reluctant, maybe even against the movement. Every few feet there were paintings, evenly spaced. I put my hand to the wall, and when my fingers touched it, the entire hallway rippled like a pool of pitch-black water. The ceiling looked like a cluttered mountain of gemstones, each with a small glowing red crimson dot at the center.

I stopped and looked closely at the first painting. It was a full-body portrait of a man; he looked familiar, but I couldn't identify him. He was wearing a blue shirt with a purple bow tie. His wrists and fingers were dripping with gold and diamond jewelry. The figure's hair shot up in wild shoots of red stalks. The eyes were dark, and I thought they were moving. But if I *focused* on the eyes, they stayed perfectly still.

I walked farther down the hallway, tracing my fingers along the wall as I moved. The ripples reverberated and ran lengthwise down the hallway, and I saw them crest into a small black wave toward the very limit of my eyesight, where it seemed the hallway stretched to the point of infinity.

When I came to the next portrait, I thought it was the same exact painting as the first one. But when I looked closer, I saw that the skin of the man was sallow and scarred, with portions around the head reddened like swellings ready to erupt; his hair was wilder, with the red shoots appearing chaotic. Behind him were the licking flames of a fire. The figure's limbs had grown longer; the man's forearms pushed through the blue shirt cuffs till they rested at mid-forearm level. I leaned in closer to examine the paint that was used. The man's skin had a porcelain hue to it.

I wanted out.

I started running, but when I did, the length between the paintings extended more and more, like in one of those old *Looney Tunes* episodes. Only when I slowed to a walking pace did I come closer to the next portrait.

The third portrait was of a freakish creature. Think Modigliani on speed. Its limbs were so long and thinned out that the blue oxford shirt cuffs were at the elbows and the hems of the dress pants were at the knees. The red hair clumped in stalks and growths, long and still chaotic. Long, open wounds sliced between the stalks. The porcelain skin was cracking, its pieces flaking off. The figure's feet were cranked up and the ankles were deformed—*a velociraptor with a congenital defect*. The fingers were as long as a man's torso, the nails half-foot-long talons, and there were extra joints and knuckles. The eyes glowed red and green, two colors mixing the way burning orange glow mixes with soupy, ashy obsidian in a lava flow. The gold bracelets and rings were rusted and covered in what looked like dried blood and mold. The bow tie was impeccable, however.

Jesus, buddy. Someone's worked you over good. The picture was fantastical, horrific. Fantastical, but it looked so real. The figure was recognizable, but for some reason I couldn't reach into my brain, into the separate lobes, to draw out and piece together the title and image.

Who are you? I heard my brain asking.

The image flickered and I jumped back. Caught by my tail, I felt myself sinking into the wall, and its black-liquid pitch started to pull me in like quicksand. I tried to move, but the more I did, the stronger the wall's grip became. I felt it seep into my pores—it washed over my face and pushed itself into my tear ducts, through my nose, into my mouth. I coughed. I gasped for air, but the black gunk rushed into my mouth—a running river of wet soot and dark muck. The bony, long hand—that freakish appendage—reached out from the painting. As each part of the hand—the tips of the fingers, the knuckles, the meat of the palm— pushed out from its canvas portal, each part of the hand enlarged tenfold.

His smile. I'll never forget that smile. That awful, too-wide smile. Like someone had fish-hooked his cheeks and ripped them up toward the top of his ears.

Hellooooo Fraaannnkieee.

The monster's voice called out from within the portrait; it spoke as half of its knifepoint-sharp chin jutted, along with the rest of the face, into the air from the painting. Gold teeth, like needlepoints, extruded from its mouth. Some of the teeth were so long the mouth couldn't contain them, and the points punched through its lip and cheeks. Its gums were rancid-pink and black and green-brown.

Fraaaannnnkieee.

My heart was exploding. It felt tight; I thought I was having a heart attack.

Where have I seen you? I know you.

The monster lifted its leg, hoisting it over the gilded frame of the portrait, and stepped out into the open air. When he did so, the black water enveloping me frothed and bubbled maniacally. The black ooze was still rushing into my mouth, and I would peri- odically try to vomit, but the stuff kept pushing itself in. There's no worse feeling, I now know, than having that vomited black slime pushed back into my body while I'm still trying to expel it, nothing worse than being suffocated by a river flow's worth of black sickness back into my mouth. Now the creature stood out here, in *my* reality, outside the painting. It must have been eleven feet tall.

Fraaaaannnnkiiie…

It laughed. High-pitched and dissonant; an awful sound. The monster slapped its knee and reached one of its overlong fingers out toward me.

Teeeellll meee, Fraaaannnnnkieeee… haaaavvve yoooouu beeeeen nauuughty ooorrr niiiice thisssss yeeaaar?

It was Christmas Eve, I remembered, as the anti-Santa specter bellowed in shrill laughter. Cruelly, stupidly, until it was rolling on the ground and convulsing.

From the corner of my eye, I saw another disfigured creature— another monster. *Good to know it can always get worse.* The new monster wasn't as large as the gold-razor-toothed abomination before me, but it was infinitely more grotesque. Elk antlers grew out of its face, which had three nose holes, but the surrounding skin had rotted off like a leper's. Its body was like a boar's, but propped upright, and it had six arms, all of which displayed an underhang of furry, loose skin. The armpit hair was braided, which I thought was an interesting touch. And it was fat. Not just a little fat. Hugely fat. Morbidly obese fat. Santa was a pea by comparison. Its fur wasn't fur, but more like patches upon patches of mange. The fingers were like bird talons, but the ends were sliced or hammered open, with a runny discharge coming out of the ends. The fat six-armed disease-elk screamed out, making a sound several octaves below a lion's roar and several times louder.

The roar inspired the bowtie-monster to spin around and face the elk-monster. Bowtie monster's posture tensed.

Pure animal fear. It's scared shitless.

The gold-toothed predator that had trapped me saw a thing more terrifying than itself. Nevertheless, the bowtie-monster turned to face its new enemy, holding open its gigantic hands and baring its needlepoint teeth. The elk-monster swiped at the other creature with its slimy talons, its furry gut swinging back and forth. The gut's girth finally hurtled in opposition to the body like a larded counterweight—and its swing missed. The bowtie monster bit into the elk-monster, sinking its teeth deep. But the elk-monster only smiled, as though it were thinking *now I've got you*. It grabbed the bowtie-monster with all six hands and bashed it against the ground. The bowtie monster tried to get loose, but the elk-monster—smiling, then chuckling in deep gales of hooting bass notes—bit into its face and tore off a chunk of its flaky porcelain cheek. The bowtie monster shrieked, and the elk-monster turned it around on its stomach with four of her arms.

Yes, it appeared to be female. I could distinctly make out four pairs of flabby, huge, furry breasts on the front of the elk-monster. She used her two free arms to latch onto the bowtie-monster's head and press her tits into its eye sockets. The bowtie-monster let out another shriek and desperately kicked, thrashing for its survival. It managed to get away and scrambled back into the portrait. The instant the beaten creature had returned into its portal, the black water let me go. I coughed up wretched black gunk until my vision blurred.

But now I was standing in front of the other thing. The elk-monster. It held up the three arms on its right side and waved to me. I was stunned. I almost laughed at the peculiarity of the situation. I waved back. Then, it waved for me to follow it. So, I did.

CHAPTER 25

Huey Purgato's essence began to coalesce back in his lab room. The very air of the room was suffused in the fading glow of a pulsating orbit of red electricity—traces of vapor rematerializing, transmogrifying. The moment that enough elements of Purgato had returned to the darkened space to form a voice, Huey screamed out "lights" in a high, foreign, monstrous shriek and a row of bulbs flashed on. As the remaining particles of the mayor snapped back into place, he shrank from the long-limbed beast back to his normal size. He bled through his shirt around his back, and his eyes were swelled and bruised. He had wounds wherever the elk-woman-thing had battered him, and he fell to his knees as the final reconstitution drew to its close. He tried catching his breath. He hacked and wheezed and spit up blood. Huey Purgato stuck two of his fingers into his mouth and fished around; when he pulled his fingers out, two teeth came with them. He cursed and aimlessly threw the teeth.

He struggled to stand and yanked on the bow tie tethered to his neck. It slipped open and fell onto his shirt in an upside-down U-shape. He pulled the purple-paisley bow tie out from under his collar and looked at it, relieved to find that there was no blood on it. He ripped off his oxford blue shirt and his dress pants; he had no use for them anymore.

Huey took an elevator up to the floor his office was on. He then crawled to the false wall and pressed an invisible indent in the plaster. The wall reacted to his touch and separated long enough for Huey to exit, and the parted construction closed behind him as he teetered on his hands and knees into his office. He came to a stop when he reached the center of the room's black-tiled floor.

Cotton Lenny sat in the chair behind his massive desk. Huey became much less concerned with his injuries when he caught sight of her. He tensed, awaiting her reaction. In truth, his fear of that elk-monster paled in comparison to his fear of Lenny.

"Yins went too soon, Huey. Huey, Huey, dear Huey." She smiled, laughed, then spit on the floor toward him. "Grown too big for your britches, you squirmy little wormy. Yins need'a partner. Been sayin' it. Been sayin' it," she cooed, undoing the button on her houndstooth jacket.

"I had him," Huey said ruefully, bashing his fist into the floor. Crimson globules of mixed spit and blood hung and flung from his mouth. He swallowed a yell and held his hand against his abdomen.

"I fucking had that son of a bitch. I just… I don't know who that ugly cunt was. That fucking bitch. That no-good mother-fucking bitch."

Cotton Lenny continued undressing until she stood nude in front of Mayor Purgato's great desk. Her body was firm, voluptuous. In her own way, her unkempt mess of hair and her hunched gait belied the unconventional sexual attractiveness of which she was prepossessed.

"My poor little ruler. My poor little Master of his Tiny Demesne," she mocked him, even as she knelt beside him and wrapped her arms around his crumpled form, pressing her breasts against his back.

"What should we do?" he asked, leaning back against her. She reached down to his genitals and started working him slowly. Huey shuddered.

"We can worry 'bout that in a minute," she replied. "First, let's get yins right again." She started moving her hand faster. "My squirmy little wormy. Get yins right'z rain."

CHAPTER 26

I don't remember how I got here.

I remember following the elk-monster, not knowing why.

I don't remember coming to *this* place.

There was a huge willow tree, and I was standing just at the periphery of it, where the branches hung low enough to obscure what was underneath in the shade. I saw a flickering glow manipulating the shadows in the darkness under the tree, and I heard a voice.

Come here, Frank.

I brushed aside a cluster of branches, hesitantly peeking underneath to find an old, ugly woman in a babushka—*Baba Yaga.*

"No, not Baba Yaga," she said with a toothless smile.

"Did I say that out loud?"

She grinned and poked a branch into the simmering fire in front of her. "No." The embers shot out sparks and a small rippling, cracking noise rose from the shuffle of the heat.

I sat on a log—there were a few of them, some gnarled and some smooth, some big and some small.

"Did... did you save me?" I stammered.

"Yes, I did. You were in deep you-know-what. *Deep.*"

"Yeah, I guess so."

Babushka had a makeshift spit over the fire with a small kettle hanging from a hook and chain.

"Tea?" she offered.

"Sure."

My arm was throbbing. Wherever we were, my arm was still slung up in the cloth and rickety splint like before. But it hurt bad now. Real bad.

"Yeah," she started, "that black water got into you. I'm surprised you ain't bitchin', the way that shit was pushin' into ya."

"Can you read my thoughts?"

"One step away. More like I been around enough and seen enough—and the details I seen; what with the devil bein' *in* the details—so I know what a man's thinkin' when he's thinkin' it."

She paused and curled her lips down. Kind of a look of maternal amusement.

"Or maybe I can. Don't know with any certainty. That's what I think about most everything, anyhow. Can't know nothin' with certainty. Not the way people want to be certain. Can't. Anyhow, maybe it's a educated guess; good enough to be right, not good enough to be magic."

"Right. I guess that makes sense."

"You oughta drink some of this...." She reached for the stick she'd been using to coax the fire and used it to pull the kettle off the spit, carefully and slowly balancing it. "Got your cup?" she asked.

I reached into my pocket, but it wasn't there. "Must've left it at the desk. Knew about that too, huh?"

"You're a war man. War men carry that tin cup around. Didn't even have to use the old spooky rays to figure that one." She grinned wide—*how many teeth does she have left? Four? Five?*—and pulled out two cups (coffee mugs that looked like clay mortars). She poured a bit of tea into mine, then hers. She was about to reach for the cups to hand me mine, but she paused, looking at me with her eyebrows raised. "A touch of the shine?" she asked.

"Wouldn't be very gentlemanly of me to refuse."

"Thought you'd say that." She reached into a pouch by her feet and pulled out a brassy brown glass bottle that seemed to change colors as she moved it. I couldn't tell if it was the fire that did it, or the light and the shadows, or if the bottle itself was just randomly cutting across spectra on its own. After pouring the teeniest touch of liquor into each cup, she passed one to me.

"That'll set you right," the babushka said. "Right as rain," she repeated, whispering to herself so that I could barely hear.

As I drank the mystical Russian breakfast tea, I could feel it coursing through me, dissipating my throbbing headache. I looked down at my broken arm; the pain had subsided completely.

"What the fuck?" I muttered.

She took a long pause to drink her own tea before answering. "The thing is that whatever happens in here happens out there, too. Do you understand what I mean by that?"

Whatever happens in here happens out there, too. I nodded my assent.

"Good. That's good. Past times, it'd make an awful mess of things; people that didn't believe when I said that. Now, judging by what I saw, we have a lot of trouble. Because what happens in here—it happens out there, too."

I nodded again.

"The trick of it is to try and listen to the folks who come before you. When I was younger, I wasn't too keen on taking advice. But I'm a lot older, and maybe a little wiser. When you get to be my age—now that I think of it, you won't; or maybe you will—you'll be sifting through the shit to find the gold. Wisdom, that is."

"You mean like the old saying about a man representing himself having a fool for his counsel?" I asked.

"*Exactly!*" She slapped her knee and smiled wide.

The visible patches of sky were filled with stars—billions of them, it seemed, brilliant and multi-colored. The wind whispered through the night. There was a rhythm of quiet vibrations echoing in the breeze. Without thinking of where it came from, I started reciting a few lines of verse:

"A quiet kept, a secret spoken

In bending breeze 'neath glowing stars

Where I keep my teeth and token

I know the things that made my scars.

"What does that mean?" I asked.

"I'm not entirely sure, Frankie, you're the one who said it." Another few moments passed before she spoke again. "I guess you'd like to know what's happening here, eh?"

"I sure wouldn't mind."

The toothless smile again. "Right. Right. *Wouldn't mind. Couldn't hurt.* Well, how about I tell you a story? Easier that way."

"However you like... Miz..."

"You can call me Runny."

"Miss Runny."

"Sit back, Frankie. Story time."

A man and his son.

The man is large, tall. The boy is beautiful. Beautiful because he is kind and loving. His father is a decent man. The mother is ill. In body, in spirit, but especially in mind. She believes in dark stories, whispers of conspiracy, grasps at the slightest end of string; to unravel, to whisper back. The family unit hails from the *Provinz Neiderrhein*. Now they live among the Pennsylvania Dutch.

All day and night, the boy and the father work alone together in the fields. The father is a mountainous heap of human machinery—the son has his father's strength, if not his stature. They plow and sow, raise livestock up to use and slaughter. The mother, home in their cabin, stews in a quiet contained fury. She doesn't understand why they left the Rhineland. At night, she comes into the son's room and tells him stories about his father— terrible stories, untrue stories: *your father killed a man in Worms, that is why we left; your father says we would be better off without you; I'm not your real mother.* Not all the stories were untrue, though. The last one was true.

One day, the father and son were out in the fields together. The sun glistened over the field and over the boy's healthy brown hair, filtering light through so that his head was backlit with the golden rays of an ikon. The father couldn't help but smile at the cherubic boy. Sometimes, the love he had for his son was unbearable—not unwanted, but too heavy for his heart. He had so much to lose. The son was his father's everything. But a son needs a mother, or so the father reasoned and argued. They sat together in the field, and the father wrapped his arm around the boy. They rarely spoke, but something more powerful than words transmitted between them. Something potent—a wild purity, a mixture of need and bloodline affection, a dire connection—kept them within their hearts' most precious, rare, closely guarded places.

Love's purity.

When they spoke, it was because something had become unclear. Something was gray. More exactly, something was impure. If they couldn't agree without words, conversation became their last resort.

"Father?"

"Yes?"

"Is Mother sick?"

The father sat quiet for a long time, hoping that truth could simply be guided by providence toward his son's heart. That hoped-for moment did not come. In somber notes, the father spoke plainly.

"Yes."

"What does she have?"

"I don't know."

They sat silently again. The father felt a deep shame for lying to his son. He knew what was wrong—the father did—and he'd been thinking about it for a long time, thinking of a way to escape, thinking of a way to make things right. And now the boy was old enough to understand that his father's presence had become more destructive than productive. And the father knew that the son knew this. The father started crying. The son had never seen his father cry before.

"Father?" The boy's eyes welled up, too.

The pain of seeing his son cry was too much. "I have to tell you something, my son."

The boy said nothing, waiting expectantly.

"The woman who lives with us is not your mother." The father paused, waiting for the son to say something. Moments that were otherwise fleeting became eons—the waiting, long waiting, for his son to speak to his sadness and panic.

"I know. She told me."

The father felt some relief. As if this was just one more revelation that confirmed his suspicions, firmed up his confidence in his plans, however loosely formed they were.

"I thought she might have."

"Who is she?"

There was another long pause before the father spoke. "I was a soldier. Your mother was pregnant with you. We had just won at Leipzig, and all of the soldiers were drunk. I was due home the next day. I was too drunk. I saw this woman—she had wild hair, and... all the... all the parts of her made in such a way that she was very attractive to me. It's hard to explain, these things. But I wanted her, to be... to *lie* with her. This will all be hard to understand, but I hope you can. I need to be clear with my meaning, but I am not good—not good speaking about women..."

The man looked off into the distance. "I was drunk, yes. Very drunk. And this woman drew me in. There was something about her. Maybe it was the light I thought I saw... some red light..."

Unholy fire. Unholy fire!

"...Some unholy fire that I saw coming from her. A temptation."

"From Satan?"

"Ah, I think it is hard to say what Satan is, who he is. But... no matter. Either way, it was—yes, it was—like the temptation of the Devil. Or maybe I say that now because I was drunk, and now I want to believe there was a reason I was so weak. I was so weak. She took me in, and she took off my boots, and drew me a bath."

She drew me a bath. Comfort and pleasure and bliss.

He wiped at the tears running down his cheeks and continued. "No man is meant to feel that, not without paying some price. I'm ashamed to say, my son, that the sins of the father are being revisited upon... *upon you.*"

The son stared at his father with a look of pain shot through with compassion. He said nothing, straining to find words of wisdom in the older man's monologue.

"I wanted to feel her—the woman," continued the father. "It was just as I said: Just the body, her body—it was sheer pleasure. Like bliss. My mind was unclear, and I did whatever she asked. Maybe I did it because I was certain that it was the end. It wasn't. I was young, and I didn't know anything about the world. I had no books. I was from a small village. The things I know now... I was foolish. I spent two nights at that woman's house, drinking, smoking, and surrendering to my lust, saying *yes* to whatever or whoever Satan is. I said yes to every temptation. At the end, the woman gave me a lock of her hair."

The father aimlessly gathered stalks of grass and broke them between his fingers.

"I came home to your mother, and I was so happy to see her. I loved your mother so much. I felt an incredible shame, and when I saw her, I said to myself, in my own mind, that I would have done anything to reverse it, to turn back and throw away the things I'd done. I would have lived through a thousand hells to undo those two nights of surrendering to temptation. But you know—you're a smart enough boy to know—there is no taking back the deed once it is done. You remember the story I told you about the slanderer and the wise old man who told him to collect all the feathers in the wind?"

The boy nodded.

"Yes, you're a smart boy. It was like that. Living with a lie is an unbearable burden. The lie either makes a man submit until he speaks his truth, or it turns him into something small and pathetic. Well, my lie made me small and pathetic. I couldn't confess to your mother what I had done. Not when I saw her face."

Tears of anguish streamed down the father's face. The boy saw his father's remorse, his pain, his fear—for everything that had passed and everything that might come—and he couldn't feel anything but love for his father.

"She looked just like you," sobbed the older man, wiping his tears with both hands. Like a child.

Like a child.

The son turned toward his father, but still said nothing.

The father continued, correcting himself.

"No, you look just like her. Your beautiful hair, your eyes. Your nature—a good nature. You are smart like her. She could read. That is how I learned. She taught me. Every time I would falter over a word, she would simply push me forward, with a loving hand. She knew the middle of me, the inside, the outside, every part. All she had to do was look at me, just as you look at me. I felt such shame. Such *shame*. I feel the same shame knowing that I've hidden this from you. But how could I help it? *How?* It is no help to see your face and it is just like hers. I can see you aren't angry. Your heart just swells with love. You are pure. Like she was. I ruined it. *Goddamn it!* I ruined her..."

Goddamn it! I ruined her.

The boy pulled closer to his father and rested his head on his chest. He spoke, at long last.

"Father?"

"Yes, my son?"

"What happened?"

"I am ashamed to say. But that is what I have earned. I have earned this pain and this shame, and it's given me nothing but a rotten soul and a worried heart. So, I will tell you. And I know you won't hate me, even though I *wish* you *could* hate me. Then I would feel that there was some punishment. But I know that G-d sees in my heart and knows my shame, and even Christ himself could not forgive my lying tongue. Knowing you will forgive me can only increase my shame, and that is what I deserve."

Instinctively, the father brushed his son's hair.

"Your mother found the lock of her hair. The woman from Leipzig. I was so sure I had thrown it away. I remember it so well —I thought I was dreaming! *This must be a dream.* I remember getting rid of it. But there it was, and it was no dream. I couldn't speak. I felt the presence of that *unholy fire* again."

"What did you do with it?" the boy asked.

"I burnt it."

"Burnt it?"

"Yes. In my disgust and shame, I set it aflame, hoping it would burn up my sin too."

Maybe the flames would also burn up my terrible memories—maybe they would turn into a nightmare?

"You know when you have a nightmare, and then you are awake long enough afterwards to feel safe again?"

The boy nodded.

"Yes, smart boy, I know you know—you've had your share of nightmares. I thought maybe that would happen. But it didn't. This terrible thing was real. Right at the same moment I recognized both that I was *right* that I *had* burnt the lock of hair; and, also, that your mother knew everything, even if she didn't know the whole story of what had happened. After that, things were not the same."

"She was angry?"

"I wish she had been. It was much worse. She was sad. *In sadness. Inside a dark sadness, and it had no end.* She couldn't feel anything but sadness all around her. Because of it, she…"

The words wouldn't come. In that dark pitch of silence, the father and son understood one another without further verbiage. In that moment both were spared having to hear the terrible way the boy's true mother had relieved herself of her pain.

"There is more. Some of it worse, some of it better to hear," continued the father. "When we buried your mother, the woman was there—the woman from Leipzig. The woman I tricked you into believing was your mother. I'm your father and I deceived you. The rest is too terrible, I can't say."

"Father?" the son asked. At first, his father couldn't meet his eyes. *"Father."*

"Yes. Yes, I will finish."

This might sound like a fairy tale, but I swear it is true, every word.

He cleared his throat and continued in a graver tone.

"The night before we buried your mother, the sky had colors in it—and strange lights—that I had never seen before. These lights changed me… in my soul. I don't know how to tell you how they changed me. I don't have the words. But they did.

"I went out to walk the streets. I remember I came to a cobblestone path going over a footbridge, and I saw the woman there. She said that I had to surrender to her, or I would lose you, too. I submitted to her again, only this submission was of a different nature. We came here, to America, in the country, and she came with us. I've told you she is your mother. I was afraid. I cannot tell you anything else from the story but what I've told you; and this."

I am still afraid of her.

The son hugged his father.

CHAPTER 27

We—Miss Runny and I—were still sitting under the branches of the willow tree. The fire had died out and reignited time and again, thanks to her prodding and feeding of the embers. I felt at peace in a way I hadn't for a very long time. I wondered how long we'd been in this place, wondered about space-time phenomena, wondered how I came to be saved by a she-beast and hosted by a kindly babushka. Then I thought that the wondering didn't do much good, so I broke out a pack of cards, which I didn't know I'd had in my back pocket.

"Hey, you want to see a trick?" I asked Miss Runny. We'd been sitting quietly for a while; it seemed she was giving me the time to think about the tale of the father and the son, and the evil woman who'd posed as the mother.

Strange. So fucking strange. I'd never been a cardsharp, never been known to carry a Bicycle deck.

"Of course," she said, smiling.

I pulled out three cards and folded them lengthwise down their midpoints. "Three-card Monte!" I announced, holding two cards in one hand and one in the other. "Follow the Joker."

"I think I already am," she replied.

We had a good laugh at that. I did the trick where I kept the card that *looked* like it was being thrown between my thumb and middle finger and did some rudimentary shuffle and shimmy.

"Okay, pick 'em."

She pointed to the middle card. It was the wrong one.

"Very good," she declared, smiling wide and showing her missing teeth again.

I got the sense that she let me get by her, that she was not deceived. That picking out the real card in a three-card shuffle was probably within her abilities. I was still happy about putting one over on her, though.

"Could I have some more tea?" I begged.

She looked hesitant at first, but poured some more, then added the touch of shine to it.

"So," I asked, "what now?"

INTERLUDE III

The world after The Long War was a happy one, though it was insecure. The world after the War was a freer one, though it was hateful. The world after The Long War was polluted, though it was cleansed of the creatures that had made it decay. For once, no reign of quantity. There were new symbols, new signposts.

Signs of the times.

The best of times, the worst of times.

No police. No doctors. Few nurses. No nations. No states. Few cities. Only people. Then tribes. Then tribes in tandem. Then some police. Now, a few cities. But still, no firefighters.

There was room enough for all. Property a-plenty. Resources to be gathered, resources to be spent. The myth of predictive-dystopian literature (that corpus from both technocrats and the literati) was wrong about how things would shake out.

Infrastructure didn't crumble as they thought it ought to. Engineers and electricians, planners and plumbers, architects and arborists; these men survived.

Why them? Who's to say?

The power stayed on, at least in the areas that didn't get bombed. Where the lights did flicker... well, it wasn't *too* difficult to solicit a specialist to spot-check and repair, so long as there were enough people living in the area to make it practical.

But still, no firefighters.

On the outskirts of what used to be Scranton, a not-insubstantial number of families had moved into a large condominium complex. The complex was new and shiny before the fighting kicked off—long after the coal industry had made the region a warren of blackened houses sinking into mine caves.

The complex was one of those places whose outlining walls were a square enclosing four smaller and identically shaped squares of apartments glued together at the seams. In the middle, there was a perfectly proportional smaller square—a commons—with a pool in the middle. The families who moved into the cubes were postwar and non-nuclear: uncles who took nieces and nephews as their sons and daughters; soldiers who gathered the enemies' children that they orphaned; sisters who married the husbands of their dead kin; tight-knit tribes of folks who lived together long enough that they felt like family.

But still, no firefighters.

The grass had grown long and high around the gardens—untended and brittle dry in the summer heat—and it was catching. Maybe a cigarette, maybe a stray match.

It caught fast—the first fire—and took up the walls. Everyone was at the pool when a huge blast of trapped heat and frying air burst the windows from the inside. The shards rained down after the big bang. For an instant, the cooked oxygen and a flush summer gale held the shards in the air, then they came down shimmering, reflecting the orange and yellow, descending slowly. Slowly. Slowly.

The children didn't know what was happening. Some of them might have thought it a phantasmagoric light show designed for their entertainment. The children hadn't yet reached that final, curtain-is-closed recognition of unfolding tragedy; their eyes still feasted on that holy, enthralling terror that only leaves with the conditioned disenchantment of time. It was the parents—uncles, aunts, and strangers; the sisters, brothers, and killers—who knew what was happening. They knew it when they heard it, even before they saw it. It was one of those moments that sifted and sorted and winnowed the brave, the cowardly, and those in between. When they looked up, the flames looked so high. Impossibly high. *How could fire rise that high?* As high as sixty feet in the air. No, more. A hundred feet. A thousand feet. More. Fire that rose and baked the atmosphere, pushing all the way up to the sky till it melted the clouds into rain.

Then, a vacuum—a blackened vortex—swelled up and ate the fire on one of the faces inside the Baroque cube. A huge figure, possibly eight feet in stature, was seen exiting the vacuum. A huge dark cloth had cast a dark shadow across the front of the figure as it emerged through the orange flames. With the blazing backdrop, the huge cloth covering the figure's body made it look like a bizarre x-ray of a kid under a white bed sheet playing Halloween ghost. The black cloth hung over two long, uneven branches at the very top of the figure. The figure looked like a huge rectangle. The only dots of color the families could see were two icy-blue lights, glowing slightly below the rough-shaped branches. The black rectangle came closer to them, moving in stalking, unnatural strides. Some screamed, others stood frozen in place. Most of the men began attacking the figure.

Then, in one swift motion—so fast that their eyes couldn't catch it, and defying the world's physical laws—the black cloth threw itself over the families in a suffocating leap.

Not suffocation, but salvation.

The families didn't remember anything except for a moment of pitch darkness. They awoke to find themselves in a field only a coal scuttle's throw from the blazing cube; they had been saved. The first to notice the calling card of the shadowed figure was a child. She picked up a coin that was lying next to her on the ground and held it up to show the others, the survivors.

CHAPTER 28

8 6 had followed Frankie and Truckie down into the sewers.
He hadn't been able to track them the whole way—
many of the rooms he'd followed them into were smaller,
and some of them were well lit; like the Tesla power plant. The
mayor had provided information to 86—old maps and official
plans for the sewer system. Consulting the documents, he figured
a way to work around the aggregation of iron doors and security
apparatuses that the little freak-man had constructed.

Earlier, 86 had been down in the sewers by himself, figuring
out how to surveil some of the unused pathways—some air ducts,
a few smaller tunnels—that Truckie hadn't yet utilized. To that
end, 86 had brought down what he thought might be necessary:
weapons, food, and a small spider-like automaton with a camera
and microphone. 86 controlled the spider-camera with a circular
remote housing a joystick, enabling him to wait in the shit and
stink of the under-city, hoping to get some useful information.

What 86 wanted was intel regarding the whereabouts and
actions of Attanasio. And the smart freak—the little one—had to
be monitored too. In fact, Frank Attanasio had been sleeping for a
good long while now.

CHAPTER 29

I was beginning to think I'd been caught in some kind of loop, or a fracture in the fabric of existence, some special place where ticking minute and second hands have no relevance, where the hourglass holds no sway. It didn't matter. Not right now—*if there is a "now" that I can recognize, then time must still exist, right?*

Once I'd woken up, I wanted to find Truckie. The layout of this place was ingenious, but beyond my understanding. I was trying to find the common hall where everyone seemed to congregate. Maybe Truckie would be there.

Sound helped steer me. The group produced a cacophony of odd syllables and vocalizations—sounded like a room full of sick people, really. But they weren't. So, I followed a sort of hallway that led in the general direction of the loogie-hocking orchestra. I felt a tug on my sleeve and looked down.

That little girl was there. Just standing, staring up at me with her big blue eyes. Her other two arms were behind her back. And though I'd had a lot of information come into my mind as of late, I remembered her name. "Jeffornessia, right?"

"Mfth pmfth," she said. She smiled at me, her small mouth crowded with very white, but very jagged teeth.

She sputtered some more words I didn't understand, though somehow, I was getting used to the jargon. The pauses and syllables. She seemed to want something from me. "What do you need?" I asked.

She turned to look, as if to make sure no one was around. Then she tugged at my sleeve again, not letting go.

"Oh. Okay, yeah," I said. I knelt next to her.

Jeffornessia removed the other two hands from behind her back. Her hands were too small to cover the whole thing. I didn't know what I was looking at, but she passed the thing to me. It was well-crafted, considering her stubby fingers and the resources she had at her disposal. The thing was a half-paper, half-aluminum-foil construction. It was like one of those fold-out papers they used to have kids make during craft time in preschool, but her craftsmanship exceeded that of a standard four-year-old. It was a perfect foldout of three snowflakes, all sharing the same pattern. Aluminum foil supported all the edges, and there was a thick line that ran across the center of the whole thing.

She was giving me a gift. And damnit, I couldn't hide my smile from the girl. When I looked closer, I noticed she'd written something in that thick part of the snowflakes. It read: MuRpHy X-mESS.

Merry Christmas.

"Jeffornessia, is this valuable garbage?"

She looked down and rocked her head in the smallest version of a nod I'd seen.

"Did you have it processed or sorted or whatever?"

Her head stayed down. The little rugrat had taken valuable garbage, hidden it, and broken rule number one. For me.

Too stunned to speak, and honestly, unable to, as my throat tightened, and my eyes dampened, I stood and turned to walk away from her. But something stopped me. Some urge that was strange and familiar at the same time. Something I wouldn't have done yesterday, I don't think. I turned back around, knelt in front of her again, and allowed a few tears to fall as I gently gripped her into a hug. "Thank you," I said. She laughed and hugged me back, then happily jaunted off to join the group. It took a minute before I was able to follow her.

The emotion in that simple act was overwhelming. I carefully refolded the snowflake piece and placed it in my pocket—hoping to transfer it to my coat later so it wouldn't get bent.

"Mrfmrf squmfth ptht," a voice came from behind me. It was the giraffe lady. She urged me forward. I wanted to revel in the moment a bit longer, but I had to be gettin' on. She led me to the hall, where a makeshift table appeared at the front of the common area. There was a special spot on the floor, next to Truckie, and it was for me. I didn't wanna be up there. I didn't like attention. But the children of the undercity were waiting to hear some words of wisdom from someone they deemed wise, from above. I didn't know about how wise I was, but I was from up there.

I stood at my designated spot at the table, gripped an aluminum cylinder with ridged sides (what used to be a can for non-perishables), and held it high in the air. "I want to offer a toast to all of you."

The murmurs and shouts of indecipherable mutant dialect quieted down, and all the children of the undercity looked to me.

"A few days ago, I didn't know anything about the world. I thought I did. But after coming down here, I guess anything is possible. I mean that in the best way. Even if I never really know anything about the world, I'm happy that I learned about *yours*—about your world. You're good people. Kind people. And if any of you ever want to come up above, you have a place to stay. Thank you. Cheers, to all of you!"

Pie in the sky when you die?

There was loud applause, praise even, then all the creatures dug back into their refuse-laced dinners, alternating between chomping down and guzzling a wash of pruno and shine to push the dinner along. We were sitting on the dirty ground, which had been cleared of refuse as one of the concessions of hospitality.

Truckie leaned in toward me. "Nice words, Frankie."

He smiled and elbowed me in the side. I winced playfully and slapped his knee. He laughed. Then I laughed. Then we all laughed.

GHB walked over to where me and Truckie were sitting. A huge man—with a faced shaped like a bulldog's—was standing behind GHB.

"Mr. Attanasio, we are all—we have all been grateful for your presence. I'm told that your Tribunal was the most successful we've ever had."

"Wasn't it the only one we've ever had?" Truckie asked.

GHB gave him a funny look without answering.

"This is Jeffers, one of our more able brethren," GHB introduced the giant with the bulldog-face. "He's going to go with you up above."

I took a sip of the boozy swill from the food can. As the drink hit my mouth, I shot a quick, questioning glance at Truckie. Truckie had a poker face. I'd decided to trust him, so I extended my hand toward the bulldog-faced thing called Jeffers. He didn't offer his hand in return.

"Oh, he doesn't shake, you see," GHB explained, "he's got some trouble with the, uh, nerves—can't tell whether you'll get a dead fish or an iron vise."

"Ah, I see."

"Yes. Anyhow, I vouch for him. Jeffersaint will vouch for him, too," GHB proclaimed.

I didn't recognize the name Jeffersaint until I remembered that it was Truckie's title in the bizarre cultish taxonomy GHB had crafted. I looked over to Truckie to see if he'd nodded, smiled, or done anything to indicate agreement. But he seemed like he was far away. Maybe in a distant land of memory, on a remote island of thought.

CHAPTER 30

ÉVREUX — 1928

The doctor stood at the bedside of the gigantic man and spoke softly; much too softly and with too much affection and warmth for a French person.

"Monsieur Uni, you should rest if you can. But you should also prepare yourself. You have lived a good life. A long life. You are a remarkable being. Not many will come along who are like you. I told my son that I was treating the famous Apollon. He didn't believe me. He is very interested in physical culture. I asked if he thought he might apply that enthusiasm to the study of medicine, but he is uninterested. *Eh bien*, what can I do?"

Louis smiled at the doctor. "My daughter never listened to me either. That is life."

The physician nodded, but in a genuine mode of assent, not feigned at all. "Well, *Apollon*," the doctor said with a cheeky grin, "is there anything else I can get you?"

"Maybe you could turn out the light. I'm weary, doctor."

The doctor flipped the switch for the light, and as he was closing the door he whispered, "Goodnight Monsieur Uni. Goodnight *Apollon*."

As the door closed behind him. Louis whispered back to the empty room: "Goodnight doctor."

Louis had been moved to a private room. An older maid, who once upon a time had a crush on Louis, pulled some strings to get the strongman a suite. Louis breathed in. The breath expanded, and a notching sound, a rattling croak, came and went with his exhalation.

What a contradictory state; the man whose strength was unmatched, falling weak before the great tranquilizer of time, disrobed from the golden fleece, sent up the River Okeanos to check in with Cronus. He had been *Apollon*; he had held near a quarter-ton over his head. Was there irony in Louis' choice of Apollon for his stage name? Apollon the god of healing and light. And yet here he was, ailing in the dark.

Fancy thoughts.

He laughed to himself, a little too hard, and he started coughing again.

Yes, stupid fancy thoughts.

And then it came. A voice from the darkness. "Why worry so much about it? You'll be prancing in Elysium, fucking every goddess whose robe isn't tied right."

Louis shot up—well, creaked up—in bed and squinted. "Wh—who is that?"

"I've come for you, Louis. Your time has come."

It was a hooded figure, wavering ominously in the absence birthed by the shadows in the corner of the room. It crept forward until the moonlight made shone on its face so that Louis could see it.

Louis smiled, involuntarily, till his face stretched and the hairs of his mustache, not following the upward arc of his smile, draped over his upper lip.

"Trucule? Is that you?"

Truculento peeled down his hood to his shoulders and stood with a somber beam of happiness curling his lips.

"*Mon dieu!* You look as young as ever, Trucule."

"And you look old and tired, Apollon."

Louis scoffed. "You should call me Apollon, too? Me? Who knew you when you could barely string together a sentence? Who knew you when you were too ignorant to know your gifts? My secret friend, who is stronger than the strongest man in the world. Come here, you fool! Come here."

Truculento, with tears bleeding solace and regret from his eyes, hurried to the hospital bed with the enthusiasm of the child-minded knave he had been when he had first met Louis. Louis cried too. They hugged one another powerfully and held that embrace. Louis pushed him back, hands gripping Truculento's powerful shoulders.

"*Trucule*, my young hero. Where have you been? I haven't seen you since—"

"It doesn't matter when. Friendships are like book-binding. As long as the beginning and the end have a backing behind them, then the whole story can stay as one."

Louis laughed heartily. "I swear to you, I've never heard someone say such a perfect thing as you have just now!"

"I've been there. From time to time. I saw you bested Batta in the overhead press."

Louis grinned. "He couldn't even get it above his head. But that's small-time for you, isn't it? Why did we never go on the road together?"

"Ah, you're the showman. Look at me," Truculento said, waving from his neck to his lower torso with the inside edge of his hand. "This isn't a body spectators want to see in a unitard."

Louis cackled. "Fair enough, fair enough."

"I heard your wife married an animal trainer."

"If you had been married to her," Louis replied, "you would know what a perfect match that was."

"She was a tigress?"

"Ha! More like a common shrew."

They burst into laughter.

Louis continued, "So, *Trucule*, tell me. I must know what you've been doing."

"It wouldn't interest you."

"Ach! You know better. You live like a prince, steal like a pirate, owe nothing to no man. You have no ballast, no big-breasted anchor to shipwreck you. You must have been to a million places, learned a million things. Come, now. Be a good sport. At least a story or two. It's been so long. You owe me that much, you know. You owe me that much."

Truculento pulled out a hand-rolled cigarette and a bottle of wine. "Well, I suppose I thought I might have to."

Louis beamed. "Yes, yes! Wait, when did you start smoking?"

"It's for you, Louis."

Louis smiled and snatched the cigarette from Truculento's hand, waggling a free finger at him, "You are a good man. A *good* man."

Truculento pulled out a match and lit Louis' cigarette for him.

"What would you like to hear, Louis? The tale of the Serbian Madman or the Secret Garden of Uruk?"

"Ah," Louis held his arms out wide, cigarette aloft the lips, *"dealer's choice."*

They sat for hours. After Truculento had exhausted his reserve of traveler's tales, Louis' excitement boiled over, and he reciprocated. They sat together, Louis smoking cigarettes—Truculento even had one; Louis said it was bad luck to let him smoke and drink by his lonesome. They depleted both bottles of the wine Truculento had brought. Only when it was just an hour before the nurses came in for their morning rounds did Louis began yawning. His eyes were sunken, and his breathing was strained. He looked as tired as Truculento had ever seen him. Too tired for an athlete. Too tired for a living man.

"Trucule, I must tell you one more thing before you leave."

"Yes?"

"I knew I would see you again. I *knew*."

"I apologize for not coming sooner."

"Ah, it's okay. You're here now. That's all that ever matters. Like you said, it's the beginning and the end of the book. What happens in the middle…"

"Fancy thoughts."

"Yes," Louis smiled. "Fancy thoughts."

Louis set his wine glass on the nightstand beside him and extinguished his last cigarette.

"It's been so good to see you, *Trucule*. It is, in fact, the best end to the Story of Apollon." Louis stared at Truculento, eyes cutting through him, straining to swim through his soul and bloodstream, eyes seeing everything and knowing everything; powers granted by the Creator prematurely before Elysium had greeted Apollon. "But no one will ever know the perfect ending, will they, my friend?"

"No," Truculento answered. "No, they will not. Only us."

Louis patted his hand on Truculento's forearm. "Well, that's good enough for me."

Truculento smiled. "I agree."

"Then let's call it. The end of the story, *Trucule*."

"The end of the story."

"I always knew I'd see you again. Don't give up on us, my friend. We are an awful lot. But there are those of us, good people, who deserve your love. And you too, Monsieur Truculento, deserve love from yourself. Fancy thoughts." Louis laughed weakly and closed his eyes.

Truculento could hear the death rattle's last ratchet expiring; he briefly allowed himself to cry, albeit with restraint. Louis had spared Truculento the pain of having to close his dead friend's eyes—he had fallen asleep moments before he expired.

CHAPTER 31

Gulraiz Gholam hadn't been very good with computers at first. His first love had been the law, and his mistress was languages. His on-the-side shtick was film. He made documentaries during The Long War. Now, he was the computational consultant for Mayor Purgato. Beggars can't be choosers, especially after the film business had gone kaput after the armistice.

Coding was kind of like linguistics. It was easy enough to learn the ins and outs. Every human enterprise, he reasoned, had internal rules and inner logic (and illogic). Computers were no different.

When Gulraiz was overseas he used language as currency—first in France, where he picked up the language in two months' time; then in the Middle East due to knowing Pashto, Tajik, Farsi, Arabic, Uzbek, and Turkish.

Young Gulraiz thought better of telling any old friends or family that he spoke Hebrew and even Yiddish.

Gulraiz Gholam was never a huge fan of the Jews—although he felt wistful when he thought of the fact that they weren't around anymore. He thought Yiddish was little more than a comedic language and a rich one at that. Gulraiz's favorites were:

er zol kakn mit blit un mit ayter (may he shit blood and pus); *ale tseyn zoln bay im aroysfaln, not eyner zol im blaybn oyf tsonveytung* (may all his teeth fall out, except one... so he suffers); *fransn zol esn zayn layb* (may his body rot from a venereal disease); and, his very favorite, *shteyner af zeyne beyner* (stones on his bones!).

When all was said and done, though, Gulraiz found himself missing the Jews. What was life without an enemy? Especially an enemy so crafty and cunning as his Abrahamic cousins, the *yidden.* To try and remember what it was like to have them as adversaries, he would seek out and read old Yiddish stories, loudly denouncing the characters as he went along. After a while, Gulraiz allowed himself to just read the stories and denounce the Jews in an inner monologue. Then one day, he found himself just reading the stories. No denunciation. Not a whit. *Well, I'm just keeping up with one of my languages—staying sharp. Nothing wrong with that.* Sadly, once they were gone, Gulraiz had stopped hating the Jews.

When he came to the Seven Points, Gulraiz tried to find a shrink who could help him with his Yiddish literature addiction. It was out of control. It was getting to the point where he couldn't get through the day without reading at least an hour's worth of Sholem Aleichem or Moyshe Kulbak. Sometimes Gulraiz would stare at the picture of Kulbak on the dust jacket of *The Zelmenyaners* and he'd feel some hot feeling in his groin and nipples. *I hate you Moyshe Kulbak.* And then he'd whisper to the picture, "*I don't really mean that.*"

Who was he becoming?

It didn't help that when Gulraiz finally *did* find a psychologist, and when he got up the nerve to admit his addiction, summoned the courage to bear himself emotionally naked before someone who'd *sworn an oath* to help the sick, to *do no harm*, the doctor laughed him out of the office after painfully extracting the nature of Gulraiz's addiction. Gulraiz was devastated.

Gulraiz Gholam finally lumbered to a conclusion. It was high time he made a radical spiritual transformation. He had to hitch his salvation to another messiah-pony.

And then, one day, he found Huey Purgato. Huey Purgato looked, in some small way, like a ginger-stained version of Kulbak, but even handsomer. Gulraiz worked on his "campaign," and Huey Purgato remembered his name *every-single-time-they-met*.

"Call me Huey," he even said to him. Swoon.

And it was a question of mutual ass-scratching. Huey needed a computer expert. So, Gulraiz figured it out. And with this specific task now laid in front of him, the disciplines of linguistics and computer science met a serendipitous confluence.

GULRAIZ HAD BEEN TEAMED up with that intimidating man known as 86.

Gulraiz didn't care much for 86. The brute reminded him of the soldiers who quietly enjoyed the fruits of war, the men who longed for prey and wept (figuratively) when the exsanguination had ceased. Men like this kept control, Gulraiz had always thought, because it made their rarer fits of evil all the sweeter. He imagined 86 not speaking for weeks on end, then being sent out on a black op, where the large soldier with that unnatural grin would rape women and children. That's what Gulraiz thought. Thank goodness he didn't have any of those repressive issues.

Despite not holding his partner in high regard, Gulraiz was a professional through and through. As soon as Huey Purgato teamed him up with 86, Gulraiz linked into his portal and brought up his mission partner on video-conference.

"86 here. Confirming transmission protocol 8-Alpha-Delta-5-Niner."

Transmission protocol 8-Alpha-Delta-5-Niner? Gulraiz thought this was absurd. If he'd wanted to be a double-agent, he would have stayed in Europe or the Near-East, not in what used to be Western Pennsylvania.

86 continued, "Brown Camel, I'm uploading E.T.S. images—erase after use."

Gulraiz hated the call sign Brown Camel. A little too on the nose. It bothered him even more, knowing that this brainless lug—these types who talked less, so there was some "mystery" to them, so people thought they *might* be intelligent—was probably hysterically laughing (on the inside, of course), thinking how very clever "brown camel" was.

"Brown Camel, confirm."

"Confirmed."

"Full confirmation, please."

Gulraiz rolled his eyes. "Confirmed, Bronze Truth Eagle. Erase after use."

A row of video files appeared in the dark drive. Gulraiz clicked on the first one. The glow of the screen cast dancing neon colors over his face. His eyes opened wider and wider. "Where did you get these?"

"Are you on a secure channel, Brown Camel?"

Jesus Christ and Allah and Mohammed, this guy is stupid.

86 *had* to have been the muscle in the black ops unit he was in; maybe he wasn't really a specialist. All these codes, all this protocol—Gulraiz knew from limited experience translating code-breakers messages—was completely incorrect. The question about the channel didn't even apply to the communication system they were using. But Gulraiz humored the man.

"Secure channel confirmed, Bronze Truth Eagle."

"I'm on a track-and-troll mission." Not a real thing. "I've got a contact who has a contact with the group of individuals who are part of the target-mission-objective's network."

Word salad.

"Ah, I see. You've acquired an inside man?"

"Confirmed, Brown Camel. The contact claims that he can deliver a high-value item, but he has demands."

"We should consult Huey."

"Brown Camel, code names only. Please repeat."

"We should consult... *Red Father* on this. Please forward description of the high-value item and the list of demands."

86 remained quiet for a few moments. "He wants all the good garbage."

Gulraiz's face contorted. "Please repeat?"

"Brown Camel, contact wants the good garbage." Gulraiz watched as 86 leaned aside, listening to a muffled voice. 86 continued, "He wants that, and more, in exchange for the high-value item."

Gulraiz needed to move this along. "Bronze Truth Eagle, please summate the information you have, who your contact is, and what they want, so that I can forward it to Hu—Red Father."

Another video uploaded into the dark drive. "Confirm receipt of file please, Brown Camel."

"Confirmed,"

"Full confirmation, please."

"Confirmed, *Bronze Truth Eagle*," Gulraiz said through gritted teeth. He swiveled his seat to a separate console and sent the file to Purgato's office. "Forwarding to Red Father."

"Just be quick about it. Contact smells shitty."

"Confirmed," Gulraiz said, before painfully adding, "Brown Camel out."

CHAPTER 32

Bulldog Face turned out to be very useful, despite my initial reservations about him accompanying Truckie and me. He was none too bright but had plenty of subterranean smarts. He learned them from Truckie, who said we cut our time in the tunnels in half by having Bulldog Face with us. We even found an old path right under the mortuary that Truckie thought he'd forgotten. That was a funny thing for him to say, after telling me that his kind never forget anything.

As we peeked out from the sewer grate near the mortuary, we discovered quite the scene. Like a carnival, a rave, and a freak-show all rolled into one. Hieronymus Bosch, where art thou?

I saw the odd couple whose osteo-and-arbor-mutilations ran through their faces.

I saw a camp of what looked like young missionaries handing out food.

I saw a huddle of African Wizards.

I saw a motor pool of hired goons in black.

I saw a choir singing songs of praise.

I saw carolers—it was Christmas, after all.

I saw a large mish-mosh of people who weren't neighborhood

regulars (whores, orphans, workaday yeomen, triune flocks of clucking hens—all put, *the works*).

Surveying this bizarre feast of fools, all three of us had looks of astonishment on our faces. The bulldog-man (what was his name again? Some kind of *Jeff*, of course) had the funniest mug. If you ever want a laugh, try and get a bulldog to smile. A bulldog's smile is a pure one, a curious smile. A bulldog-*man*'s smile is something else altogether. I can't overstate how much I recommend seeing a bulldog-man smile.

"What should we do?" Truckie asked.

Bulldog-Jeff shrugged, as did I. We surveilled the scene for a few moments more, taking it all in. We observed one of the drunker goons, who had accumulated freebies from the proselytizers-cum-vendors-today. Wearing a shiny Lion of Judah hat, the goon was holding pamphlets and books he'd acquired from several of the faithful. Some toothless old man with straws of desiccated hair puffing out from under a duckbill cap was juggling flaming batons. A few other attractions had set up shop.

A carnival. Just an impromptu effing carnival. Feast of Fools.

"I say we just walk right in," I said.

Truckie curled an eyebrow. "*Really?*"

"Yeah, why not?" I asked. "Look at all that shit, Truckie. Ain't nobody gonna see us through with all that noise goin' on." I shifted my manner of speech back to my own. "Look, it's either that or nothing. Whether we come out here or the remote ass-end of the tunnels, we're going to have to get through that door." I shifted my eyes to indicate the mortuary's entrance.

Truckie sighed. "I suppose you're right about that."

He thought on it a moment longer, and then rolled his head on his neck while letting out a grunt. "Alright," he said, "let's go."

We crawled out from the sewer grate. No one noticed us in the commotion in front of the mortuary.

So far, so good.

A bag lady rushed by us, yellow stalagmites and stalactites jutting, rotten-gummed, from her mouth. She laughed and pointed at Bulldog-Jeff, still not enough to draw attention. We came closer and closer to the mortuary. Just as I was about to pull the keys out of my pocket, just when we were about twenty yards out—an equal distance from the pagans but a double-length from the mayor's goons—I saw, out of the corner of my eye, one of the goons slap his buddy's arm with the back of his hand and point his index finger at me. Most of the goons were ex-military types working as private contractors; the type that would otherwise grow fat and soft. *Or lean and hungry?* The merc who spotted me whistled—I couldn't hear this sound clearly, but I saw him put two fingers to his lips while making a helicopter-rotor motion with his other hand. *Wind 'em up, move 'em out.*

"Fellas, we may have trouble," I told my tagalongs.

The drunk goon in the goofy headdress was closest. He pulled a pistol from his holster, but his fingers—numb from the cold and dulled by the booze—slipped as he brought it up to fire. His errant bullet struck the latest True Hebrew to take up rotation atop that tribe's soapbox.

The other goons had their weapons out, rifles at their shoulders. Before any of them could take a clear shot, the muscle for the True Hebrew pulpiteer—he looked a combination of weightlifter and wrestling coach—tackled the drunk goon so hard that the muscle's headdress fell off and the goon's ribs crunched. As his goonly bones broke, he emitted a ghastly sound that startled his henchmen-comrades.

One of the teenagers who'd been talking to the True Hebrews grabbed the pistol as soon as it dropped from the goon's numbed hands, and he aimed it at the other henchmen. At this moment, I screamed.

"No! Kid, don't!"

My shouted plea caused Bone-Nose and his troupe to notice that me, Truckie, and Bulldog-Jeff were near the mortuary door.

"Don't let him in!" Bone-Nose screamed, as several of the pagans let out beastly howls and plowed through the crowd of bystanders.

The snow still came down in monstrous layered sheets of white wind; a vast white shroud that all but obscured the sight and sound of the scene.

Truckie grabbed me by the arm. "Frankie, we have to get inside," he sputtered.

But I saw the kid raising his gun and aiming it straight at the mayor's goons. I knew that this was how a firefight turned into chaos. And I also knew that chaos with rifles and handguns usually meant that innocent blood would spill alongside the shooters.

The kid fired just as that pagan woman, Bark-Brows, ran across his line of sight. One fast critter she was, trying to reach us before we got inside. The gunshot hit her smack in the temple, and she fell over in that classic dead-weight slump that I recognized as the gravity of being instantly fatalized.

Shocked, the kid tried to drop the gun, but the trigger snagged on a loose string from his knitted glove. Truckie and Bulldog-Jeff were both pulling my arms. I realized I had been struggling against them and trying, in vain, to get to the kid before something bad happened. I wouldn't have made it anyway. Before the goons could make heads or tails of what was going on—the snowfall grew thick enough to cloud their vision—another choir of angel-demons kicked in: the Assembled Chorus of Glory. In a single, sweeping move that seemed choreographed, they pulled out their daggers and started attacking the pagans and the True Hebrews (I later found out that there has already been some tension between the camps, and this was simply an opportune moment for some sectarian bloodletting).

Yellow fire burst through the turbid mixture of sparkling snow and the gray sky. The dark and light melted into each other, and a millisecond later I heard a thud. The look on the kid's face turned to dumb confusion, and then to awful desperation. He fell to his knees—the victim of a shot from behind that had pierced his heart. I knew he would be dead in less than a minute.

All of this—*all* of it—happened in a time span of about fifteen seconds.

The snow was falling so fast it quickly covered any evidence of what had happened. No bloody entrails, no discarded weapons, just white. Pure white. Pure, dizzying white.

Bulldog-Jeff slapped me in the face and Truckie screamed; "Frankie! You can't help them. But you can make sure a lot of people don't get hurt. You have to open that door, Frankie. *Now!*"

I nodded and pulled the keys out of my jacket with deliberate speed as we made for the door. In a single motion, I jumped forward and jerked the key into the lock, a hastened iteration of a motion I'd completed a thousand times before. Just as I was swinging the door open, one of the Assembled Chorus of Glory zealots heaved a dagger down toward my neck. Truckie hadn't seen the blade or the woman wielding it. Bulldog-Jeff, who was the first inside the mortuary and was facing me, spotted the woman. He let out some animal howl.

I'd had my back turned. Rule number one. *Watch your back.*

CHAPTER 33

Aloud pop cut through the air.

As I stood in the mortuary entrance, I turned to see what, or who, Bulldog-Jeff had howled at.

It was a primped-and-polished zealot, frozen with a dagger above her head and blood spurting from her mouth. I heard two more gunshots—loud reports, unlike the silencer-suppressed thuds of the goons' weapons. Without a word, the zealot crumpled and fell dead to the ground. The would-be-murderer's body fell to reveal a striking blonde woman holding a gun.

I recognize you.

It was the woman from the bar. She pushed me inside—I stumbled and fell face-first to the floor inside the entrance, yanking Truckie along. She quickly pulled the key from the outside lock and slammed the door shut after us. I was dazed but in a mind to survive; I jumped up and locked the door, sliding the bolt and the armor-arm into its iron holster. We were safe.

"Jesus," I said breathlessly. "That turned into a clusterfuck pretty fuckin' quick."

Bulldog-Jeff gruffly garbled some half-human sounds of agreement. But Truckie was completely quiet. I looked over to him and the blonde woman and noticed that they were staring at each other. Staring with purpose, intent, and most surprisingly, with recognition.

"Uncle Trucule!"

"Hmph," Truckie responded.

"You two know each other?" I asked.

Bulldog-Jeff looked confused, too. (To be fair, Bulldog-Jeff's face was such a fuckin' mess that he could have been confused, happy, angry, and infantilely stupefied all at the same time, depending on how the shadows caught his snout.)

"We do," Truckie answered.

"Who are you?" I asked her.

"Deedee Meador. I'm Dreck's daughter."

CHAPTER 34

ox Oculii, the Eye of the People. We're the channel that's watching the stuff you want to watch so we can make it into news you watch. On the hour, Darcy Gantz with special guest Wendy Morphy and Seven Points Mayor Huey Purgato.

[Darcy Gantz:] Hello, and welcome back to GANTZ! With Darcy Gantz. I'm your host, Darcy Gantz. Joining me is our panel, of which I am a member. First, in my spot is Darcy Gantz, host of GANTZ! With Darcy Gantz. Me! To my immediate right is Mayor Huey Purgato, who I must say is looking incredibly smooth in his gitup. Take a look at you!
[Huey Purgato:] Darcy, you're too kind. You better not butter up my biscuit too much, I'm liable to start smearing some jelly on yours.
[Darcy Gantz:] Oh, he is just a hoot, isn't he folks? You know, Mayor Purgato—
[Huey Purgato:] You call me Huey, Darcy. I ain't much for titles, and I'd rather have the world-famous Darcy Gantz callin' me by my given name than pretending we's strangers.
[Wendy Morphy:] [*Coughing sound*]

[Darcy Gantz:] Oh, yes, before I forget, at the end of the
table we have Wendy Morphy, our resident expert in
anything and everything and every-any-thing. Wendy, say
hello.

[Wendy Morphy:] Hello, I'm happy to be here as always,
and may I just say—

[Darcy Gantz:] That's enough of that, Wendy. Don't be
rude. Let's give Mayor Purgato—

[Huey Purgato:] Huey, please.

[Darcy Gantz:] Let's give Huey a chance to speak without
you running all roughshod all over him, Wendy.

[Wendy Morphy:] I-I-I Just thought that, Darcy, we're
a tea—

[Darcy Gantz:] That's enough of your yammering.

[Huey Purgato:] Now, now, Darcy, let's not be so harsh
with your co-host. From what I've seen, yins got a nice
rapport.

[Darcy Gantz:] It's my me show. Me mine. My show about
me. Now what were you here to talk about, Huey?

[Huey Purgato:] Well, Darcy, it's this whole mess with the
death of Dreck and this feller Frank Attanasio who runs the
city mortuary.

[Darcy Gantz:] Why, I didn't know we had a city mortuary.

[Huey Purgato:] Well, strictly speaking, we don't. Heck, we
didn't even have a city until but a few weeks ago when I
became mayor.

[Darcy Gantz:] That's right. That's right. That is right. Can't
have a city without a mayor.

[Wendy Morphy:] Yes, that's—

[Darcy Gantz:] I already said it's right, Wendy.

[Huey Purgato:] Well, anyhow, this feller, Mr. Attanasio, he
won't cooperate with the Seven Points municipality or its
leadership, and he won't turn over Dreck's body neither,
for examination. Yins oughta know, it's right tough the
position he's put me in.

[Darcy Gantz:] And am I right in saying that Frank Attanasio is a murderer and a sex predator?

[Huey Purgato:] Well, as Mayor, I wouldn't ever say nothin' that would harm the impartiality of our justice system, but I can say to you that I don't *not* think that Mr. Attanasio is a diddler and a killer of women.

[Darcy Gantz:] I called it, a hundred percent, bingo! Okay, Wendy, now you may speak. What can you tell us about the sex-molesterer and murderer Frank Attanasio—is he in cahoots with Dreck?

[Wendy Morphy:] Well, as you know, Dreck is dead.

[Darcy Gantz:] Mmm-hmm, mmm-hmm. Quite right.

[Wendy Morphy:] So, any potential conspiracy charges against Dreck and Frank Attanasio, done *in tanglemite*, would be complicated by the fact that Dreck is, in fact, not a living person. 'Cuz he's a dead person.

[Darcy Gantz:] Yes, I believe you're right on that, Wendy. Is she right on that, Huey?

[Huey Purgato:] Right as anything.

[Wendy Morphy:] Further complicatering the proceedings is that we don't have a judicial system, per se, in place, per se. You know, per se.

[Huey Purgato:] Actually, Wendy, I'm gon' have to correct yins on that 'un. I've consulted with my judicial system experts, and they informed me that they have found a way of consolidating the court system under one judge—sort of like a Supreme Judge—who can oversee all controversies and disputes. And I've found the perfect candidate.

[Darcy Gantz:] Well, that's great news. That's wonderful news. And who is the candidate?

[Huey Purgato:] Believe it or not, Darcy, it's me. Huey Purgato.

[Darcy Gantz:] Wow. Wow. I mean, wow.

[Wendy Morphy:] This is just *so* wow.

[Huey Purgato:] But I have better news than that, Darcy.

[Darcy Gantz:] Do you now?

[Huey Purgato:] Indeed, I do. I'm gon' ask yins ri'now—Darcy Gantz, would you be Deputy Supreme?

[Darcy Gantz:] Yes! Yes, I would love that more than almost anything except for hosting GANTZ! With Darcy Gantz.

[Huey Purgato:] Excellent! I now pronounce us judge and judge.

[Wendy Morphy:] May I kiss the bride?

[Darcy Gantz:] Shuddup Wendy! Anyhow, our next segment focuses on the difficulties we've faced in the last several weeks and begs the question: Where is the Anonymous Hero? Mayor Supreme Huey, will you hold on for our next panel after the segment?

[Huey Purgato:] I'd love to.

[Darcy Gantz:] Roll it.

For several weeks now, the Anonymous Hero has been missing...

CHAPTER 35

fter we'd settled a bit in the mortuary, I removed Jeffornessia's gift from my coat pocket. It had gotten a little wet, but it was still intact. I grabbed some tape from my desk and began adhering the gift to the wall. The urge to do so was impulsive. It was like I was hanging up something my own kid made.

"What the fuck, Frank? Where did you get that?" Truckie said, eyeballing the paper snowflakes.

"A gift."

"I see. Was it sorted and claimed?"

"Nope," I replied.

"You bastard," he yelled. "You bitch of a bastard. Three fucking rules. That's all you had to obey. You broke rule *number one!* Did you break rule number two as well?"

"What? No. And fuck you. You said rule number two was discretionary, if I recall correctly, and at my own discretion, I decided to not engage in mutual masturbation. So, I only broke the first rule. Sorry. It was a gift. I took it. You would've done the same."

"Fine, fine," Truckie said, obviously still annoyed. "We have

193

other things to deal with. Such as this 'clusterfuck' as you've so eloquently dubbed it."

Everyone went all quiet again. Once I finished taping my gift to the wall, I pondered a flurry of existential questions, most of which revolved around Deedee.

Why did this woman follow me? What did she know about me? Why did she save me—or us—from that maniac outside the entrance? How did she find me? Where did she come from?

There were so many blanks to fill in that I didn't know where to begin. So I decided on a query that let me check her against what I knew already; start with the simple shit.

"How do you two know each other?" I asked her while looking at Truckie. Truckie looked away from me, and she looked at him.

"Uncle Trucule, *tell him*," Deedee said, but Truckie gave no answer. "Uncle—"

"Quiet!" Truckie bellowed. "You left, Deedee. You left. You don't get to… you don't have the right to tell me what I should or shouldn't do."

"I *left* because I'd never had a normal life! Never! And that's all I wanted. Maybe it was selfish of me, but once I was able to be accepted by society… that was something I needed. I needed it. I didn't want to go back underground." She shivered. "It's hard for me. You know that."

"But you still left us. After everything you've been through— that we've been through—all of us tossed aside, you wouldn't *stay*," Truckie kept on.

"I don't know that you'll ever understand or that you'll forgive me. I don't even know if I want forgiveness. And it doesn't matter. Not right now. We can fight later. I'm not fighting with you right now," Deedee announced. She stood and walked over to my desk. She reached for the bottom drawer and opened it.

"Please don't go riflin' around in there," I said, but she paid me no mind.

Deedee apparently knew there was a false bottom in the desk drawer, too, because I heard the telltale click of the panel being unlatched. I was surprised to see her pull out the purple bag I'd lost in my initial scuffle with Truckie. She untied the yellow-gold rope that closed the cloth satchel and violently cast the bag in a fishing-line motion, which should have sent the coins spilling out onto the floor. Instead, the coins levitated mid-air, in the same formation I had seen before: A tetractys pyramid orbited by three coins. Every few seconds, one of the orbiting coins would switch places with one in the tetractys pattern, and a hum would emanate from them.

"Tell him," Deedee repeated, but Truckie wouldn't talk.

My eyes and head ached something fierce. I had been running on either no sleep, or lousy sleep filled with nightmares.

"Frankie," Truckie started, "we think that—that you're going through something."

"Okay. Meaning…?" I asked.

The coins hovered closest to me. My head still felt terrible. There was some feeling in my bones, some *stretching* feeling. My patience was thin.

"Stop beating around the bush," Deedee said. "I'll tell him."

She came up to me and took my face in her hands—her cold hands, slender and beautiful. "Mr. Attanasio, when the storm is out, you're not going to be you anymore. You'll be Dreck."

"What do you mean?"

"I mean," she answered, "that for whatever reason, forces beyond our control, and quite beyond our comprehension, have conspired to put Dreck's corpse in *your* mortuary, to put the coins in *your* hands, and to make *you* into Dreck."

"What? No. What's… what?"

"It's true," Truckie said.

Deedee looked at the coins and so did I. Those fuckers had shot right through my flesh, into my body. Some shit was going down here, and it had to do with Dreck, and it had to do with those coins. I found the coins inside Dreck, then they decided to live in my palms for a while. There was a connection there. One I had glossed over because of so many indescribable reasons that could only be attributed to feelings which have no words to tether them to speech.

I heard myself murmur, "The Father and the Son. This has to do with the hex, doesn't it?"

Deedee and Truckie looked at one another.

I went on. "It all makes some sort of sense. Not perfect sense. But there are little clues. When I picked out the bag to put the coins in, I felt a strong urge to find *that* specific little purple bag, the one I thought my father had favored—even though I didn't know my father. But I knew that about him, and I knew, or I thought I knew, which purple satchel was his. And as the coins spilled my blood, the blood went into the bag. Kind of the seal to go along with the sign, huh?"

They nodded and I went on.

"The evil stepmother is a nice touch; it made me think of my own life. I hadn't thought about that part in years, though. The fact that some random cunt—pardon me, but that's what she was —divided me and my father, till he ran away. And then I was left with that awful woman. Not for long, of course."

It was a lot to remember all at once. Wasn't lying when I told them I hadn't thought about that in years—I hadn't. But I couldn't determine whether I hadn't thought about it or I'd just blocked it out because it was a painful memory.

"You've been chosen," Deedee said, finally. "We don't know why. Uncle, why is it happening now?"

Truckie looked down, as though staring into his own chest, and took a surprising, sharp breath. For a moment I thought he was breaking into tears, but it was a hiccup, or a tic. Truckie finally said, "I don't know. I can't say why. But if it's started, then we have to keep Frankie and Dreck's body safe. We're playing with inhuman forces. This power is too strong to be altered, and we've got to protect it. Like a great river and a dam."

I thought I understood what he was saying, but at the same

time I was bewildered. *Sign of the times.* This was new territory for me. I'd never become something like this. *I was living through human events such as I had never seen.*

I was shocked, of course. Felt like shit. Scared. Not scared of being hurt—I'd rid myself of that fear a long time ago. *This was a fear I didn't know or understand. The fear of becoming.* And then I thought of how universally loathed Dreck was, and that scared me too. But a part of me, a reactionary part of me, said *fuck them,* and I felt a sudden pride—even though the fear of becoming didn't leave me. In that moment, I felt the honor of being chosen, chosen by some cosmic process beyond my understanding, beyond the temporal reckonings of mankind. *Still, this was heady stuff.* I could only issue a faint whimper in response to Deedee's news.

"Your father is… Dreck's your father?" I asked Deedee.

"You tell him, Uncle."

"No, Deedee, it's better that you do," Truckie said, removing that book—the *Kromee-Ohm*—from Bulldog-Jeff's backpack. "I'll go through the Book and see what I don't know already that can help us. Frankie, can we have the keys? We'll want to look at the body…"

I gave Truckie the keys to the cold room and watched him and Bulldog-Jeff disappear into the vestibule. Against the quiet suffusion of the snow still falling outside, I heard them undoing the series of mechanisms and latches. Then I heard the cold room door open and close behind them.

Deedee and I were sitting alone together now.

"She told you the story?" Deedee said as she looked at me, her eyes loving and scared, motherly and innocent, eyes lighted by uncommon knowledge and guided by purpose. Eyes that spoke of love for the stranger, and pity for none.

I nodded.

"All of it?"

"No," I said. "No, I don't think so."

"What don't you know?"

"The old woman told me about the Father and Son getting ready to leave. And the Hex."

"I can fill in some gaps, I think," Deedee said.

She told me about the false-mother—the one I started thinking of as the Evil Stepmother. Everything she said matched up with the folk and fairytales, and my own experience. Such as the Evil Stepmother who cursed the Father and the Son so that they would transform into monsters.

Deedee told me the story of the black device of the Evil Stepmother's hex: That the curse's power was strengthened a thousandfold when the Father and Son were together, and—the worst part—that Father and Son's memories of one another would slip away faster when they were together, so that the very existence of their incredible love would be the cause of their pain. Their love, which could allow neither the Father nor the Son to live without the other, would bring them the worst pain of all, as they fought against the impossible force of erasure, as they struggled valiantly but futilely against forgetting.

She told me how the forgetting was made all the more powerful by the Father and Son transforming into their cursed forms. This story was too horrible, I thought, too much to bear. Too much for the soul to countenance without damaging itself.

But she kept on. *She kept on.* She told me that the Son would become immortal—the Evil Stepmother guaranteed this—and it was all due to her hatred for the boy. The Evil Stepmother wanted him to relive his pain forever, until the end of time. And the Evil Stepmother's hex guaranteed that the Father would be reincarnated, again and again, as Dreck, to wander through the world with all his painful misremembrance, searching for the Son whom he would never find. It was a cosmic madness in which the Father, Dreck, could only stupidly claw about, wanting to do something about the existential pain that gnawed at him but that he knew nothing about, searching for a solution to a problem he did not know existed, seeking in vain a cure for a spiritual malady whose name would never be utterable from his forgetting lips and memory-less tongue.

"Do you think it will happen, Father?" the Son asked.

The Father thought to himself: *Jerusalem, if I forget you, let my tongue cleave to my palate.*

"No, my boy. No, I don't think so. She is just an evil woman. She is not G-d."

"But is she Satan?"

The Father had no answer for that. "Let the two of us think on this problem—even though it is not a real one. You are a very smart boy, very much like your mother. Your real mother. Let us think of something to do. So we never forget, yeah?"

"Yes."

"How did they remember?" I asked.

"I don't know that they did," Deedee answered. "Even if they could for a little bit, it was all but guaranteed that eventually they forgot how to not forget; if they were ever capable of working a way out to remember. So, the Father became Dreck. And one day Dreck wandered away. He became confused—stupid and perpetually confused."

It was a lot to take in. A lot of sorrow and heartache that one Evil Stepmother decided to cause just because she had to have one man's soul all to herself.

"What happened to the Son?" I asked.

"Nobody knows," she answered. "It's possible he's still out there, doing Lord knows what."

A long pause, then Deedee said, "We are his children."

"Yeah," I replied, "I guess we're all the children of Dreck in one way or another—unwanted, unloved; Island-of-Misfit-Toys kind of thing, right?"

"No," she answered. "*We*," she said, pointing to herself, and then toward the cold room where Truckie and Bulldog-Jeff were. "*We* are his children."

"Well, what do you mean by that?"

Deedee was viciously overtaken by an unknowable force. Her body trembled and her voice became unsteady. She was crying, and it seemed hard for her to contain that sadness.

"It's just really fucked up, isn't it?" she asked. "Do you want to know what he did? What he's been doing to try and get his son back?"

I shook my head.

"Dreck has spent his whole life finding women who look like the Son's mother and impregnating them. What a poor, dumb creature."

Though my eyes stung, and my heart ached from seeing her in pain, from the pain of the story she told, I couldn't help but think inappropriate things. Amazing how a person can feel devastation, sympathy, and still have such banal questions they should never ask another soul. Intrusive thoughts cropped up, and before I could suppress them, my mouth had already opened.

"Wait a minute. Wait. So, Dreck's got all these kids, but... how? He's... he's not, you know, he's not exactly what women would find to be *cute*, if I'm not mistaken. Is he... is he... are these women consenting to these, uh, these relations?"

Deedee's face was a mixture of confusion, pain, and intrigue. "What?" she asked.

"What I'm asking is how did *that*..." I gestured in the direction of the cold room, "create progeny? I mean, no disrespect here, but as the stories go, and yeah those are maybe wrong, but they all say that Dreck's a threat to humanity, so I can only assume—"

"Oh Lord, no." Deedee interrupted. "Dreck's representation has become twisted and regurgitated. Appearance can implicate one in so many forms of wrongdoing simply because, as you said, the person isn't 'cute.' No, Dreck didn't... he couldn't have... he didn't have sex with these women against their will."

"Okay, so how, then, were they persuaded to have sex with him?" I asked.

Deedee groaned. She threw her arms up in the air. "I don't know, Frank. Pheromones? The point is," she continued, her rage and internal pain flowing outward, "that he did awful things, even if they were consensual. I never knew my mother. Probably took one look at me and decided I should be dead, and maybe she was right, but someone allowed me to survive. As a newborn, I was just... dumped at a Catholic orphanage. They kept me hidden, on some low basement-level floor, away from the other children. I never interacted with anyone until I figured out ways to hide myself. And it's all Dreck's fault. He wanted that son *so desperately*, he cared nothing for the consequences of the daughters, or the other boys. The 'wrong' boys. He spent years just going around, stupidly fucking lookalikes. And do you know why?"

I shook my head again.

"Because he knows nothing. He is a moronic brute—or," she said, wiping snot from her nose, "I suppose he *was* a moronic brute. Uncle Trucule, GHB, all the 'Jeffs' as they call themselves now, they're all Dreck's children. I am, too. That's why we're all deformed, all monstrous, all abominations, affronts to nature, however you'd put it."

"But—" I started to speak then realized I had nothing to say.

"I've been over it in my head a million times," she went on. "I say to myself *why*? Why would he do that? I came to the conclusion that there must have been something in his head. Something left over. Maybe some memory of scripture—wanting G-d to make his offspring as plentiful as the stars of the sky, like Abraham. Or maybe he thought he was so abominable that he believed that if he could have a child—a perfect child, a *Christ* child—that he could maybe be redeemed. Or he was too stupid to know that the new child wouldn't be the Son. There was some good innocence, or some awful ignorance, so that no matter how many children he had, he would think, every time he tried, that the Son would come back; even if he didn't know who the Son was anymore, even if he didn't know himself anymore. That's what I tell myself: that somewhere inside of him, he never gave up on that."

"But—but what about you?" I asked.

"What about me?"

"You don't look—you don't look like…" Deedee stared at me, waiting for me to say something substantive, but I couldn't, even though I knew exactly what I wanted to say.

She smiled. "You can say it."

"But you're not like them," I said to her. "You're not short and scarred and weird like Truckie, your face isn't fucked up like Bulldog-Jeff. I've been down below, and I've seen them. They're all disfigured pretty severely. But you're not. You're almost—you're almost perfect."

"Can I show you something?" Deedee asked.

"Sure," I said.

"Just sit still. I'm going to do something, and I don't want you to misinterpret it. It's better if you're just silent, and you let me get all the way through. You'll understand when I'm finished."

"Okay," I said.

Deedee sat on the milk crates and pulled off her galoshes, then her socks. She unbuttoned her winter coat and let it fall to the floor. She disrobed: her shirt, her pants, her bra, everything but her underwear. I could only sit still, dumbly gazing at her, hopefully not so slack-jawed that I'd looked like an idiot. There were wild scars all over her body, deformed breasts hidden by prosthetics. As she removed the polyurethane straps of the prosthetic breasts, I could see red marks that had turned into scars from the long wear of the prosthetics. When she removed them, I saw two concave burrows leaning into her chest, deep enough that I wondered whether the scarification reached her heart and lungs—but then, I could clearly see the outline of her breastbone and ribcage pushing through her skin—the skin of where her breasts were supposed to be, skin that looked like it had melted.

Finally, Deedee removed her underwear. She had no genitalia. Instead, where a vagina would be, there was what looked like a stent and a catheter coming out of a hole fashioned by, I can only assume, a surgeon.

I wanted to control myself, but I couldn't. I felt pity, even though I tried to remind myself that I had no right to, even though I hadn't felt pity for any living thing in years.

"Almost perfect?" she asked.

I wanted to look down, to look away, but I didn't. Something in me forced me to meet her gaze. I thought to myself, wondered whether it was worse to be a plain mutant like Bulldog-Jeff or to be hiding in plain sight like Deedee. *What a fuckin' paradox, man.*

She stood there naked, shivering. In all the chaos, I hadn't yet turned the heat back on. The snow was still falling outside. Like a shroud. Like a bridal gown. I said nothing as she slowly dressed herself.

CHAPTER 36

Jeffersaint handled all the above-ground business. GHB had never, in his memory, come above ground to the city.

There were several reasons for that. First, he had very poor spatial intelligence, a disability that married poorly with his cocksure appraisal of his own smarts. He had roughed it alone through the underground network, due to the secrecy of his current undertaking; he was now a very lost, arrogant fool trundling through the sewers. It took him about twelve hours running down and up dead ends and looping through the same places. After he passed the same intersection of sludge and slime for the fortieth time, he finally started marking off where he'd been and consulting one of the maps Truculento-Jeffersaint had made up for him (but that GHB had never used).

When he finally poked his head up above, it was like the legendary groundhog. Only he didn't see his shadow, he saw snow. Lots of it. Snow piling down in white mounds on the ground. He'd never—once again, in *his* memory—seen snow. GHB started laughing like a fool, dancing, kicking his feet in the cold white powder, then taking long leaping strides before bringing his sideways foot swinging down into the drifts. He dropped the small gym bag he was carrying but grabbed it before it became buried in the still-accumulating snow.

"You must be GHB," a tall bald man in a polar jacket said.

"Oh, I didn't see you there."

That was true. GHB's eyes had to adjust to the light, even in the cold dark; but it wasn't really dark, not with the glimmering ivory falling from the sky.

The bald man, who stood beside a Crusher, waved GHB over to the vehicle.

"Ah," GHB said, "I know what this is. This is a *vehicle*."

"Yeah, sure is. Hop on in, Mac."

The bald man opened the back door, revealing a man waiting inside, holding a pistol. GHB didn't know any better; he just smiled. "I know what that is, *too!*"

The goon with the pistol said nothing. They drove off toward the city center.

When they reached their destination, the tall bald man opened the door of the Crusher for GHB and ushered him in through the underground service entrance of the building. They went up via the elevator, which opened straight into the mayor's huge office.

Huey was waiting, smiling. He extended his hand to GHB. "Sir, very good to meet yins, come'n in, naw."

"Very good to meet you, Mayor. *Mayor?* What does that mean?"

"Well, it's kind of like—go ahead and sit down now—it's kind of like..." Huey explained while the tall bald man pulled out a seat for GHB to sit across from Mayor Purgato, "kind of like we're a little family here in the Seven Points, and our little family has chosen me to take care of the important decisions in the household. You take my meaning?"

"I take nothing that doesn't belong to me, Mayor. But I do understand of what you speak. I am, in my own way, a mayor."

"Oh, yeah?"

"Yes, I am. You know, I pick out the clippings from the magazines, decide who gets to eat the good food—sometimes we even get cat food and dog food—that comes fresh because it's stored in the good cans. And I put on classes."

Huey smiled. "Classes, huh?"

"Oh, yes. Personal enrichment stuff. We're having a poetry slam workshop next week."

"Poetry slam? Can't say I've heard of it."

"It's a performance artform from the late twentieth and early twenty-first centuries."

"Wow," Huey responded, "sounds like you have a pretty good bead on things, better than I do, at any rate."

GHB stood up quickly, knocking into his chair so it fell backwards onto the floor. The big bald man reached for the inside of his jacket, but Huey discreetly held up a hand up to signal him to holster whatever he was packing there. GHB struck a pose.

> *"Mayor. We both be's mayors.*
> *And being mayors: It's gots layers*
> *Knock-knock, who be there?*
> *It's me, with the Alpo*
> *Knock-knock, who be there?*
> *It's me, makin' yo' mind grow.*
> *Am I a tree? Am I a root?*
> *Am I a choo-choo, goin' toot-toot?*
> *Only one thing's clear*
> *Only one thing's certain*
> *When I drop my fresh skillazills*
> *Yo' ladies be squirtin'."*

At his poem's end, GHB reached down, propped his chair back up, and sat down. Huey started clapping, first slowly, and then rapturously.

"Sorry about the chair," said GHB.

"Oh, come on, now! Forget about the chair. That was fuckin' beautiful! Yins sure're an artist, boy!"

GHB smiled. "Thanks. I'd like to say it comes naturally, but honestly I do work at it a lot."

"I bet you do. Now, how about we get down to business. Do you have what I asked for?"

"Oh, absolutely."

GHB opened up the small, ratty gym bag he'd brought with him—the one he nearly lost in the snowdrifts—and pulled out a large binder filled with magazine clippings.

Huey looked at it. "What is this?"

"The Book of Prophecy, as promised."

"But… but this isn't the… Mr. GHB, this isn't what I *need*."

"Well, why not? This is the mighty and sacred Holy Book of our people."

"But… but I need the book that yins sent those images to us from."

"The *Kromee-Ohm*?"

"The—the crummy what?"

"The *Kromee-Ohm. That's* what you wanted?" GHB laughed.

"Yes."

"Well, that's no problem. No problem at all. Though I can't imagine why you'd want it," GHB said.

Huey sighed with relief and gave a nervous laugh. "Thank you. Much obliged."

"But you're going to have to wait a couple of days."

"Why's that?"

"Because Brother Jeffersaint and his new friend Frankie are using it right now."

Purgato smiled, though it was a fake smile. He had trouble composing himself at the revelation of this new piece of intel. He placed his hands together to form a little chapel. "Excuse me?"

"You're excused," said GHB. "But don't worry about seeming stupid, Mayor Huey, these sorts of things can be very confusing to those inexperienced in leadership, such as yourself. You are not a stupid dummy idiot at all. I just have a much wiser head and a steadier hand. Not because I'm anything special, mind you. Just experience. Just good old-fashioned experience."

Huey tugged at his collar, already drenched in sweat. "Mr. GHB, my understanding was that we had a deal: I give you your own penthouse apartment in the city, a personal guard, and, in your words 'all the good garbage.' Then you would provide me with the book I sought."

"Well, sure," GHB replied, "that was the deal. But how was I supposed to know you meant the *Kromee-Ohm*? I mean, that thing is completely useless. Once you touch it, you have everything you need from it anyway."

Huey raised an eyebrow, still tugging at his collar. "How's that?"

"Well, it speaks to you. Well, not to *you*, Mayor Huey—and I'll remind you that this is, once again, not because you are a stupid dummy idiot, but because *I* am the one who has had the contact with the *Kromee-Ohm*—and it speaks to *me*."

"What's it saying right now?" Huey asked with a skeptical tone to his voice.

GHB closed his eyes and concentrated, like a swami at a state fair. "It says, *rishon, rishon, bereshit, ze karov*."

"What the hell does that mean?"

"Hell if I know," GHB said. He looked into the mayor's eyes and asked, "So when do I get to see my new apartment?"

"It's a *penthouse*," replied the mayor. "Maybe too far above-ground for you."

GHB did not miss a beat. "As you can see in the Book of Prophecy," he replied, "there are several excerpts from an ancient periodical called *Penthouse*. Naturally, I'm very curious and excited to see what a penthouse apartment looks like. In the words of the *Maxim* scribes, the idea *tickles my pickle*."

"Wait, wait, wait, wait. Hold on a minute. Can you just write down some of those things you hear?" asked the mayor.

"Sure, why not? But, I have to tell you, I am *awful* hungry.

Perhaps before attending to more business, I might get some of that good garbage?"

Huey looked at the tall bald bodyguard, hoping for some sort of cue, but the big man only shrugged. Huey Purgato stood and walked over to the trash bin next to his desk and brought it over to GHB. GHB enthusiastically sifted through the trash bin's contents and pulled out a half-eaten sandwich and a used prophylactic. He ate the sandwich and then dangled the used condom above his waiting mouth. "Ah, time for dessert."

The tall bald man started retching and made for the bathroom stalls.

Covering his mouth with one hand, Huey picked up a pen and a pad of paper and handed it to GHB with the other. "Now do me a favor and write down whatever that *Kromee-Ohm* thing is transmitting to you."

"Sure thing," GHB said. "You want me to do the doodles, too?"

"The doodles?" Huey questioned.

"You know, the funny symbols and stuff."

"Yes. Yes. Everything."

GHB made as if he was going to start writing but stopped just as the pen was about to touch the paper. "I'm going to need more of that good garbage."

"Absolutely." The mayor whistled loudly and had two men sent out to the dumpsters next to the garage.

CHAPTER 37

L avalle didn't know how long he had been lost in his world of perversion. He had never indulged himself in that type of pure animal escapism before.

Pervert, sicko—those words flashed on and off inside his mind. He'd kept strict control over his behavior for the majority of his life, only to lash out with vigor—indulge in escapism—when given the opportunity.

As Lavalle wondered how many hours or days had passed, Cotton Lenny appeared in the room. She approached the bed where Lavalle was unwinding from his latest adventures of feet worship.

"Yins have'd y'self a good ol' time, sick-boy?"

Lavalle grew pale as chalk.

"Com'n on, now," Cotton Lenny added, "we got's t'go."

Lavalle's brief recollection only allowed a short memory of him and Cotton Lenny walking down the stairwell, then his eyes flashed, his memory hit a fuzzy spot, and he found that they were entering the mayor's office. It was a very strange scene.

He saw a man, freshly bathed, wearing a silk bathrobe while he picked through garbage bags. The man removed a rotted, half-eaten sandwich wrapped in aluminum foil and ate the sandwich along with the foil. While chewing, he attempted to write out something, but was doing it at a slow crawl. The mayor looked frustrated until he stole a look in Lavalle's direction.

"Lavalle, my boy! Thank goodness yins're here. We got a little project for you."

Cotton Lenny gently pushed at the small of Lavalle's back with her spindly phalanges, moving him closer to the odd scene.

"Go'head naw, darlin,'" she cooed.

"This is Mr. GHB, by the way," Mayor Purgato said to Lavalle by way of introduction. Lavalle extended his hand to the freshly shampooed GHB, which had left his long hair and his beard a frizzy but smooth forest of static chaos. GHB did not extend his hand but simply touched Lavalle on the head in an odd anointing ritual. Finally, GHB spoke in a hip-hop chant:

> "Your name is Lavalle
> Nigga, you be pale
> I got the rhymes
> I got the Times
> Of New York
> Salty, like jerky made from pork
> Here's the news, read tha paper
> If I had to guess your M.O.
> I say yous a raper."

GHB smiled and slapped Lavalle with a downward high-five. Huey smiled and, tongue-in-cheek, explained, "Mr. GHB has been teaching us the old historical practice of slam poetry."

Lavalle's cheeks turned bright red. *Raper.* He was fresh off the shame from the brothel. "Mr. Mayor—"

"*Huey*, boy, you know that."

"—*Huey*, how may I assist you?"

"Mr. GHB has been kind enough to record some important information for us, but unfortunately his... typographical skills are not of the same superior level as his historical and artistic abilities."

"I'm a creative," GHB interjected.

"Oh, yins sure're. Lavalle, would you mind sitting with Mr. GHB and transcribing the sounds and images he describes, as they come to him?"

GHB had already moved to a far corner of the room and lifted the back of the bathrobe up high around his waist, like a lady lifting the hem of her dress before stepping over a puddle. He was engaged in an act of defecation.

Lavalle looked at Mayor Purgato quizzically. "And this is for…?"

Purgato excused himself, Lavalle, and Cotton Lenny from GHB and led them to an office corner for a private conversation.

"I know, it looks… strange. It is. This fellow claims he does not need the *Kromee-Ohm* because it speaks to him directly, but," the mayor paused to glance back toward GHB, "I must say, while I believe this fellow, I have come up with a backup plan, if you will."

"An' jus' what's yin's backup plan, Mister Mayor?" Cotton Lenny asked.

"My associate, Mister Lavalle here, did not do anything about the Attanasio fellow when he had the opportunity. I am going to right his wrong," Purgato claimed. "Yes indeed. By any means necessary."

CHAPTER 38

Exhaustion got to me, and I fell into a deep sleep in my office chair. Or I fell into a reverie.

For the first time since I started slipping into the nightmares—not knowing when I was awake, not knowing if I was asleep—*I knew where I was.* More specifically, I was better able to grasp my level of awareness and my conscious state.

A great edifice loomed in front of me—a building that was a hybrid of an old continental parliament building and a golden mechanical clocktower. Moving gears covered the structure. Pulleys were attached to gigantic sheets of iron, steel, silver, and gold that shifted and churned in a continuous game of Tetris. Some portions of the sheets would meet at their edges or overlap, shielding the clocktower-building's interior, while others rotated and lifted away to reveal the innards of the great machine. There were moving gears and pulleys inside the living building as well.

I know that I am here. Here must know that I am. This place must know that I am—what I am.

For the first time, I was unafraid of The Becoming. Out of curiosity, I waved a hand in the air. The mammoth machinery stuttered—*I made that happen.*

"Pretty neat, right?" a familiar voice asked. Old Miss Runny was standing next to me.

"Hi!" I answered effusively enough to surprise myself. "I was hoping I might see you again."

"Likewise, sonny. Likewise."

"What is this place?" I asked.

She only laughed; it was a friendly laugh. "Hard to say, since it's yours. I was hoping you might tell me."

"What do you mean by that?" I asked. "It's my dream?"

"It's not a dream."

"Then what is it?"

Miss Runny shrugged and pouted her lower lip in response. "Don't be a sour little baby," she replied. "I said I didn't know what it was. I didn't say I wouldn't help you find out."

"My apologies."

Miss Runny pointed up at the mechanism. "Look," she said, "It's not exactly ship-shape."

She was right. Some of the pulleys were attached to ropes that had snapped from weather wear, and there were rusted-over chains with missing links. Some of the gears were lying on the ground, as if they'd been removed for maintenance and then never replaced. That explained why the shimmering plates of precious metals stuttered every now and then in their Tetris block scheme.

"Hey, let me ask you something," I said.

"Shoot," she replied.

"How does time work in here?"

She smiled. "It doesn't."

"Meaning...?"

"Meaning this isn't a dream, it's something else. So's'far as I know, that whole dream cycle temporal relativity thing don't apply. No, it don't."

"Meaning...?"

"Jesus, boy, just say what you want to say."

"Are we losing any time being in here?"

She pulled out a clutter of necklaces from under her cassock:

talismans, amulets, and other doohickies, each one tied to a leather string. "Let's see," she intoned gravely as she sorted through them with a consternated glare. "Nope... nope, not this one. Fuckin'ell, I don't remember even having this one." She stopped shuffling and held one of the trinkets up. "Ah, here it is."

She fingered the amulet, tapping on the glass shell over its face. It looked like a combination of an astrolabe and a miniature telescopic device set into a calculator. Miss Runny fiddled with a few buttons then brought her eye right up next to the device's face.

"Nope," she answered. "No time in here."

"So, we can take as long as we need to."

"Strictly speaking, we're not *taking* anything, long or short, time, space, or otherwise. We just *are*. In this place. Here."

It made perfect sense to me, in my animal soul. My rational mind started itching, but considering everything I'd seen and heard in the last couple of days, I decided rationalism couldn't play any part in my decisions.

I concentrated, waving my hands as I had before, and the rusted gears and cogs lying on the ground hovered briefly.

"Hey, pretty good," Miss Runny said, "but try this." She showed me a few fluid hand motions. "It's not about fighting it—you look like you're fighting with it. It's about moving with it."

Miss Runny rotated her arms in sync with the giant cog now floating in front of her, then sent it spinning toward the great building. With a loud *clank,* the cog found its way back into the machinery. Following her lead, I gave it a shot. Three of the gears spun up all at once; pulleys snapped back into place as their ropes rebraided. It was like a film running backwards.

ON THE COLD SLAB, Dreck's body began to move. A small jerk, a tiny movement. A glowing in his dead blue eyes.

Truckie turned to look at him.

"Is it doing anything?" I asked Miss Runny.

"Does it matter? You in a hurry to get back to that shitstorm you was in?"

"I guess not," I muttered.

There was a lever, I think, that must have switched on in my brain, because the next time I brought my hands around, I did it with a sureness that engendered an incredible spectacle: the precious metal panels flew outward from the building, then hovered in the air, fully exposing the machinery underneath.

BULLDOG-JEFF LET OUT a howl and jumped back. Dreck's body was twitching. Fucking twitching.

"EVERY GOOD TURN DESERVES ANOTHER," Miss Runny said.

She thrust her hands outward; her arms stretched and strained then transformed into bundles—thousands of them—of thick, ropy strings. The string appendages held the panels in the air. She nodded to me as if to say *get back to it, boy.*

I smiled, then mimed a great tidal wave with my arms, which shook off the verdigris from the copper and the grit from the cornices, cleaned the dirt from the dials and washed the soot from all the surfaces. The gears and cogs of the golden clocktower abruptly thrummed and hummed with a deafening sound—like church bells, only a thousand times more… *more harmonious, more pleasant, more powerful.* Miss Runny yanked back the strings, and the thousands of strands flew back and transformed back into her hands.

"Now," she bellowed. *"Now!"*

I don't know how I knew what she meant. What the word

"now" meant. But I did. I can't remember what I did next, but it sent all the cleansed and well-working parts back together—a colossal crash sounded as everything shot back into place. There was nary a gear—let me tell you, *nary-a-fuckin'-gear*—that wasn't working perfectly after that.

The golden clocktower gleamed.

DRECK'S BODY shot up on the cold slab, sitting upright. Truckie and Bulldog-Jeff, terrified, jumped back.

"What's happening?" Truckie screamed.

Deedee rushed into the room. She didn't look afraid. She knew that the vessel—the body—had resurrected. Yet, there was still a nothingness, a void, behind the blue eyes.

"WELL, THAT WAS FUN," Miss Runny remarked.

Performing telekinesis in a place outside of time forced my adrenaline up higher than it had been in a long time. Higher than it had been since the War, anyhow. How I had adrenaline, how my pulse beat as an indicator that time still went on—that I didn't understand. But I had *control*. And it was not minimal. These actions would yield results. My actions. Over which I had control.

What happens in here happens out there, too.

"Fuckin' hell yeah," I said, out of breath. "How about we go take a look inside?"

We walked in together.

Inside was an old leper. The skin fell off his mangled and hideous body. The poor creature was so odious that even Miss Runny recoiled from him. I did not. Because he did not repulse me. His appearance offset the good that resided within him, and I didn't know how I knew that he was good. Maybe the time I'd spent with the children had shed a few years or centuries or decades of judgment off of me. But the leper was simultaneously a leper and something else. Some*one* else.

I tried to remember the last time I had to open a conversation with a living human being I didn't need something from. The memory wouldn't come to me, so I decided to wing it.

Miss Runny spoke first. "Leper," she said, "whose tower is this?"

He rasped uncomfortably, lips half-paralyzed and mind unpracticed in the art of language, or maybe just communication. But he did do it—he did speak.

"It is a greater construction, ma'am, than any man can claim ownership of. Celestial. Outside of time and space, and all that rote nonsense. I suppose its steward, though, is the boy with whom you came." The leper flashed a lingering glance in my direction.

"My name is Frank Attanasio, sir," I said. "We would like to help you, if we can."

The leper wheezed and wobbled. I caught him when his knees buckled.

"No, no. You wouldn't be helping me, son. You would be helping yourself."

"What do you mean?" I asked.

The leper rose unsteadily to his feet and limped away from us, calling back, "You're welcome to do as you like, my son. Surely, you know that there is no hour here but the holy hour, no clock hands to point you to your appointments. Be well."

I thought I saw him disappear into the dark shadows at the far end of an arched walkway—like a cloistered courtyard in miniature. But when I squinted, there was no trace of the leper. Not even a piece of flesh fallen from his decaying form.

My elderly companion cracked her knuckles. "I say we get started."

I looked around the massive interior, which seemed impossibly larger than the already monolithic exterior that we had fixed. "Where would we even start?"

CHAPTER 39

"And verily, the person who hath touched the trunk of the tree: that person shall have sap upon his hand, and the hand shall be alike unto the stickiness of the sap, as the tree was alike unto the earthiness of the earth."

GHB recited his translation of the *Kromee-Ohm* to Lavalle. GHB's language was so classic, so formal—*so King James-ish*—that even in conversation, his words came out in a way that made one visualize italic slants to them.

GHB abruptly veered into vernacular as he envisioned an illustration from the book. "And there's a doodle of a couple triangles with the face of a dog on top of it," he blurted out.

"What kind of dog?" asked Lavalle. "Any kind of dog? I mean, there are *hundreds* of canine breeds. Could you be a little more specific than that?"

GHB leaned over Lavalle's shoulder and ran his fingers across the doodles the young man had drafted over the past few hours. "Ah, my child, I see that you are trying to use your thinking brain to translate the prophecies of the *Kromee-Ohm*. No, no, my child— that is all wrong. You must use your heart brain. Your *heart* brain."

The two had been at loggerheads all day. Lavalle had been

transcribing, translating, and illustrating for hours, and his hands hurt. GHB had insisted that because the Book itself was written in ink (or so he said) that any writing and pictorializing could not be done with the aid of a word processor or animation program. Lavalle had retorted that since the *Kromee-Ohm's* images transformed as they were revealed to GHB's consciousness, they should use animation to replicate them more accurately. But GHB had only laughed and called Lavalle a "toolie tool."

"Shall I continue?" GHB said this with his nose upturned and his arms spread out sideways in a messianic pose.

"I guess so."

GHB went back into his italic-speech mode.

"The spheres of wisdom are very much like a drum set. For the largest sphere, it is the bass drum; and the floor-tom, it is the medium-sized sphere; and the smaller tom-toms—they, according to their sizes and how the drum-key tunes them, they are smaller spheres yet. Moving on to how the Harmony of the Spheres is like the wikka-wikka-wah sound of the wah-wah pedal..."

Huey broke the spell by barging into the room wearing his signature smile, the painfully-upturned smile, that Glasgow smile that reached for his eyes. "How's it comin' along. Yins chugga'-chuggin', movin' along?" he asked.

"Oh, yes," GHB answered. "Lavalle has been most instrumental in transcribing my prophetic visions to the written page. I must admit to you, Mayor Huey Manperson, that I was skeptical of your desire to record the contents of the *Kromee-Ohm*, but as young Lavalle and I have moved along, we have discovered that the process has been most efficacious. Like the mongoose and the snake, we work in perfect harmony. Like the brooding teenager and her mother, we are perfectly aligned in our goals. Like the turd and the toilet bowl," GHB continued, solemnly clasping his hands together, "we have become one."

"Well, that's great, sir. Yessuh, that's fine, real fine," Huey cooed in his best politico voice. He peeked over Lavalle's shoulder to look at the notebook his aide-de-camp had been scribbling into. There was a picture of a dog—more like a stick figure—with big, oval ears and a squiggle-line for a tail.

Lavalle turned to his mayor-boss and said, "Mr. GHB has taken the liberty of explicating some of the verses. His exegesis has proved... voluminous."

Huey looked nervous. Lavalle reassured him, "But, I took the liberty of separating the main body of the translation from Mr. GHB's interpretation using color coding."

Huey sighed in relief. "Good thinkin', Lavalle. Real right good thinkin'."

At that moment, Cotton Lenny sashayed in, though she didn't look her regular whimsically maleficent self.

"How they doin' at it?" she asked.

"Real good. Some real right good thinkin' they got to 'em," Huey replied.

"Is it ready?" Lenny asked.

"I should say so," GHB answered. "You can give it a spin."

Cotton Lenny yanked the notebook away from Lavalle. She held it up to her face and started reading, rapidly flipping through the pages, muttering excerpts as she read. "This—this can't be all the right shit."

"It has footnotes for ease of use," GHB replied, completely unaware of the irritability bleeding through Cotton Lenny's speech. "It's... it's *footnotorious*."

His witticism did not register with Cotton Lenny, who let a scowl creep across her face. "But—but it's all in some kind of meter. Like poetry," she complained.

"I know," GHB replied, impressed with himself. "Easier to remember. You can thank me later."

Cotton Lenny looked like she was going to smash the notebook down onto GHB's head, who had his back turned. As she yanked the notebook in a violent downward swipe, Mayor Purgato grabbed her by the wrists and pulled the notes away from her. Just then, GHB turned to see Huey holding Lenny's arms, and smiled.

"Ah, young love," GHB said. "You two make a lovely couple."

Huey smiled. "Thank yins."

He let go of Cotton Lenny's wrists as he whispered to her, "Why don't we give it a try 'fore we go bashin' folks in they heads, hmm?"

Cotton Lenny's glare pierced through Purgato. "I need results *now*," she said in a hushed, biting tone. She ripped her arms from his hands. "Get me somethin' workable, *god-damnit!*"

Happily taking the opportunity to look away from the woman, Purgato addressed his ancient-texts-garbage consultant. "Mr. GHB, wouldn't yins mind walkin' with me?"

"Absolutely."

GHB followed Huey as he walked over to one of the three elevators that opened onto his office floor. They stepped into the largest one, an industrial-size lift with doors that opened and closed from the top and the bottom like a cavernous jaw. Huey held down the emergency call button and punched a code into the floor-level buttons on the interface. The elevator descended, then stuttered after a few levels. Suddenly, it shivered and hiccupped, and the lift started moving horizontally instead of vertically. GHB marveled at this, beaming. After a few minutes, the industrial elevator opened into a large, poured-concrete bunker, high-ceilinged and the length of a football field.

"Welcome to the lab," Huey pridefully spoke.

"I don't know what to say. This secret laboratory..." GHB replied with a grave look on his face.

Mayor Purgato looked nervous.

"This clandestine location," GHB went on, "is... *awesome!*"

Huey let out some nervous laughter. "Thank you kindly."

"So, what are we doing down here Mayor Huey Manperson?"

"We's gon' see if that book yins crafted up has got the same... properties as the, uh—what'sat you called the original book?"

"The *Kromee-Ohm*."

"That's right, the *Kromee-Ohm*. We's gon' see if they's the same."

GHB walked over to one of the manifold mechanical control boards. His hands flew over them, twisting buttons and yanking levers.

"Now-now don't do that yet!" interrupted the mayor. "We gotta get Cotton Lenny down here 'fore—"

But before Mayor Purgato could finish speaking, the assembled gears and gadgets, computers and contrivances, whirred on in a harmonious consonance of sound, very much like the tuning of a symphony orchestra.

Huey's face displayed pure awe. "How did you...?"

"Oh, Jeffersaint has a few of these different thingamaboobs down below. He showed us how to work them in case of emergency," GHB said.

"What kind of emergency?"

"You know—like... hmm. You know, actually, I *don't* know. But it seemed real important to him that I know how to work this stuff. Something about a *portal*. But I might be misremembering. So, what did you have in mind?"

Huey was tongue-tied for more than a moment. Finally, he turned to GHB and said, "Why don't yins show me one of them passages from the *Kromee-Ohm?* You know, just so's I can see it in operation."

GHB smiled. "Sure. What do you want to see?"

Huey leafed through the notebook and stopped when he saw one of the illustrations.

"What's this one? It looks like a glass of water with gold flakes in it," Huey asked as he held up the notebook for GHB to see.

"No, it's Goldschlager."

"The booze?"

"No, no," GHB laughed, "that's just the word we use for it. It's actually a glass of water with gold flakes in it. But don't feel like a stupid dummy idiot—these are just things I've learned; it isn't your fault that you haven't done the learning, Mayor Huey Manperson."

Huey shook his head. "Well, what does the picture and the writing—what does it *do*?"

"Alchemy."

"Turns water into gold?"

"Yes indeed."

"Wow. Have you ever tried to use that before?"

"No. Why would I need to do such a thing?"

"To... to turn water—to make gold."

"What for?"

"You know, to have something valuable, so you can buy things."

"I've never bought things," GHB said.

"But... but in case you *want* to buy things."

"I've never wanted to buy things."

"Then how do you get what you want?"

"I find it."

"How?"

"By getting other people to do it."

"And how do you get them to do the things you want to do?"

"By giving them things."

Huey thought he had finally cornered GHB. "Aha! And *what* do you give them?"

"Songs. Knowledge. Personal enrichment classes."

Huey could only sigh. "Fine. You don't need gold."

"That's what I was trying to tell you, but you wouldn't listen. It's really not your fault. Don't think that it's because you're a stu—"

"You know what, that's okay," the mayor insisted. "Let's just see if it works."

GHB shrugged in response. "Whatever you say, Mister Mayor Manperson."

Huey Purgato was surprised to find that GHB didn't have any of the reservations of normal socialized people, wasn't hesitant to get his hands all over other people's property, and didn't care much for the things other people cared greatly for. And boy did he ever look the part of the eccentric—his unkempt hair and Brillo-like beard jutting out all over the place, as if the first bath he'd ever taken made his body hair messier than when it was filthy and matted down. GHB placed the notebook in front of him, looked around, patted the sides of his robe to check the pockets, and smiled to himself as if sharing a joke.

"You know what we could use for this one, Mayor Huey Manperson?"

"What's that Mr. GHB?"

"A glass of water."

"Ah! Of course." Huey walked over to the full bar he kept down in the laboratory and poured a glass, then returned and held it out for GHB.

"Don't hand it to me; set it on the aluminum table over there."

Huey set the glass down and stood next to the table.

"Now walk away from the table!" GHB chastised. "Jeezy creezy Japanese-y, now you *are* acting like a stupid dummy idiot."

Huey wanted to throttle him.

"Well, turn it on," GHB said.

"Turn what on?"

GHB sighed in exasperation and held his head in his hands, fingers pressed against his temples like he was self-soothing a headache. "The thing you use for your bad stuff. Do you want me to do this or what, stupid dummy idiot dum-dum?"

Inside, Huey was fuming. He was sure he would kill this imbecile when all this was over. Nevertheless, he turned out the lights and switched on the machinery that controlled the shapeshifting electricity. He switched on the looping perpetual motion machines that conducted that energy.

GHB seemed to be in deep concentration. He held up the book, image facing the motion machine, and his lips moved in vibrating murmurs. Finally, he screamed out, "Shut it down! Shut it down!"

Huey ripped the kill switch and turned the lights on. He

walked over to look at the glass. There were tiny little flecks of gold in it.

"*Fuckin' fuck me,*" Huey exclaimed. "You really did it."

"Fuckin' fuck right I did."

What Huey didn't see was GHB sneaking a vial of gold flakes back into the sleeve of his bathrobe.

CHAPTER 40

Apart of me felt like I'd been inside the golden clocktower my entire life; a safe, steady backdrop to my childhood memories. My friend Alex would always talk about the two homes he remembered as being constants throughout his youth and adulthood. The first one belonged to the woman he called his Nani, who lived near Lebanon (in Pennsylvania, not the Middle East).

Nani lived out in the sticks, although by the time Alex'd grown up, even Lebanon had condo complexes and strip malls dotting its periphery. He told me stories about riding the tractor over the fields, just past the chain link fence that closed off the part of her property not used for planting crops. He remembered going out with his neighbor—the one he was supposed to stay away from because his family were *low* people—to shoot rabbits out by the creek—no, the *crick*. And then there was the old Victorian house in Harrisburg, where his studious uncle and brilliant bohemian aunt lived. His aunt and uncle would host celebration after celebration in that old Victorian house, becoming the locus for all family activity.

Most of Alex's stories of childhood revolved around those two places. And I remembered those places from those stories with clarity. A clarity that my own life's remembrances—especially those from my childhood—lacked. Strange how I can barely remember anything from my childhood at all. But maybe I'm remembering those places because the very *essence* of memory is what the inside of the golden clocktower gives me. Memory. Memory that I haven't had, memory that is new but old at the same time. I begin to see things in my mind's eye; I can see these memories that aren't mine while I'm trawling the walkways of this infinite palace within the gleaming gear-machines—walking and chewing gum, as it were. Floating memories, like what the Japanese made in their *ukiyo-e* prints before the earthquakes and then The Long War—hell, isn't that what *ukiyo* means? Transience?

Even though this place is not a dream, it has the quality of a dream. Many times, I can't remember how I came to be in this room or that room. At one moment I'm repairing beams and refinishing the old walls that have grown cold and cracked, and in another moment, I'm sitting silent in an empty and dark room. This is a peculiar place. Miss Runny has been very helpful while we've been here; a span of time that, for all I know, could be ages. I wouldn't be surprised to return to the physical world only to find that I'd missed a few millennia of human events. Memory lapses.

As the repairs move along, I see the leper again here and there. It's hard to get a direct line of sight on him. When I do, I swear that the mutilated portions of his anatomy have, in some small measure, repaired themselves. And when I try to look at him, I'm unable to do so directly, as the attempt only ends, at best, in a peripheral glance. It's a lot like having floaters, or little dark or light spots that overlay one's vision—try to look directly at it and it slips right out of direct view. I've tried to follow the path they take, or to control them, but no matter what, they always evade my attempts to lock in on them. That's what it's like with the leper. I can never quite *see* him, even though I always see him.

There are no days in the clocktower. There are something like hours that fold in on themselves and restart in this place where time doesn't exist—that's the reason I sometimes can't remember being in a place, or can't remember how I'd come to *be* in that place.

But there are other memories, memories from beyond this place, that aren't mine. And they are as vivid and real as any other memory I'd had, and as real-feeling as any experiences I've had in my life. Strangely, the more Miss Runny and I repair this place, the more those ever-clear foreign memories invade and dominate my consciousness.

I saw a field, golden rows of wheat, a wooden fence in the distance. I saw a man, he looked like me, but he was stronger, broader, taller. I smelled these memories, tasted them. I saw a home in some wooded hinterland, and remembered winters that came and passed, never seeing a television, or taking a sip of alcohol. I saw a granary and a dairy, and remembered the bearded farmers raising and nailing homes. I remembered laughing with the tall, broad man. He was my father. I was remembering my father.

But how can that be? These aren't my memories. That man— he is nothing like the father I've been told about (although, the one I never knew).

MISS RUNNY TOUCHES MY SHOULDER. It's been minutes and it's been a thousand years.

"We've finished," she tells me.

And I know she's right, because I can feel it in the steely veins and metallic tendons of this place, in its clusters of organs: court-yards and tapestries inside the golden clocktower. I feel music. Its tones are unfamiliar—dissonant but not unpleasant; the sound of every conceivable tone and half-tone sounding out in unison. If tones could be light, it would be a beacon.

We follow the sound, and walk into a grand theater, baroque and drenched in the blood of the silkworm, golden-roped and well-lit with the appurtenances of the stagehand's trade, a glow pouring below the proscenium, washing yellow and bright over the stage's floorboards. At the bottom of the seating area, directly in front of the orchestra pit, there is a glass box with the leper inside. But he's not the leper anymore. He's a handsome man with a persnickety facial-hair trim—a tight, dark-dyed Van Dyke—and penetrating blue-green eyes. He is done up in some Orientalist's vision of old Persia, wearing a great big Ottoman turban with a peacock feather and a precious jewel set as the third eye. The glass box encasing the Ottoman Leper-who-was is set atop an arcade thingum, with a slot for coins and red rectangular buttons. There is gilded lettering across the top of the glass box.

"It's Zoltan," Miss Runny said.

"Who?"

"You know, from the movie *Big*."

I shook my head, unfamiliar with the reference.

"*Big*," she repeated. "You know, with Tom Hanks."

"No idea."

"G-d, I'm old," she replied. "So twentieth century."

We walked down the red carpet runners lining the lanes between the curved squares and rectangles that made up the orchestra seating and mezzanine. Once we reached the bottom, the theater lights dimmed so that only the glass box was backlit; the glow alternated between a vivid purple and emerald haze. The color-lights bled into one another, swirling ethereal and bright against the backdrop of the darkened auditorium.

A ticket-dispenser buzzed, accompanied by the whirring sound of one being pushed out. It was a yellow pulp-paper ticket, but larger than usual. It read:

The Fisherman has his catch.
The feeding for the yellow wretch.

ADMIT TWO

The moment I'd finished reading the slip of paper, Miss Runny and I found ourselves back at the entrance to the theater.

"Has this ever happened to you?" I asked her.

"Not quite like this. This is... specific. If a bit odd."

I scoffed "This stands out as being odd? Then what was all the rest we've gone through?"

"Off-color but run-of-the-mill."

"That's a hell of a mill."

"I suppose," she answered.

A ticket-taker, dressed in coat and tails, stuck out his white-gloved hand in expectancy. "Tickets, please."

I looked at Miss Runny inquiringly. She was now dressed in full gown and pearls, stemmed footwear and gleaming earpieces. Her physiology had rearranged itself so that she evinced a beguiling, dark, mysterious beauty, something remnant in her body.

The look on her face was, I imagine, very similar to my own expression. I looked down and saw that I was cleaner; not only that, but I also felt younger, stronger. I noticed some treatment in my hair. My eyes felt clearer. And, I too, found myself mysteriously dressed for a night out on the town. We smiled at one another, and I handed the yellow pulp-paper ticket from the Leper's arcade machine to the ticket-taker. We walked into the foyer area and there were theater-goers speaking and shouting, listening and laughing, creating that low-hum background chatter that peaks every now and again with a sharp titter or a guttural *harumph*-or-something-other.

Miss Runny took my arm. She was looking around the crowd. At that moment, I noticed something in her eyes that I hadn't seen before—delight. She was overtaken with that phenomenon of *what's-catching*, and as she heard loud and boisterous laughter coming from the pockets of friends gathered here and there, she began laughing too.

I turned to her and asked, "Can I buy you a drink?"

She smiled and nodded through her laughter.

Her pure delight was contagious, and I found myself chuckling. "Why don't you go mix it up and I'll get us a round?"

She obliged and I went over to the bar.

I looked toward the barman and raised a finger. "Gin on the rocks and a glass of white wine—the good stuff, not the swill you give to the marks."

The barman smiled and said, "Right away, sir." As he moved swiftly—and he did move swiftly, as professional tenders do when trying to avoid a bottleneck—he spouted the normal patter of a practiced barman. "So, where are you from?"

"I'll be honest, I'm not even sure anymore." I didn't normally brook ice-breaking chatter, but I was long across and away from that familiar river—humanity—and thought the better course was to play it as it lay.

"Well, that's better anyhow," he replied. "We're all from nowhere, or from somewhere we forgot. Either way, you're going to have a great time tonight. You'll *love* the show." He placed both our drinks on napkins (the outside of the glasses were bone dry; he really was a professional barman).

"What'll it be?" I asked.

The barman smiled. "On the house, sir. Your money's no good here."

"Why's that?"

"It's *your* show. Hasn't anyone told you?"

I shook my head.

The barman gave an incredulous laugh. "Then, boy oh boy, are you in for a treat!"

Just as I was about to ask what he meant by that, Miss Runny touched the crook of my elbow.

"Frankie," she cooed, "I want you to meet someone. This is Zoltan. The one I was telling you about, from the Tom Hanks film."

A swarthy Fars (or maybe Hindu) was standing next to her, dressed in loud silk and sporting the same headdress the healed

leper had been wearing. He bowed to me and said, "Mr. Attanasio, *sahib*. Truly, it is an honor to be here on the night of your
Rememorial."

I extended my hand to shake but he paid it no mind.
"Rememorial?" I asked.

"Yes, *sahib*. It is quite the event."

"Never mind that," Miss Runny interjected. "Show him one of
your tricks."

Zoltan smiled and said "Miss Elizabeth is quite enthusiastic
for legerdemain. Simple illusions, mind you, but I must admit,
sahib, that I didn't learn them in order to *not* entertain."

Miss Elizabeth? I questioningly mouthed that name to Miss
Runny—*Elizabeth?*—to which she only shrugged. "Go ahead!" she
prodded Zoltan. "Come on, now, *show him*."

Zoltan held out a deck of cards—half-foot-long squares, ornate
and hand-illustrated, with some Italianate print along the border.
Not your typical deck. Very old tarot, maybe. He snapped his
wrist, the cards spread out into a fanned half-circle, like the wing-
span of a falcon tipped in ink.

"Take your pick," he told me. This was easy, as one of them
produced somewhat of a drawing energy, something that called to
me. The card had a picture of an old fisherman sitting on the bow
of a fishing boat (the boat was so tall and narrow I thought it
would be impossible for it not to tip over in the water). The fisherman was holding a pole with an apparatus that looked like an
antique telescope with an arc of electricity running along its housing. A great green-and-yellow behemoth—I think from the Book
of Jonah—was leaping after the bait on the hook while a pinkish,
red-eyed monster, some great thing made of moonstone and ether,
looked down from the sky; its monstrous hand rising next to the
too-tall boat in the unnatural blue-and-white ocean. Zoltan
nodded, grinned, and held the card between his hands; the rest of
the deck disappeared, I can only assume into his large, billowing
sleeves. He rubbed his hands together, concealing the card I'd
picked in his large palm, and when he opened his hands, the fish-

erman was sitting on the tips of his fingers, and the green-and-yellow Leviathan leapt between the lines in his hands.

Miss Runny—no, Elizabeth—clapped in delight, and spouted, "Incredible!"

"That's quite a trick," I added.

"Thank you, *sahib*," Zoltan said. "I'm glad you enjoyed it."

"*Zoltan, you old dog!*" Someone called out from across the room. He answered, "Coming!" then turned back to me to say, "I have to mingle. If you'll excuse me, *sahib*."

Miss Runny—no, *Elizabeth*—took my arm and we walked over to where the house-merchants were hawking their wares. There was a gift-stand with *Playbills* and other twentieth-century memorabilia. I pick up one of the *Playbills* and examined it: *Frankie Attanasio Rememorial—ONE NIGHT ONLY*. Weird. Then I saw the keychains, cups, and t-shirts for sale with pictures of my face on them, and the same title from the *Playbill* in bold and blocky lettering.

"What do you make of all this?" I asked.

"I say we just enjoy ourselves," Elizabeth purred, and leaned in to kiss me on the cheek.

A bell chimed and the five-minute-warning was announced. We finished our drinks and headed to our seats, which were right next to the orchestra pit, all the way in the front. I peered over the barrier between us and the orchestra and saw musicians playing instruments that I didn't recognize.

There was a boy in a copper exoskeleton, like the ones the bomb experts wore in The Long War. His limp limbs made him look like he was quadriplegic; his long unkempt hair, with two lustrous curls at each temple, gave him a peculiar mystique. The exoskeleton beamed with innumerable small lighted pits, each one a tiny spotlight that projected vaporous hologrammatic constructions of stringed and percussive instruments, which in turn were operated by projections of vaporous hologrammatic appendages. The ephemeral instrumentation and appendages produced a complex symphony. There was an old man leaned over a pedal-steel guitar whose strings glowed a neon blue. When he picked at the strings, an echo of tessellated shapes puffed out into the air, visible vibrations, and then hovered before slowly disappearing as steam would.

The swell of the orchestra, closing in on a universal harmony, ebbed and flowed with the organic addition and subtraction of pre-performance participants down in the pit.

Finally, the lights dimmed. As the curtains opened, the murmur of the cheery spectators also shrunk to nothing—silence. A spotlight projected a brilliant spectrum over the first character to appear: an unidentifiable man wearing a mask. A slow dance between woodwinds and strings began, and the man in the mask spoke in rhyming but mangle-metered verse.

> *The Gleaming Clocktower having reached its repair*
> *And the ten worlds now gathered, Empyrean fare*
> *The harvest of spirit, plowed for the souls*
> *Collected for us to bear witness—Rememorial*
> *Tale-bearers bereft, in times before the quill*
> *Where ink-stained hearts within could not spill*
> *A memory palace; a Golden Clocktower*
> *So the Son's completion heralds this hallowed hour*

A circle materialized behind the man, around it were numbers, arrayed about outward-pointing triangles demarcating the outer boundary of the shape.

> *Through our wisdom we have but retained*
> *The most paltry grain of the Father's remains*
> *And in this hallowed hour we discover*
> *The means by which one thought becomes another*

I then saw a young boy onstage. The boy looked like me, but handsomer. He looked human, but some features of his anatomy looked like origami, and his joints moved like a marionette's. An amber backlight floated and created an ethereal haze behind the boy's head. The marionette-boy looked out to the audience—no, looked to *me*—and said:

> *We and I were made undone*
> *Until this becoming, by the Hun*
> *That many-guised sorc'ress whose gaze belied*
> *The blackest spirit; the Devil's eyes*
> *Then the man in the mask spoke again:*
> *In the boy's forgetting did come a rot*
> *A declining cell that spread throughout*
> *And Father's memories could not be spoken*
> *Until Another healed the clock so broken*

The marionette-boy replied:

> *I have forgotten his name, my lips once knew*
> *And in this shelter, forgetfulness grew*
> *In living, I did so, in eternal motion*
> *But for Father: one life of forgotten devotion*

A simulacrum of Dreck, shadowy and flittering—a fleeting phantom—appeared from the darkness at the back of the stage. His voice moaned, in a low animal sound.

> *I, once the Father, have found this tower*
> *In which each eternity I've lost but an hour*
> *And in my suffering forgetfulness*
> *Suffered all that is Man that pulsed 'neath my breast*
> *The golden walls and ropes and circuits*
> *I could not repair by my circumstance*
> *Cursed forever—remaining impotent, feeble-minded*
> *Remedy out of reach—nothing kept for the finder*

Though the verse was often insipid and the meter ragged, the effect made my hair stand on end. Elizabeth gripped my arm tightly as the show went on—there was a pained look on her face. The man in the mask spoke again, as though casting a spell on us all:

> *So destined, Father and Son, to never be in their ages*
> *A Book of Names never mended, torn out of middle pages*
> *Until this last harvest, till the plow for the souls*
> *And here, we are gathered, for Rememorial*

The marionette-boy *transformed into me*. He looked *just like me*. Shaken to the bone, I saw myself transformed, walking to grasp the hand of the phantom Dreck. And I heard myself speak upon the lighted stage:

> *Father, I am Son, though I've lived countless lifetimes*
> *Now our flightless route has crossed — your life, mine*
> *If only one could remember that harvest of souls*
> *I yearn for the day of Rememorial*

Dreck answered in a deep, flesh-throbbing voice:

> *I cannot but waste you in the blood of my spirit*
> *Your much-loved remembrance, I cannot come near it*
> *Possessed of Man's soul but as an animal numbered*
> *No longer two spirits, and joined through their hunger*
> *Observing the works of the great, gleaming tower*
> *I know not the name and I know not the hour*
> *Yet I hope with the lingering remnant of spirit*
> *You shall know how to mend the tower once near it*

Then, the man in the mask spoke again:

> *Here we discover the devil in the writing*
> *For years, a blind battle the Son has been fighting*

And even without knowing, could repair the hours
That run outside time, in the gears of the tower
Groping in darkness the Son has discovered
The means by which his Father's soul is recovered
And so ends our tale of the harvest of souls
May we forever celebrate this Rememorial

The curtains smashed together, closed forever. But part of me thought I could run up there and reach through them, part them again if I wished. Nothing would come of it, but I could try. That would be a feat greater than refurbishing the clocktower. The *swish* of those curtains closing did not lend the feeling of an end. No. It was something more, something that my mind could use to simply *know*. And it did. The unknowing unwound. That lifelong, unknown unknowing unraveled, and I understood at once. I understood. *I wasn't who I thought I was.* Dreck wasn't who he thought he was either—he didn't even *know* who he was. Deedee wasn't who I thought she was. Truckie wasn't who I thought he was. They were closer in blood than in word or deed to my lineage, closer in bond than in time or memory.

They were mine. My family.

CHAPTER 41

G HB peered warily out of the floor-to-ceiling glass enclosure that formed the wraparound length of his new penthouse apartment. As *Vox Oculii* played in the background, he espied several prostitutes walking either naked or in semi-nude lingerie get-ups. One of the girls sashayed up to GHB. She was in the nude. She handed him a cup of brown water, a blurry mix of sandy liquid.

"Excellent, Twyla. Excellent," he said as he sipped from the cup, "What do you call this again?"

"Sugar."

"Really? That's it?"

"Well... brown sugar?"

"Ah, yes. Brown sugar. My, oh my." GHB drank deep, staring with meaning into the glass. "How good you taste," he purred.

Twyla looked on, perplexed, but kept any outward display of surprise in reserve. "You sure you're alright just drinking that sugar water?"

"It's *brown* sugar water, Twyla," he replied, looking at the glass and then out to the smoggy skyline. "Brown. Sugar. Water."

GHB walked over to the couch—a gigantic old sectional he'd seen in the dump, that wondrous new place Huey had shown him. He'd fallen in love with the couch of questionable origins the moment he laid eyes on its rusted springs peeking through the tatters of torn cushion.

With a tremulous voice, he plotzed down in the middle of the couch and called out to the perambulating prossies. "Girls, come sit with me, for I am having a vision."

The hookers gathered around him, a half dozen on each side, till it looked like a lascivious sacrilege of the Last Supper. In a prophetic mode, GHB laid his hands on the women on either side of him, and grilled them solemnly, with furrowed eyebrows.

"Girls, what do you know about slam poetry?"

They looked at one another in confusion. Their communal body language—shaking heads and weird shrugs—indicated that they knew absolutely *nothing* about slam poetry.

Finally, one of the girls broke the silence. She wore knee-high socks and a plaid shirt that could contain neither of her breasts. "What is it?" she whispered.

GHB, who had long insisted that "breastial exposure is the spirit's utmost precaution against the demons of the world," was into full prophetic mode by now.

"Behold, for I will prophesy," he proclaimed, turning sideways and draping his legs over the girls on one side and placing his head under the ample breasts of the first girl on the other. He adjusted her breasts so that they rested on his forehead and pointed, like an infant, to the woman on the other side of him to massage his legs and feet.

He intoned: "In the time before man knew of lyrics and musical comedy, it was a dark land. Many people went from home to home eating dogs and cats. There were some dogs that had vocabularies of over three-hundred words, and cats that could play piano, but even those magical animals were eaten. For a crappy darkness had descended upon the world, and, verily, people had become dicks.

"Then, from amidst the blackened clouds of the shitty-dick-world, came a man. Verily, that man's name was *Slampapi*.

"Slampapi surveyed the rules of man—his institutions, his structures—and said of them, 'these shits are stupid.'"

GHB repeated the quote with gravity, *"These shits are stupid."*

He continued thus: "Verily, Slampapi's wisdom was great. And so, Slampapi took the unjust laws of man—and you must remember, girls, that unjust laws are not laws at all; a wise woman named *Oprah* said that. So Slampapi eradicated the unjust laws through the force of bearing witness. And yea, didst Slampapi bear witness to his own great workings, and he called them *slam*. And it was good."

Some of the girls looked confused, while others looked enthralled. More than a few looked bored. One way or the other, though, they were a captive audience as GHB waggled his finger at the sugar water and pointed to his mouth. Twyla took the cup and carefully poured the liquid between his open lips, to much smacking and aahing.

"Can we hear some?" the very youngest girl spoke.

One of Huey's goons had found her in the streets, and she matched all GHB's criteria for his "muses": early twenties, large breasts, red hair, and she knew how to operate an industrial trash machine. Her name was Elsie. GHB sat up quickly, bashing his head against the breasts that had hung over his forehead, causing their owner to wince.

"My child," he proclaimed, "nothing would give me greater pleasure than to demonstrate this great and mystical art form."

GHB stood on a podium he had installed in the center of the room for speech-making. He had *demanded* that podium, had told Huey that he wouldn't help decipher the Book unless he had *that* podium—and began, in a meter that fractured as he went along:

> *"When I sees your boobies*
> *I think to myself*
> *Them be's some nice boobies*
> *I think I'll put them on a shelf*
> *Knick-knack, paddy-whack, give a dog*

Give a Dog
Give a Dog
Give a Dog a bone!
Nah. Dog. Dawg. I think I'd rather give myself a boner
When I look around at these marvelous mammaries, I say
they ain't loners
None of these nipples are loners for when your titties are
in the shop
When I was a child, I dreamt I would grow up and
become a cop
Woop-woop! 'Tis the sound of police
Wang-dang-doodle, it's the pigs on the creep
Don't come around here unless you got brown sugar
water
Cause I got it dribbling on my tongue, bein' fed to me by
your daughters."

It had become more of a poetry slum than a slam. GHB closed his eyes and rested his hands on the podium, a perfect picture of serenity. Twyla looked at him with a glimmer in her eye. There was absolute silence in heaven for half a moment, until Twyla started clapping her hands together furiously, as did the other girls.

It was at that moment that Huey Purgato and two of his henchmen walked into the penthouse apartment.

"Ah, Mr. GHB himself! How you enjoyin' yins accommodations?"

"Ah, very well indeed, Mayor Huey Manperson. Very well indeed. I was just instructing these low-born harlots—and I do mean that, girls, in the very best sense possible—on the importance of slam poetry."

"Yins heard GHB do his slam poetry, did'ins?" Huey asked the girls. "Well, what a treat that must have been. Yins are lucky, right lucky, to be in this feller's stable, tellin' yins what!"

"So, my mayor friend, how may I help you?" asked GHB.

"Ah yes, business. Is there a place we could speak privately?"

"These girls won't understand of what we speak, Mayor Manperson. For, yea, they are innocent, uncorrupted, and verily, have many large breasts and various other lady-parts."

"Well—well now, I don't *disagree* with you, GHB. It'd just be a favor to me. And anyhow, you got to have man-talk, just like these girls have their girl-talk. Ain't that right, girls?"

A few of them nodded. Others sighed or rolled their eyes.

"Very well," GHB replied, haughtily. "Twyla! Bring the mayor and I to the Rectangular House of Sartorial Tribute!"

Twyla went over by the door. She grabbed the brass hotel-grade luggage cart by one of its horizontal bars and started to haul it over to them. The luggage cart had a fold-out chair duct-taped to it.

Purgato eyed the luggage cart, feeling that it was a less-than-practical means of transportation. "Oh, that's alright, GHB. Why don't we just walk there ourselves? You know, like the common man."

"Ah yes, the *common man*. I like that. It's earthy. It's homey. It's three syllables. *Com Mon Man*. Very good."

They walked together down the long hallway connecting one side of the penthouse to the other—it spanned the width of the entire building. When they were halfway through the hallway, GHB ceremoniously knocked on a door. A young girl's voice sounded from the other side.

"My, how the weather is nice out today."

"Yes," GHB responded in a stilted and rehearsed tone, "I like the way the clouds look."

"I agree. The clouds look like milky potatoes."

"Yes. Milky potatoes that look like breasts."

Huey heard several bolts, latches, and chains being undone. The door opened into a coat closet. There was a pants-check girl inside wearing over-large eyeglasses and black panties but nothing else. She had red hair and freckles.

"Welcome to the Rectangular House of Sartorial Tribute. May I take your pants?"

GHB slipped out of the silk pajama pants he had been wearing. Nude from the waist down; he looked over to Huey, who said, "Nah, I'm good. Yeah, I'm okay just how I am."

"Suit yourself," GHB replied, and walked into the closet. "You coming?" he asked.

Huey hesitated, but figured that it wouldn't help any to make GHB feel strange. Not that he thought he *could* make GHB feel strange, not that GHB had any normal gauge on what strangeness was, anyhow. So, Huey squeezed into the closet behind GHB, and they sat in the very cramped space, so close their legs were touching, with the freckle-faced redhead sniffling as if she had a dust allergy.

"Do you mind if she leaves?" Huey asked. "No offense, sweetheart, but we're discussing some important and confidential government business."

"It don't bother me," she said, "s'long as it's okay with GHB."

GHB was sitting in some strange cross-legged contortion, with one hand on his knee and the other hand on the redhead's thigh.

"My child, go mingle with the others," he told her.

The redhead pouted, "But they don't *like* me. That's why you said it could be just you and me in the closet!"

Huey whispered to him, "Do yins sleep in here?"

"'Course we do," the redhead interjected. "GHB cain't sleep in big beds 'cause the space isn't properly accommodating to his lumbar. He needs to curl against three different walls!"

Huey scoffed disbelievingly.

"The other girls share rooms. *I'm* special so I gets to stay in the Closet Temple," the girl added.

"The Rectangular House of Sartorial Tribute, Lucy?" GHB corrected her.

"Fine, yeah—*that*." she pouted.

"Hey. *Hey*," GHB prodded her.

"*What?*" Lucy answered.

"Who's my little toaster oven?"

She looked away, petulant, refusing to give him what he wanted. "I don't know."

GHB reached out, lightly gipped her chin, and turned her face toward him. "I said who's my little toaster oven?"

Lucy couldn't help it. She smiled. "I am."

"That's right. Now go out there and try and make nice. Remember, to err is human, but…?"

She poofed out her lips and painfully said, "But being naked together with other women is great."

"That's right. Now run along."

Lucy scampered off and closed the door behind her.

"This sure is… private, GHB," said Huey when she had left.

"I know," GHB answered, reaching into one of the trench-coats hanging on the rack around them. "Nice, isn't it?"

"It suits you. So, listen. Cotton Lenny's been having some trouble operating out of the notebook you made for us. And we sure do appreciate you helpin' us out, but is there any way you could transcribe it in a less… personal language?"

"What do you mean?"

"Well, it's just some of the notes in the margins—the directions, or whatever yins call 'em—they don't make much sense to her. Or to me, if'n I'm bein' honest."

"For example?"

Huey pulled out a notepad where he'd bullet-pointed three separate passages, having anticipated this stopping point coming up.

"Okay, so on page six, there's a diagram of a giraffe eating a tuna fish sandwich."

"Mmm-hmm."

"And next to that picture it just has the words 'EAT LOTS OF MILK TOO' in all bold lettering."

GHB hummed. "That's not clear?"

"No, not particularly, GHB."

ALEX GRASS

"Well, I'm sorry for that, Mayor Huey Manperson. I feel like I've failed you. I feel like *I'm* the big dummy stupid idiot."

"No, no! Not at all. But maybe you could explain this one, just as an example."

"Sure. The giraffe is allegorical. It's meant to direct how to calibrate your red-light portal. So, you push all the levers to max power. And 'EAT LOTS OF MILK' should be transcribed into proto-Hebraic, and then you take the Gematria values—do you know the numerological correspondents for the Aleph Bet?—and those are your coordinates for the Arc Continuum."

"Arc Continuum?" Huey seemed truly mystified.

"You don't have an Arc Continuum?" GHB asked.

"Buddy, I don't even know what that is."

"Okay, well then *I'm* sure embarrassed, because then I should have written EAT LOTS OF MILK, TULIP so you could complete the operation without an Arc Continuum. Does that make things any clearer?"

Huey sighed. "Not particularly."

"Hmm. Well, there is *one* other alternative. It would make things a lot easier. You need to instantaneously populate your mind with the knowledge from the *Kromee-Ohm*, and then you wouldn't even need to consult me. Would you be interested in that?"

Huey sat for a moment, stunned and slack-jawed. "Yes. Yes, I think that might be easier."

"Great. Then all that's left is the vision quest."

"Vision quest?"

"Yes. I can explain, if you want."

Huey suddenly felt an overwhelming sense of unease. He felt like he was trapped in a confessional with a predatory priest. He swallowed hard before he replied. "No, no. That's alright. Let's just go ahead and do it."

"Right." GHB said as he clapped his hands together.

Huey tried to avoid looking in any direction toward GHB that would bring his own line of sight into viewing GHB's exposed member. Then GHB reached up into one of the other jackets hanging along the rack, picking out two plastic cups and a bottle of port. He poured a glass for each of them.

"Why don't we have a toast first?"

"Hey, I never say no to a drink, GHB."

Huey didn't notice that GHB artfully managed to dose the mayor's cup with a hallucinogenic. One that would have Purgato off his ass for a few hours, at least, and GHB could return to his breastful sanctuary.

CHAPTER 42

Dazed. Discombobulated. Drecky.

It was the same feeling I used to get when I would doze off for a few minutes at my desk and startle myself awake, surprised that I'd nodded off.

Truckie and Bulldog-Jeff walked back into the office from their visit to the cold room. In my blurry state, my eyes swept over the room, and I saw that Deedee was fully dressed.

Images of that strange theater were still in my head, memories of the golden clocktower, memories of Miss Runny, elderly and toothless, who became the beautiful Elizabeth, and most importantly, the revelation of who I was and who my father was. I thought it would all dissipate in a post-dream vapor; that I'd gain awareness, and the details would peel out of my memory like weathered paint peels off an old rain-beaten wall.

But that isn't what happened. Instead, I remembered *absolutely everything about the dreamscape*—every detail, as though there was not even one minuscule bit I could suffer to lose. I reached for my tin cup and one of the closest not-too-empty bottles of shine and poured myself three fingers, then gulped it down.

My memory remained mostly as it was before, only now I knew more—not everything, but *more*—about my story. About *this* story. But there were little spots of life that had emerged. I now understood that I was *not* forty-seven years old. My cynicism was a carryover from centuries of engaging in worthless wars, watching governments lie to their citizens, then crumble, only for a new charade to be erected in place of the old one. Details were hazy. And maybe I didn't have the specific memories to fit my life, but I had the memory of the memory. My life wasn't so important. Not on its own. The most important things revolved around my father. I remembered my father. But there were still blank spots that revolved around our other relationships and connections.

I felt different—physically, internally (not just physiologically, but the internal and inscrutable part of man that sits at the seat of his soul). Even the alcohol tasted different to me. I felt a sharp pain in my gut, something like the feeling you'd get after eating a bad tuna sandwich. Something like food poisoning.

Was my soul now so purified that simple pleasures had become corrosive?

Deedee stood in the corner, barely paying me any mind, but I spoke. "You're my family," I said.

Her head turned so fast, and her eyes bore into mine. "What… what happened? How…"

"And Truckie and all of them," I said. I wanted to continue, but the phone rang.

Somehow, answering the phone, after everything that had happened, seemed to be the strangest thing that I could do in that moment. I picked it up.

"Mr. Attanasio, sir. It's—"

"Agent Aggie, how you doin'?"

"Well, that depends on how you answer the same, sir. I've called in to check on you."

"I'll be honest, Aggie. There are some strange things goin' on here. The bizarre-o quotient just upped itself by a fuckin' solid eight-thousand-percent."

"Yessir, I understand. ReCo has been… monitoring the situation on the ground. It certainly doesn't look good. Anyhow, we still can't *remove* Dreck's body until—"

"Aggie, I don't think that removing Dreck's body is the most important thing you're dealing with right now. I gotta tell ya, there are some new—uh, uh—some new revelations that make me think that the whole Dreck corpse obsession is sort of low-burn."

"Yessir, we understand that too. And that's why we're sending a team in for extraction and sanction. You'll pardon me for the bureaucratic wrangling; I know it's been the cause of some pretty ham-fisted secrecy when you could use the info. I swear, we're not known for being all thumbs—actually, it's the high priority rating of this operation that's sort of gummed up the works, caused a lot of—um—nervous indecision."

"Agent Aggie, I think that's just about the most I've ever heard you say."

"Well, Mr. Attanasio, sir, I am just awful sorry about how this all must seem to you. ReCo really isn't the type of—well, whatever you want to call us, we don't have a habit of making obscure non-promises and leaving the folks that do us favors in the lurch."

I listened to him talk. Every word. Before, I would have thought he was bloviating and waved it off. "Aggie, it's alright. Not your fault."

"No, sir, it's not *directly* my fault, but culpability is a little more complicated than just black and white, and I'll own my part of the miscommunication and confusion that's been caused to you."

"I appreciate that, Agent Aggie. So, when can I expect this sanction-extraction team?"

"Well, that's the bad-news side of things. It's still going to take them about seven hours. Mr. Attanasio, do you think you can hold tough for the next seven?"

I thought of everything I'd learned while I was away—for a hundred years, for two hours?—in that plane of celestial mechanics and mystic theatricality.

"Yeah, something gives me the feeling that I'll be just fine."

My newfound patience dissolved; despite my spiritual rebirth, I felt myself getting angry. I was tired, beat down, done wrong.

Despite knowing what was best, and knowing that this all had to end somehow, and that the body had to be taken in a safe manner—I was angry.

I didn't want anyone to come in here and take him away from me.

Agent Aggie must have heard something in my voice. "Mr. Attanasio, I'm sorry I have to ask this: you won't try to do anything now, will you, sir?"

"Aggie, I ain't promisin' shit. I'm mad as hell, and if I feel I have to do somethin', then somethin' might get done."

There was a long pause before Aggie spoke again. "Mr. Attanasio... I understand. You do what you need to. Just—"

"Yeah, Aggie?"

"Just don't *lose*, sir."

That last bit gave me something to think on.

Seven hours. Where's the clocktower when you need it?

CHAPTER 43

Mayor Huey Purgato, having failed to glean much from GHB's "vision quest," arrived at the snowy fairgrounds with his usual politico bravado. It was an all-sorts mob gathering, and he decided it was about time to take this motherfucker by the reins. He brought in all the goons, every monster mercenary and by-the-hour-bully the city's payroll would accommodate. Huey's goons had corralled the crowd so that there was some semblance of order; they bought the mob's good will by handing out free booze. Huey was an expert glad-hander, too. It wasn't for nothing that he'd become mayor. He went around shaking hands with the pagans and the Mormon-Manicheans, the True Hebrews, and the rest of the riffraff.

Through all this, it seemed like the Ice Age had cycled back to wallop the city with snow—drifts of it. To accommodate the festivities, Mayor Purgato had brought in a crew of workers to shovel the triangle outside the mortuary every half hour or so. Then he had a makeshift podium and PA system installed. Despite the harsh weather, Darcy Gantz had come down all the way from the *Vox Oculii* studio—Huey had sent one of the goons in a Crusher to go fetch her. Now she stood beside Huey on the makeshift platform.

"Citizens, yins are here on a momentous occasion," the mayor orated. "A very special day for us Seven Points citizens. You are here to see the first trial conducted by the Supreme Judicial Panel. Now, for you of those who don't know me—and if I done my job right, there won't be many—I'm Mayor Huey Purgato. I will be serving as Supreme Justice in this tribunal, and likely in many future tribunals pertaining to other controversies of such a… delicate political nature. And to my right—yins know her, come on!—is *the* Darcy Gantz; why don't yins giv'r a round of applause?"

Huey spoke with such a silver tongue that he could move the masses with ease—all the way from the basest dolt to the sharpest wit. The smarter people were actually easier to dupe because they had the luxury of savoring his fanciest thoughts. It worked. He knew instinctively that Darcy Gantz's show was immensely popular. There are few things in this world that people love so much as unmerited, passionate persecution (especially when conducted with no foreknowledge of a subject). She waved and Huey made room for her at the podium.

"Hey yins. I am just so happy to be here today to conduct some justice," Darcy began. "How many of yins are ready to see justice done tonight?"

The throng offered a full-throated, mindless cheer. Causes were to be celebrated, regardless of what the aim of the cause was.

"Now, as you know," Darcy went on, "it's very important that we be objective in our trying of Mr. Frank Attanasio. So, the fact that I was a prosecutor in the post-war tribunals will not be admissible as evidence against me, and everything I say isn't hearsay. Hoot-a-toot-toot!"

(Point of fact, Darcy Gantz was never a prosecutor; she had only been a legal clerk to one of the attorneys assigned to research the motions for pre-trial.)

The crowd cheered loudly again as Darcy strained to speak over them.

"Now, as an *objective* persecutor—and yins should know that objective means that I will not look at Mr. Attanasio as an object, but as a person. I will not pre-judge any of the things that I'll be judging on before I judge them as a judge. For example, I will not hold it against Frank Attanasio that he is a sexual predator who, according to my research assistant Jimmo, has raped many of *your* children."

The crowd jeered loudly and rawly then turned their venom into approval of Gantz.

"Now, now, hold on," she continued, "We can't hold it against Mr. Attanasio that it's his job to clean all the poop and pee out of dead people's buttholes. That wouldn't be right of us. But we can use evidence. *Evidence*." The crowd fell quiet until Darcy whipped them into frenzy with her parting shot.

"Seven Points, I love you!"

Darcy sat down and Huey reassumed his position at the podium.

"Alright, now I'm gon' have the charges read. But first, we gotta know what they are. So, I'm going to ask the folks that have been here the longest to raise their hands, and we'll assemble the charges. My man Lavalle here will record the charges for the indictment as they're assembled. Now, who's first?"

"He's ugly!"

"He's a rapist!"

"He kept the body from us!"

"He's using Dreck to make money!"

"He's using Dreck to make a monkey!"

After several minutes, the charges were gathered, formalized into a written document, and read out loud by the mayor.

"Alright, folks," Huey announced, "my Deputy Justice and I are goin' to examine and deliberate, and we should have a verdict for you as soon as we can. Prol'ly about ten or fifteen minutes."

True to his promise, a verdict was swiftly rendered. The crowd was solicited, absurdly, for a voice vote—deputized as judge-jurors forwarding the nonsensical noise of populist democracy against a solitary and uniquely strange man.

Justice waxed cacophonous as Huey bellowed at the crowd, egging them on toward the door of the mortuary.

"With judicial sanction, yins're gon' tear that motherfucker down!"

As the mob lunged toward the mortuary entrance, they were surprised to see that the door flung outward before they could greedily pry it open with their angry little democratic appendages. At that moment, Frankie Attanasio stepped out to face the crowd.

"Yins lookin' for me?"

Some in the crowd hooted and hollered at him, but most, surprisingly, held back with an attitude of restraint, like dogs around an unfamiliar creature; like children waiting on the caprice of an abuser; like an animal confused by its own reflection. They didn't make a move, and Frankie smiled as he turned toward the mayor.

Huey Purgato stepped away from his podium and slowly approached Frankie. "Well, well, well. If it ain't the man himself. You causin' an awful lot of trouble out here."

"Yeah? Well from where I'm standin', you're the trouble with this whole thing. You're the trouble with this whole city," Frankie shot back.

"You aim to do somethin' about that?" Huey asked in response.

Cotton Lenny appeared from behind a wall abutting the mortuary entrance. With a high shrill scream, she leapt at Frankie. Taking a cue from her, Huey also went for him. But before they reached him, Frankie did something he wasn't even sure he had meant to do. He pulled them—all three of them—into a silent void that opened in the air, where the snow couldn't reach. The cosmic portal inhaled them and took them to a plane quite removed from the streets of Seven Points.

CHAPTER 44

Huey and Cotton Lenny—now the reluctant inhabitants of a dreamworld—found themselves in a huge, seemingly endless black space, ankle-deep in black water; though they didn't know how or why. They looked the same—at least they thought so—but their bodies didn't feel the same; it was as if their souls had been poured into clothed vessels several sizes too large.

The place they were in was somewhat familiar. But this place wasn't malleable, like the nightmare world had been. When Huey tried to bend objects and transform their surroundings, nothing happened. Cotton Lenny tried, too, but found herself to be similarly ineffective. The nightmare world would have been a paradise compared to this.

"Where is he?" Huey asked.

Cotton Lenny shushed him, listening intently.

"Why can't I change anything?" Huey asked, frantically.

But Cotton Lenny didn't answer. She simply scanned the endless blackness, hoping to find some subconscious artifice—something outside of Frankie's control—that she could latch onto. But it looked like Frankie had complete control. This did not bode well.

Then Huey realized that his body didn't look the same, after all. Huey-in-dreamland now manifested as a demonic elongation of himself, with blood-flecked porcelain skin and his mutilated, carved smile set in his cheeks, and sporting grotesque thin, stretched limbs. Cotton Lenny looked the same, though.

"The notebook," hissed Purgato, "do we have it?"

Cotton Lenny pulled it out of the inside of her jacket. They'd lucked out in that way, in that they had the precious knowledge of the Book—the *Kromee-Ohm*—that GHB had transmitted and that Lavalle had transcribed. "Will it work, though?" Huey asked, "We don't have the motion machine, or—"

"It'll work," Cotton Lenny answered with confidence. "These places are different from the world as you know it. It all works in here, as long as it works with the machine out there."

At that precise moment, a burst of beige and pink and shimmering corn-kernel yellow flashed past Cotton Lenny.

"What was that?" she exclaimed.

"I didn't see anything."

"Open your fucking eyes, you fool. Keep your wits!"

There was a Teutonic, guttural twist in her voice, a percussive throb to the vowels and a harshness to the consonants that Huey didn't recognize.

The flash of colors went by her again; this time, Huey saw it, too.

"What was that?" he howled.

Then, a child's laughter. But not a merry titter. No, it was the sound of informed deviltry, the cunning laughter of a mocker.

The flash of colors zipped by Cotton Lenny again as a small but muscled hand—a farmboy's hand—reached out and slapped her full and hard in the face. Absolutely shocked, she caressed her pained face.

"You rotten little shit! A lifetime of pain isn't enough for you! *I'm glad, you hear me? I'm glad.*"

The blackness surrounding them began shifting and melting. Liquid colors fluctuated like globules in a gravity-less space, and then glommed together in lumps that hardened while oscillating between translucency and a copper-brown, and then a beige-yellow, and then a navy-black with sprinklings of grayish neon. The globules of seemingly random color organized themselves until the whole of them blotted out the blackness. Huey and Lenny found themselves in a cornfield, with stalks so high they obscured vision of anything other than more rows of stalks. Even Purgato, tall as he was, couldn't see over them.

A great yellow moon hovered above them; it seemed to hang so close that they could touch its surface. Huey started to shrink, his skin flickered—the way a television might—and hues of his humanity channeled through in pixels of white noise. Although this wasn't quite the dream world, or the nightmare world, it was something similar—something interstitial. As an experienced lucid dreamer might tell you, once you lose your grip on lucidity, once you lose your grasp of the unreality of midnight reverie, you might not realize you were dreaming and so you might never make it back. *Huey was forgetting what they were doing there, who they were, forgetting his sense of mission.*

He turned to Cotton Lenny, asking "Who are you?"

He shrank down more, until he was back in human form.

He heard a whispering in his ear—it was barely audible so Cotton Lenny couldn't hear it as Huey did, but she heard it well enough to know that *something* was whispering: *"She's after you, Hugh. She wants to put you in a pot and boil you. She wants your skin. She wants to rip off your scrotum and make it into a hat. And then you'll be in trouble, Baby Huey. You'll be in BIG TROUBLE for being a bad boy."*

Huey mumbled, child-like, "No, no, no, no…"

At the same time, anger boiled inside Cotton Lenny. Her eyes glowed red, bleeding crimson that was something like blood, but much older and far gone in its rottenness.

"Get a grip, you fucking dullard!" she yelled at Huey.

Immediately, he bolted, running across the field, the swaying husks slamming into his face as he ran blindly through the field.

"Hey!" she screamed after him, "Huey, come back here!"

"No, no, no, no. Can't get in trouble. No, no, no."

And then he was gone. The child-like laughter rang out in the night air again, but the open air didn't operate as it normally would; instead, it sounded to Lenny like she was in a small sound-proofed room, where the laughter pierced her eardrums and excruciatingly bounced off the walls and back into her head, bombarding her until her hearing could take no more.

"You rotten little *arschloch*!" Her Teutonic sound was no longer concealed. "Come out here and face me, you *scheisse*!"

As deftly as a boa constrictor, more than a dozen cornstalks wrapped themselves around Lenny's limbs. They quickly brought her down to the cold, hard soil, lacerating her with abrasions and exposing her to the petrifying winter air ripping through the night. The stalks wrapped tighter and tighter until she couldn't breathe anymore—one of them at her neck; it seemed like a million more erupted and lashed every graspable part of her, from her fingers to her knees. Finally, a pincer of vegetation reached with surgical care and precision to hold her eyelids open. It was only then that the boy appeared.

"You took something from us," the Son spoke, but with Frankie's voice. *"You took something from me, and I want it back."* The cold air whipped through the field and shot springing jolts of pain into Cotton Lenny's eyes as the gust dried them out. A tiny green sapling reached into her eye and pierced it.

She screamed, *"Fuck you!"*

"You took it from us. Why? I don't even know my father's name because of you. I know nothing about him. Nothing. Nothing except that I loved him and that you took that away from me. Why?"

"Because I *could*," Lenny said, grinning evilly. "Because, *boy*, I am the darkness. Because there is no part of your world that I cannot reach. Because I will corrupt everything that is good, even if it takes a thousand years, even if it takes a million bloody eons! Eons, and I'll still tear your worthless, awful little souls to your blood-soaked insides, to shreds! You hear me, you little twerp—you *arschloch*—do you hear me?"

TRUCKIE LOOKED out the door of the mortuary that Frankie had flung open. The horde was frozen in fear—something unfamiliar, something dark to them, wouldn't allow them to interfere. There was a circle; inside the circle was Frankie, Huey, and Cotton Lenny, and they were all frozen. Frankie's hand was on the knob of an open door that had materialized. Peering inside the door, Truckie could see only blackness. It was a rainbow of obsidian, its black parts swirling into one another, like an opaque ghost engine. Maybe the others couldn't differentiate between black and black, but it was there.

Deedee sat next to Dreck's body, desperately clutching his gigantic arm. She was murmuring quiet devotions, fervently pleading, "Please. Please help. Please wake up. Please help him."

COTTON LENNY CACKLED. "The truth is, your father used to be handsome. That's why, *boy*, I made him into that disgusting mutilation. Because I wanted to. Because I can."

Frankie now appeared as an adult—himself as he was, or as he knew himself to be. There was a sober cadence to his speech, "I don't believe you. But if you're not going to give me your reasoning, I suppose that's the way it is. I don't need an answer. I just thought I'd give you a chance." Frankie's limbs grew, hardened, became wooden and unyielding. Skin shed from his face and was replaced by furrows from which jagged growths of bark grew. His legs carried him higher and higher—he sprouted as he transformed, until his arms reached mammoth proportions, his fingers becoming gnarled and knotted cords of poison foliage, dripping with a dark red-purple sap. Neon bulbs, glowing yellow and

263

orange and green, bloomed, mushrooming all over his body. Cotton Lenny was surprised at the power Frankie had gained.

This is centuries of conjure; how can he know it? Still, she cackled —brazenly. Frankie was taller than a house. But still Lenny laughed.

"Impressive, you filthy little twerp. But I'll still have you. And when I do, I'm going to put the Hex on you and your father again. I'll revive the both of you for centuries, just so I can do it again and again."

By this time—though time was inconsequential and fluid— Huey had run off into the field; lost after leagues of sprinting. Lenny closed her eyes and let out a banshee wail that split the air, surprising Frank. The sound shot out in ripples of air-bending vibration, and reached Huey Purgato, splitting his eardrums. A loud *pop* cracked through his head before there was silence. Huey screamed as blood ran from his ears down the sides of his face.

HUEY SHOOK his head in delirium. There was a loud single-tone ring that pulsed, unbroken. He reached to touch his ear. When he pulled his hand away, he found his fingertips covered in blood. Purgato tried to concentrate and saw that he was inside an electric-fire-lined circle—a conjure of demarcation. Lenny was frozen still, and so was that bastard Frankie Attanasio. He heard Lenny's voice in his head, barely audible through the painful ringing that was rocking him.

Can you hear me, Mister Mayor?

Yes.

And can you see that Attanasio fucker standing there?

Yes, he answered again inside his mind, *I see him there. You too. You're both frozen.*

Kill him. End it now.

"But that doesn't make sense. All this time we've been trying to reach either of them and *you have him right there with you*,"

Purgato spoke out loud in frustration. "We have to end him *in there*. We can have his soul, his powers!"

No, he's learned too much. Kill him!

"But I can beat him, I can do it!"

Listen to me, Mister Mayor—either kill him now or it will be too late.

Truckie could see Mayor Purgato's movement—it looked like he was talking; to himself perhaps? Then, through the turbid clouds of wind-whipped snow, Truckie saw the mayor pull a stiletto from his belt.

I NOTICED the witch's arms starting to shake, buckling against the cornstalks. Her limbs inflated, so rapidly that her paper skin burst in tiny slits that then oozed a brackish green coagulant. The vine and branch manacles that held her started to shatter in dry, brittle pops and cracks. She broke through her constraints easily and transformed: Her skin desiccated and gray, covered in pustules, open sores, and hardened black-blood wounds; her fingers wreathed into keratin branches, longer than her infected limbs; her hair now cobwebby, sticky and stringy and delicate enough to break with the slightest touch or by the slightest turn of her swaying head; her neck creaked, broken and on a swivel of surplus vertebrae that pushed through her back like porcupine quills. Her body lengthened until she was two-thirds the size of my own massive form, bursting the seams of her clothing so they fell from her. Her eyes remained that awful crimson color, and they bled their alien fluid in gushes. Her breasts drooped down past her navel—which wasn't really a navel anymore, but a gash through which a ghastly rotted cluster of burst intestine protruded.

During this transformation, the woman-turned-beast muttered words in some language—some odd German dialect?—and a silver mercurial liquid accumulated on the tips of her freakishly long talons. Everything happened so quickly, I didn't have the wherewithal to react. She sank her silver-tipped talons into my toughened hide while screaming in a horrid multi-tonal chorus— it sounded like a thousand voices of agony calling out in a bloody choir: "*Fair zur Hölle, der Mistkerl!*"

My pain was indescribable. In my excruciation, I fell to one knee, my tree-sized appendage sending a crashing, reverberating *boom* across the dream-field as my shin hit the soil. I let out a low-octave, beastly wail. The ghoulish woman cackled at her victory, her laugh reminded me of a choked pipe filled with muck, its brackish ooze sloshing and splashing out of her mouth as she laughed. As she dug her venomous talons deeper into me, my awareness slipped from me. I deflated, reverting to my earthly form. But it was more than that. The deflation happened in my mind as well; my focus narrowed, and panic steered my movements and thoughts.

I'd lost control.

I tried to move, but I couldn't. The silvery venom must have had some paralytic in it. But we were in *my* world, the plane of visions whose waves of movement and sound resonated to my rhythm and mine alone. It didn't matter, though. The more I tried to reason, to think rationally, the more paralyzed I became. And soon, I fell further into vulnerability, into humanity, becoming the golden-haired Son, infinitely smaller than the powerful behemoth I'd just been. And

just

like

that

I was too small to hurt anyone.

I wasn't smart enough to not be scared. I was a child. And I was *in pain*, and I couldn't move because all I could do was cry.

"Father!" I yelled, but the lady was bigger now; she was so big she could scoop me up in her hand. She had claws and those reminded me of one of my barn kittens who scratched a lot at things that should've broken its claws. But the kitten's claws got stronger, and so did the mean lady's. She lifted her twisted and horrible hand before she smacked it into me. But that wasn't all because one of the claws went right through my leg. She picked me up like that—just by her nail in my leg—and all I could do was cry and cry and cry and cry for Father.

Moving hurt when I was stuck on that claw, but I couldn't stop moving. Things got dark and she hung me upside down. I saw the whole cornfield, and it was pretty. Calm. I just wanted to stay there in the pretty calm field forever.

TRUCKIE SAW Huey stumbling and falling, still weakened and hazy, but with the needle-sharp stiletto in his hand as he circled toward the still-frozen Frankie.

Inside the mortuary, Deedee cried, no longer quietly. She squeezed Dreck's arm, her forehead pressing violently against his body, like she was a wounded and confused animal, unable to comprehend mortality (and fatality), trying to revive her kin by simple force and painful longing.

She began sobbing uncontrollably, pounding on Dreck's chest, screaming. "Help him! Help him, you fucking bastard! He came back for you, do you hear me? He fixed it. Now wake up and help him. *Fucking wake up!*"

THE BAD WOMAN held me upside down. I still didn't know what happened. I was so big, and my mind was much bigger, too, before, and I could have beaten her, but now I was small again. Her claws really hurt me. I knew there was just more about every-thing, but I couldn't think of the more because I hurt so much. Her whole nail was in my leg and out the other side. And she was laughing the whole time. It was a happy-sounding laugh, but I knew she was *not nice* and she wasn't a happy person. She was *mean,* and I was still crying. I wanted to ask why she was hurting me.

"My dear boy, have you ever heard of the expression, *the house always wins*?"

Her claw twisted in my leg. I wanted to say I thought so. Should I still respect my elders when they're hurting me?

House always wins? It's about cards! Or a casino! I was happy I remembered that, and I wanted to tell her that I knew those words. I thought maybe if I did, she'd let me go. But I was in too much pain.

"This place," she went on, "is *my* house. You think just because you learn a few tricks that you can come and upset the order of things? *I* am the one who haunts dreams. You're a fucking tourist."

Her rotten hands squished her nails deeper into my skin, and I cried very loud because I couldn't not cry. I couldn't stop it. She scared me. She hurt me.

TRUCKIE SAW something pushing against the inside of Frankie's pant-leg, and then a spatter-pattern of blood leaked through. Truckie ran toward the rim of electricity, aiming to take Huey down before he could run Frankie through with the stiletto. But, as soon as Truckie's body hit the electric circle's outer demarcation line, it shocked him and sent him sprawling back.

I CRIED AND CRIED, which made me remember other times this woman had made me cry, had made me hurt. And finally, I knew who the mean woman was. And I was mad at her. I *hated* her, and that made me madder at her. So mad that I could ignore her hurting me for long enough that I could yell at her. I could say words to her I wanted to say for a long time, so I did.

"You killed us," I said. The mean woman still smiled, but she looked like she was listening, so I tried to tell her more. "You took my father away from me. You made him a monster. You're evil. You're Satan."

"Oh, darling… I'm much worse."

She squeezed my head, making it feel like it would just pop. I was screaming and shaking and I couldn't talk anymore because I was so scared of what she was doing to me, and I was so scared that she would hurt me even more. I screamed and screamed and screamed.

"Father!"

IN THE MORTUARY, Deedee held Dreck's hand, accepting the finality of it all: the disastrous end that meant Frankie's death, the unknown future, the sadness of this bleak moment on the horizon. She kissed Dreck's cheek delicately, pressing her face softly against his, and said, "It's okay, Father. It's okay. You can go if you want. You don't have to hold on. I'm sorry I didn't find you sooner. It isn't your fault. What that awful woman did… it isn't your fault. You deserve peace. Close the eyes of your soul, then, and in its slumber find your eternal rest."

Then Deedee whispered in Dreck's ear, "I know there's some part of you still there. And if you can hear me, then hear this one last thing: Your son has started to break the curse. But he needs your help to destroy it. And you can see him again if you just wake up. But if you don't, the woman who killed your wife is going to kill him too. Do you hear me?"

MAYOR HUEY PURGATO MOUNTED UPWARD, pressing his hands against his knees to raise himself upright. He stood nose-to-nose with Frankie, who was now bleeding from his head, and whispered to him, "Say hello to your father."

"Yes. Hello," came a deep voice from behind him. Huey whipped around, and as he did, Dreck pushed his hand through the mayor's abdomen, ripping his bowels out through his front. Then Dreck took Mayor Purgato by the hand—the hand that held the stiletto—and ripped it off at the wrist. Bleeding from the mouth, Huey fell to his knees and looked up at Dreck in abject terror.

The restored Dreck opened his cervine maw and devoured the mayor's head. He spat it out into the rainbow of black beyond the threshold of the door-portal.

Dreck stared into the roiling abyss, letting his rage quell. After a few moments, he turned around, his blue eyes landing on something of a kindlier Pietà: of Deedee caressing a badly burnt and injured Truckie. Dreck stared at them longingly, with great shame, and said, "If I don't see you, I am sorry for what I have done, and I'm sorry for everything that came after." Deedee's eyes were streaming with tears. It looked as if she was going to jump up and embrace Dreck, but he held up his hand as if to say, *no.*

Truckie could not approach him, but Deedee did, and then he came close and held her; and then he spoke:

"*Seht mich nacht an, daß ich so schwarz bin; denn die Sonne hat mich so verbrannt. Meiner Mutter Kinder zürnen mit mir. Sie haben mich zur Hüterin der Weinberge gesetzt; aber meinen eigenen Weinberg habe ich nicht behütet.*" Dreck kissed Deedee's cheek, drew away from her, and waved. "Goodbye, my children."

And then he stepped through the door.

MEANWHILE, Cotton Lenny had raked Frank's scalp with her needle-sharp nails, and licked the blood from almost every inch of those razorblade talons.

Seemingly out of nowhere, Huey's head rolled to her feet. It was crimson red around the open hole of the mouth, which had frozen in a contorted gaze of horror. She yanked her claws out of little Frankie's leg and let him drop to the cold, hard soil.

Not long after, something in the air shifted. Lenny could smell it; she sniffed at the air. She turned around.

There he was.

"My darling," she said nervously, "I'm so glad you're okay."

Dreck, having had his memory restored, the curse diminished by Frankie's time in the golden clocktower, still couldn't remember who this woman was.

"Do I know you?" Dreck asked.

He didn't notice the Son, Frankie, who had crawled out beyond the shadows of the cornhusks to escape the witch. Cotton Lenny had transformed, turning not into herself as she had appeared in the Seven Points, but as she had first appeared to the Father all those years ago—lissome and dark, voluptuous and awful. The most sensuous evil.

"Lena…" Dreck muttered, a mounting fury rising in his voice. "Where is my boy?"

"Darling, you have to understand—"

"WHERE IS MY BOY?" Dreck's voice had become a roar, reverberating through that endless field, shaking the leaves and stalks and husks. Cotton Lenny shrank back and pointed through the husks. Dreck walked out to where the boy—Frankie—was. He knelt beside him.

"My son," he said. He'd never been great with words in tough moments, and this was easily the hardest moment of his life. But he spoke through his tears. "I am so sorry. I wish there was more time. I wish I'd had more time."

SANCTUARY. To be enfolded into the embrace and the promise of *sanctuary*. Of the Father. The Father who I'd not known until the gleaming clockworks; the Father who dumbly roamed the four corners of the Earth, impelled by a half-instinct to copulate, to restore.

Father had come for me. Father had come... to save me. My heart sang. I wanted to reach up, to embrace him, but I was stuck in the mud, mucking blood on the ground with each lame half-movement.

"I knew—" I breathed the words raggedly. It was difficult. " ... I knew I would see you again. Even before I remembered anything. *Father*." I almost whispered the last piece, like a silent devotion.

He smiled at me, but did perforce, as a reaction. Through the smile, though, he looked sadder than I'd ever seen any creature, man or beast. Then anger overtook him, righteous indignity, undirected fury to our misfortune. "You're dying."

He began to yell. "Lena, what did you do to my boy? *What did you do to him?*"

He turned to face the succubus—the witch? The horror?—but she was gone. Father looked back at me, and his anger was gone too. His eyes, thick and rheumy like a blinded elk. His eyes—and he cried when he looked at me.

"My poor boy. Come with me." He picked me up. My mind expanded, turning cogs to create capacity for extra-sensory comprehension, allowing me to understand not just the gravity of the moment, but the strange place in which our reunion had come. My body transformed as well, as the sanctuary that was my memory, my father, carried me.

Despite my wounds, I felt lucid, capable of clear-eyed expression:

"None of it was your fault, Father. I know that. I always knew. And here we are. We've made it. We remember now. We remember each other. I remember that I was never mad at you. Never," I said. So much blood had drained from my body—black spots swam in my eyes. Unlike the floaters, I could catch them and look at them. Look through them to see my father. There were tears rolling from his eyes. Mine were still damp as well, but they were damp of solace, the freedom of relief. Freedom. A long-binding chain… finally broken. And even if I were to die then and there, I was happy.

"You should be angry," Father said, his voice cracking. "You *should*," he haltingly whispered.

"For what? For—why? To what end? I loved you. There was nothing to forgive. You were always a good man. She just… she hurt you. Both of us."

"I'm so sorry, Son," he said.

"Enough. Our time—who knows how much we'll even have? We're joined together again. The rest…" I trailed off, noticed he hadn't stopped walking, hadn't slowed his pace since he picked me up from the ground. "Where are we going, Father?"

"We must enjoy what time we have left, but Son, there are two things I must do. The success of the second is contingent on the success of the first. I do wish we had all the time in the world, and were it not for other powers here, we would. I need you to do something for me. Quickly. I need you to do something *with* me," my father said.

"Yeah. Of course. Anything," I replied.

His eyes were glossy, and he pointed one three-fingered hand, palm splayed, into the distance. He smiled.

That distant point was not so distant—perhaps sixty or so yards. But it seemed far enough, the state I was in. The air crackled with lightning, bolts that diverged initially, but remerged to form a singularity. From the spot on the ground where that great bolt struck—appeared the great edifice with the clocktower. In all its glory from the makeover Elizabeth and I had given it.

"How did you… I… I made that," I said. Little crackles of static erupted here and there, webbed together around the structure, and I could see it—there was a barrier surrounding the clocktower.

"Such a smart boy. Yes. You did amazing work with it. You made it what it is now. *We* created it, so long ago. Perhaps you'll remember, perhaps you will not, but we did."

273

It was hard to reply to this. "H-how?" I asked.

"I cannot take us to it. We aren't strong enough, but I can bring it here. Not for long. But Son, where it is matters little. What this building is… it matters only what we allow it to *become*. Let us go. I need you to stand up, can you do that for me?"

My legs were useless—leaden and locked in place due to my wounds. "I-I can't. I'm sorry," I replied, still in his arms. I scanned the horizon for Lenny, Lena—whatever the hell she was. "What about the woman? She's still here, isn't she?"

"Never mind her. She will not be able to interfere with our efforts, so long as we work together. Quickly," he said as we approached the clocktower.

The static bursts in the distance became more prominent the closer we grew to the structure. "Close your eyes," Father instructed. I did. He took one step forward, and the tick-tock of the timeless clock echoed throughout the barrier that Father had created. He moved forward with me in his arms, and I never once felt as though we were walking. The gravity here… the gravity was unique. But it was hard for me to focus.

Father placed me on the ground and looked up at the grand construction. There were some panels on the front of the tower where he was able to gain footholds. He began to climb.

About a third of the way up the monument, there was nothing for him to grab onto to continue his ascent. "I need your help, Son," he said, and his voice was not miles up in the air. It remained close to my ears.

"Father, I can't. I cannot climb," I replied. The sadness in my consciousness dripped into my voice.

"You're a very smart boy, Frankie. Very smart. You created this. I do not need *you* to climb. I only need you to help *me* climb."

"I'm not strong enough," I said quietly.

"You are. You restored the entire structure. Without much effort—physical effort, even?"

"I did."

"It's a similar concept. You do not need physical strength, my boy. You need another type of strength. All I know is that we must do this together. I created a barrier around this structure to ensure that no one can interfere, but I cannot keep the building in place for long."

The Father was loath to press the Son, so injured as he was. There are, however, some things that must be done.

He looked down at me and then over to the side of the clock-tower. He still wept. His tears fell on me. Weightless raindrops or snowflakes. "Perhaps you can move some of these panels. I must reach the clockface."

I tried. How I tried. Father watched and simply told me to keep trying, that we must both connect to the clock. I did not think to ask what we were doing, whether the edifice would return to its home—nothing. I wanted to help my dad. I strained to recall the past in which I had been able to sweep layers of rust off the beams, rearrange the gears, and produce a functional, new clock. Without touching it.

I surveyed the array of panels directly above my father, and below the clockface. The panels were large heavy sheets of metal that shielded the innards of the tower. If I removed or rearranged them, he'd have a way up.

I focused on a single panel above him, trying to free it. With my hand outstretched, I screamed as I tried to rip it from the tower. Adrenaline coursed through me; a massive *thud* echoed like metallic thunder throughout the area. The panel flew off to reveal the structural supports inside.

"Wonderful! Now, I need you to rearrange the maze of beams so that I have footing. You must. You must..." his voice quieted and fell away like an echo while repeating his instructions under his breath.

I concentrated on where Father stood, on the gaps between the varying horizontal and vertical steel and gold bars. Willing them to move so that he could climb. They shifted. No creaking. No sound at all. One part of the tower would disappear and reappear where I intended it to. In this way, Father was able to climb to the top.

"Very good!" he said, and again his voice was not distant from me. It was omnipresent. And so was the muffled sound of a woman's harsh cackle. That sound was the scrape and shimmer of a rusted, dangerous edge on an overused razor. And outside the visible, constant sparks of light, flashes of a black mane pacing the area outside us, taunted... *haunted* my peripheral vision.

AFTER A FEW MOMENTS of rearranging varying parts to suit the areas in which my father wanted them, he stood on a small perch, now directly in front of the massive clock's face. He reached toward the center, the nexus from which the hour, minute, and second hands all ticked forward.

The glass surrounding the timepiece alighted in that marigold hue—it was like staring straight into the sun—the moment Father touched the outer glass. He'd broken through the glass, but this time, the glass did not shatter. He reached *through* the glass as though it was not there at all. He gripped the hour hand with both of his, and though he strained, he wound and wound and wound the hand until he could finally let go.

The hour hand began to spin, whirling at speeds thousands of times faster than it had before. The clicks were so constant they became ambient background noise. He did the same with the minute hand, only this one he spun counterclockwise. It moved inexorably forward, nearly invisible at the speed at which he'd set it. The second hand was his final goal. I could not *see* his hands through the brilliance of the luminous gold—what is *seeing*, even, after all this illumination?—but I could discern the effect they'd had on the steely stems of the clockface's hands.

The second hand, he wound and spun clockwise. This hand moved with such manic energy that it must surely have been traveling faster than the speed of sound or light; but, there was no sonic boom to indicate such speed. I certainly couldn't *see* it. *Illumination. What is… seeing?* The gold surface transmogrified to a transparent albeit reflective glass, with the clock's glass face intact, the moment Father removed his hand from it.

TRUCKIE AND DEEDEE surveyed the scene outside the mortuary. A harsh and abrupt silence enveloped them, followed by a howling wind that picked up and blew continuously through the night's air. Drifts of snow blew in small, white tornadoes, decimating tents and podiums.

The blizzard, however, had ceased.

I HELPED my father climb down from the clock just as I'd helped him climb up.

He scooped me back up into his arms, instructing me to close my eyes as we stepped out of the barrier he'd created. Once on the other side, I glanced back. The clock was gone. The crackling, purple sparks were gone, and sound and gravity functioned as they had before. As though the other-worldly presence of the clock had no bearing here. The evaporation of the scene happened within microseconds, accompanied by the same lightning with which it had appeared.

"What did we do?" I asked.

"Ah, well… to be seen. But, in theory… those hands will never stop spinning—in different directions, all at exactly the same speed as one another, both backward and forward, so that no matter how time moves out there," he continued, pointing a hand in a vague non-direction toward the "real" world outside this dreamscape, "our clock is safe."

"Safe," I repeated.

"Our memories are safe," Father replied as he gently lowered me back down to the earth. The woman's cackling was distant but audible. It halted so abruptly. I hoped that whatever my father had done had killed her as well.

The cackling had stopped. But the distant sound of a howling wail of a rage untethered—that replaced the laughter. She was not dead. Not even close.

And that evil bitch was *pissed off*.

"YOU'VE HELPED ME, and I thank you, for this is of the highest importance to me. And to you. I am sorry if it seems that I valued an action more than I valued my time with you. I do not. They are one and the same. Now, please, share with me. Anything you would like to say. We are here now. We are together." Dreck wrapped his hand around his son's.

Frankie's chest moved in quick bursts, as though he could not inhale enough oxygen. Time was slipping from them. He was not the same as he had been moments before. He was weakened. Wounded. But he smiled and said, "I... when I started down the road that brought us here, I thought I didn't have a father. I thought you were long dead. My life was an unhappy one. Now, my life is over, but I've gotten all I've ever needed from it. We both have. The thing we were searching for without knowing for so long. I remember you. I know my father, and I am happy."

Dreck cradled Frankie's head in his massive hands. Frankie looked into his father's eyes, happy at last. Dreck's tears continued to fall. Tears of joy and of sorrow.

Suddenly, a red dot appeared through Dreck's chest; it enlarged and became a hole.

Lenny had transformed back into the demoness and had run through Dreck with her claw.

"*NO!*" Frankie screamed.

Supported only by what Dreck saw as his son's own fury, Frankie grew into a great monster, but Lenny only laughed. A laugh that was the dark howling of a desperate beast. Manic and insane.

"You can't do anything. All your impotent rage. All your stupid, insipid self-righteousness. I'll find your little watch and destroy it. You can't—"

Before she could finish, Frankie—the tree-trunked, neon-lit, towering monolith of a dream-monster—picked up Dreck's body, and roared into the open air that verse he'd heard in the theater, but hadn't understood until now:

> "Possessed of Man's soul but as an animal numbered
> No longer two spirits, and joined through their hunger"

Lenny understood what she was seeing, and her body went limp. Frankie, whose tears fell down to the cold, hard soil of the dream planes like comets crashing to the earth, took the body of his father, Dreck, who had shrunk so much that he could fit into his son's palm. Dreck's form dissipated until he was nothing but a gold-glowing liquid in Frank's hands. As the gilded liquid absorbed into Frank's palms, the veins in his hands became sunlit streams, allowing the liquid within to spread through veins and arterial nerves—all illuminated until Frankie was no longer visible as a monolithic being. Dreck's body—much like the coins back home—had become one with Frank's own in an effervescent display of relief and reconciliation. Frankie had become *something else*.

A great flash of light, like a nuclear explosion on a far-off horizon, blinded Cotton Lenny, and she fell to her knees. When the light cleared, there was no longer Dreck and Frankie—Father and Son—as two separate entities. They had become one unity, assuming the qualities of both. They were not merely doubly powerful, but multiples of multiples of their own powers had made in them a potency of conjure and cure that had no equal in the dream world.

The creature they had become looked down at Cotton Lenny.

She looked up at them, baring her claws. But before she could do anything, they simply dreamt her out of existence. And so the great witch that had haunted and expunged them from one another's hearts, died there in the dream world. The will of their unity was more powerful than she was awful, and it erased her from existence.

THE WORLD OUTSIDE WAS SILENT. A few of the folks who had surrounded the area before now wandered aimlessly. Calm. Ever so calm.

The two watched for a while as the chaos of humanity moved on from this latest episode, as the snow settled and melted.

Deedee turned to Truckie and asked, "Was that German? That thing Dreck said to us, earlier. What did he say?"

Truckie, still staring out the window, answered, "It was from the Song of Solomon."

"Do you know what it means?"

"Oh, I know it very well," he replied. "Our memory being what it is."

Truckie translated: "Let not your eyes be turned on me, because I am dark, because I was looked on by the sun; my mother's children were angry with me; they made me the keeper of the vine-gardens; but my vine-garden I have not kept."

They again surveyed the scene outside the mortuary. The body of Cotton Lenny was no more: it had dissipated in the air. And with the mayor having been slain so gruesomely by Dreck, the goons had simply abandoned the area without the demagogue to guarantee their pay.

The air grew still. The wild wind had died. The storm was over.

CHAPTER 45

The mayor's body was dead, but once Dreck had spit out his head, Huey Purgato's mind finally comprehended the impact of Cotton Lenny's demise. His mind, at long last, came to grips with all her insidious manifestations: as a deformation, as a grotesque mutilation, as a slick-skinned monster, as a freak with reorganized anatomy—this she-monstrous afterbirth of millionfold defects.

Still, Huey Purgato had remembered the very first lesson of malodorous black science that Lenny had instructed him on.

The parachute pull.

He remembered how he had pulled the parachute and came out the other side. That is, he came out through the motion machine in his secret laboratory hidden beyond the walls and beneath his floor-long mayoral suite.

There had been hardly any time at all, and Huey had only pulled the parachute once before.

This time, though, Huey was just a head—his body had died in the real world after Dreck had decapitated him. So even though the mayor found his way out of the darkness, even though he'd ridden the great ghostly river out of Frankie's phantasmagoria, Huey didn't come out of it whole: he didn't know how to re-materialize as expertly as Lenny did. Even so, it was a miracle that Purgato managed to find his way through the streams of extra-dimensionality and the sluices of space-time that brought him back to the real world, whole or not.

But he was not whole. No, not at all. Huey lay naked on the floor of the secret laboratory; a soupy, odd-appendaged freak-show. His inexpertly crafted organs were on the outside of him, bleeding. His face drooped, and his vision was terribly blurred. When he strained to see more clearly, a terrible pain shot through his eyes. His limbs were bendable in all the wrong places, his skin was inside out. Huey managed, despite the mechanical ineptitude of his self-reconstruction, to crawl toward the control panel of the motion machine.

With Herculean effort, he reached into one of the aluminum storage shelves and pulled out one of the three copies of the *Kromee-Ohm* that had been transcribed. With appendages nerve-less and ill-suited to the task, Huey desperately fumbled through the pages, leaving behind wet patches of sanguine slime. He finally reached the page describing the Process of Restoration conjuration. Huey turned on the motion machine and tried working his way through the words once, twice, three times. But it didn't work.

Then, he heard a voice; "Having some trouble, Mr. Mayor Manperson?"

Huey gurgled in response, "Plischz khellph meeee."

GHB smiled and walked over to the sodden remains of Mayor Purgato before rendering his judgment.

"Oh, I wouldn't bother with that conjuration, Huey, dear sir, good sir. It's what we in the leadership business call a *placebo*. There's nothing to it, you see. Oh sure, it has artistic value. I mean, the high value of artistic vision for my prophecies and songs has a premium that is, I think, inestimable. But artistry aside, I don't think that book is going to do you any good."

And that's when Huey finally—*finally*—realized that he'd been had. This man, who Huey thought was a moron, had hoodwinked him.

GHB reached down and lightly patted what was left of Huey —a deteriorating, soupy amalgamation of body parts. Thin strings of mucous-ooze stretched from GHB's fingers as he pulled his hand away from the slimy man.

"You're not bad at the game, Mr. Mayor, but I've got a few years on you. And a good deal more experience."

At that moment, Huey heard an explosion and the clattering of iron against cracked marble. It was the ReCoRU team breaking into his office. They shouted orders at one another as the echo of squeaking and stomping combat boots resounded from the open floor into the secret room.

"He's in here!" GHB yelled out.

Then, he leaned in and whispered in Huey's ear. "Slow and steady wins the race, Mr. Mayor. Slow and steady wins the race."

CHAPTER 46

Inside the mortuary, things were calmer and more merciful. Once Cotton Lenny and the electric field had dissolved, Frankie fell into the snow, still asleep. Bulldog-Jeff had gently placed him inside the mortuary at the instruction of his two siblings.

"What do you think happened to him?" Deedee asked Truckie, looking at Frankie's body.

"I... I don't know."

Truckie sat quietly for a moment before pulling out the *Kromee-Ohm*. He scanned through it assiduously, searching for one of the waving, vibrating pages with living, moving colors. He finally found what he was looking for. Deedee leaned over his shoulder and placed her hand on his back as they watched the moving picture together. It was a visual retelling of all that had happened between Frankie, Dreck, and Cotton Lenny—the transformations, the torture, and the final triumph. The picture replayed itself a few times before fading.

"What does it mean?" Deedee asked.

Truckie was silent for a long time. Deedee prodded him again.

"*Well?*"

"I'm *thinking*. Just give me a second."

While Deedee waited, they watched Frankie's body. It healed. Rapidly. So rapidly they could see the salutary changes as they occurred. The gold coins floated around his unconscious form and periodically transmitted a salve—an energetic marigold glow—into his wounds.

"Do you think he's okay?" Deedee asked Truckie.

"I think… I think he's probably dreaming."

CHAPTER 47

I looked around to get my bearings. I could tell by the colors and sounds that I wasn't awake. Through everything, I always made a point to sharpen my wits to be able to distinguish between the real world and the other spheres of consciousness—dream, nightmare, what have you. But this time I couldn't tell which side of the coin I was on. All I knew was that I was in the forest outside of Seven Points, standing by a door whose other end led to the mass graves in the Levant. There was still fresh snow on the ground, mounds of it.

And Dreck was there.

"My son. My brave, incredible son."

"Father. What's happened?" I asked.

"Something beautiful. I remember you. I can see you. I can *speak* with you. I'm no longer an animal. Don't be a doubting Thomas. Reach here and touch the wound where my antlers used to be."

"But you still—"

"Yes, I am still Dreck. The curse was a binding on the mind and our memories. But you must know that the good that was in me was kept alive by Dreck. I don't know if I was ever Dreck all those years ago—that stupid, unknowing animal Dreck—but I wear his mask now."

No words could escape me. All I could do was listen and stare at his open mouth as Dreck continued.

"It's a strange idea, but I've been wrestling with it. Is it possible that inside this body, inside this mind, and in all those thousands of trips into nightmares and the ether, that I have become more like Dreck, that he became more of a man—a good man—even if he didn't know what that was?"

Revelation poured out of him like a cascade of stars.

"It's all so much. I don't know how to sort it out. But I know that *he* is in *you* now, too. And we shall always remember this, our together-remembrance. We will remember the moment we were reunited. Maybe, too, we did something good to save this place. This *city* as I have heard it called. You carry my memories, save one, from when I was Dreck in my mind. I retain a singular memory that must be resolved, but the rest are now yours. I know because I don't have them anymore. There's an absence, a great void in my mind, but in its place, there's clarity. I am only me, my soul, and this body will be gone soon."

"I... I don't understand," I sputtered. But I did understand the ceaseless wandering, roaming of the earth for hundreds of years. My once-limited memory recall now spanned centuries, and it was hard to place the individual pieces in time, space, in the patchwork of my remembrances. Were they mine?

Alex's face was clearer in my mind's eye. A happy association sprung from within. Genuine happiness that I'd had a good friend. This was a union of emotion—mine and my father's. There was pride, too. Pride for me. Hope for me.

But there was pain, too. Desperation, dumbness, a lost ability to recall what I was seeking, but seeking it nonetheless because the finding was more powerful than the reasons behind it.

Pain. Pain from watching my son (myself) suffer beneath that horrid woman, and shame from doing nothing about it, but I could not. I was unable to. I forgave my father (myself), because neither of us were capable at that point of breaking through the wall the stepmother had placed between us.

I placed symbols hoping he'd find them. I placed them wherever I could, throughout time and space. Signs I hoped he would discover that would lead him to remember...

This recollection was new and old. Mine but not mine. Images of me/Dreck plotting placements of people and things, small symbols throughout the earth, throughout The Long War—*don't let them*—literal signs mixed with symbology, some of which I'd found and forgotten, some I'd never discovered. Starred patterns in the sky that aligned with the strange formation the coins had created—an unknown and undiscovered constellation. Had I seen it? That, I did not know. I had seen it because I carried the memories of Dreck, but as the Son, I didn't recall having noted the pattern. It did not matter. Sorting through the vast expanse of a combined millennia's worth of memories was not my goal at the moment. Those would fall into place later. The only thing that mattered was that I was here, and he was here. The reunion was complete.

"I must leave, Son. All this... all this terror and torment I've caused—is the price I have to pay. Sadly, you too will be paying a price. You will have to carry on with Dreck's memories, and with your new conjurations. You must remain here now, aging as you will—I know not whether 'twill be as man or monster—until the day your soul ascends, as mine will now."

"No!" I pleaded. "No, please. Not now, Father."

He watched me lovingly as I bit back bitter tears.

"I know it isn't right, my son."

Without another word, his three-fingered hand opened the door, allowing us to gaze more clearly through the portal, into the Levant, into the vast sandswept wasteland where the dead remained unburied.

"But those boys over there, those dead but unburied, they are also sons of fathers, and fathers of sons. They did nothing to deserve their desecration. It is my curse—my curse's unknowable effects, its awful character—that has kept them there. And their souls wait. In anguish, Son. Do you understand? In anguish. *They must ascend*. Can you understand that?"

Tears streamed down my face. I didn't want to admit that I knew my father was right. But I knew. Was it kismet, this turn of events—that I should be a death-worker in a mortuary? One who knew better than most the importance of burial, of finality. That I should be there when my father's undead body, his near-living corpse, was delivered to my door?

"You have to go now?" I asked, my words wavering and tear-muddled.

"I am sorry, my son. But yes. I must go now. I do not know anything with complete certainty. But I believe that the moment our souls fused together, the sands of an hourglass began their tumble. There isn't much time to set it right. I must free their souls before it is too late."

"But we missed so much time," I sobbed through gritted teeth. And the tears were mine and the tears were Dreck's. "We missed so much time."

He smiled sadly before speaking again. "Yes, we did. We missed too much time. But there is always what comes *after*. The life of the soul reborn. And I promise you, my son—I *promise* you —I will be waiting when your days come to their natural end."

"But, how can you know? *How?*"

"Simple, my son."

He smiled at me once more.

"Faith."

We embraced and held one another closely, for a very long time, but it wouldn't—couldn't—ever be long enough, that last embrace. After we had broken back from one another's grasp, he waved to me and said his farewell.

"Take care of your family. Tell them I love them, too. We will all be together soon enough."

I nodded. Then, my father, Dreck, walked through the door—

the door in the forest whose exit was on the other side of the world—and closed it behind him.

The very next blink I took wiped it all away, and I was back at the mortuary, with Truckie standing over me. He looked sad, angry, annoyed, but his relief was palpable. I wondered which emotion he would open with as his lips parted.

CHAPTER 48

"I had a father. His name was Louis. I don't need you," Truckie said to me.

I sat forward and leaned toward my son/brother. Odd, that was. "I understand," I replied.

"And those kids—I'm all they had. Okay? It was me. GHB is just there to... do whatever it is he wants to do. He's an opportunist at best. We'll deal with him as needed. But you will not take my place. I taught the children, and I will continue to do so. That said, they need their father."

"Look, I'm not trying to take anyone's place. I just want *a* place. If you'll have me. You can keep teaching them. That's fine."

Truckie sighed. "I don't know that I want anything to do with you. But you should visit once in a while. Your children... they need you. You can teach them, too," he said.

"I... I'll try."

"Perhaps I can help, Uncle?" Deedee asked.

"Wait... are *you* going?" I asked her.

"Yes. I think... I think I've lived enough up here. I've lived and lied, just like my father—no offense. I'm still angry, too, you know. All those women..."

"Four hundred," I said. It was the truth. Four-hundred

women. Of those women, only some had produced children. "I'm imperfect, and so are you, and words cannot convey the depth of my sorrow for what I've done to you. But we've got another chance. It'll never be perfect. But it will be better."

I was surprised at how I could collect memories and compartmentalize them. I did have two sets, but they were not necessarily all interwoven. I could speak as Dreck, and I could speak as Frankie. And while they knew the difference, I was still learning it.

As we were finishing up in the mortuary Deedee ran in and ordered me to put the *Vox Oculii* feed on my computer. I pulled my laptop out from my drawer and set it open on my desk.

"Jubilation today, as we've received news that the mysterious electrical barrier surrounding the mass graves in what used to be Syria has disappeared. The door that appeared in the middle of the electrical barrier was closed, witnesses say, sometime around midnight, and then, according to those witnesses, the door 'evaporated.' The bodies of the War dead—men who fought in The Long War—can finally be secured and properly buried. There is much speculation as to the cause of this fortuitous turn of events, but the most popular theory is that the Anonymous Hero somehow discovered a way to break the curse that had prevented the bodies of those men from being saved and interred. That speculation is based on this: one of the coins typically left at the sites of the Anonymous Hero's good deeds was found at the site of the disappeared door that the monster Dreck walked through all those years ago.

"In other news today, Geoffrey Hammond Bimmelberger, the Seven Points official who was responsible for helping to orchestrate the capture and execution of disgraced former Mayor Huey Purgato, has been named Interim Mayor of Seven Points until the next election, which will take place in another three years."

I logged out and turned to Deedee.

"He did it," I said.

She placed her hand on my shoulder. Truckie didn't say anything. He simply took out my tin cup and two more glasses and poured us all a drink.

Right at that moment I heard a voice, and saw a clean-shaven, broadly-built man with a crew-cut appear at the entrance of the mortuary.

"What are we celebrating, Mr. Attanasio, sir?"

"Agent Aggie?" I exclaimed. It was rather *nice* to meet the man behind the phone. The man behind the transport. I'd finally met the stranger who had become, somehow, somewhat of a friend.

"One and the same, sir."

Without even asking, I took another cup from my drawer and poured Aggie a drink, too. "Boy, I can't decide if your timing is perfect or complete shit."

He laughed at that. We all did. We toasted one another, and I retold everything that had happened, no omission and no embellishment—not that a story like mine needed any extra luster—from the very beginning to the very end.

At various turns, Aggie laughed, sat silent, looked at me in open-mouthed astonishment. We sat for several hours getting right—and I got a little *too* right, as I tend to do. By the end of it, it was the twilight of morning. He decided to take his leave. I extended my hand one more time and shook Aggie's.

"Will I be seeing you around, Mr. Attanasio, sir?"

I smiled. "Oh, you might catch me here and there."

He held up his hand in a salute. I gave him his, and he saluted in turn. As he approached the mortuary's exit, I called out, "Hey, Agent Aggie!"

"Yessir, Mr. Attanasio, sir?"

I took one of the coins out of my pocket. Holding it on my thumb and against my curled index finger, I flicked it high in the air—it spun and spun, gleaming and throwing glistening, ethereal hues across the bland white walls of the room—the bland, pale faces of my friends and family. The coin seemed to suspend itself, in slow motion, until it finally arced down and landed in Agent Aggie's waiting palm. He looked back at me, stunned.

"Just in case," I yelled back to him. "It'll tell you how to find me. I won't be staying here."

"What if I don't know how to work it, sir?" Aggie bellowed back.

"Don't worry," I answered with a smile. "It works through you. Even in spite of you."

"So, you will be coming with us?" Truckie asked me. This time, the anger in his voice was minimal. There was almost a hint of hope in it. I hid a smile.

"Way ahead of you," I replied. I gathered my things together—I had the snowflakes Jeffornessia had made for me (*as if she was my own kid. She was now*) in hand—and placed them into a small box, which was fitting for my world before. It had been so small.

I paused to look at my family. My children. "And for what it's worth—if anything… I'm sorry. I'm so very sorry."

Deedee's eyes dampened and she turned away. Time. It would take time. Here, now, I was unable to escape time. But I wanted to earn their trust.

"But, uh…" I stuttered a bit. "Look, I'm okay with Rule Number One…"

Truckie's head tilted up and he shot me a look of frustration. "Rule Number Two is *discretionary*."

"Uncle Trucule, he's right. It's just… it's, and please forgive me for my lack of better phrasing here, but it's gross. It should change," Deedee added.

Truckie acquiesced. "Fine. Grappling is now a practice done on one's own. Discussion of grappling, however, remains permitted."

"Fine with me," I said.

A silence that I could only interpret as strained and annoyed followed as the two helped me gather the rest of my sparse belongings. My / my father's bags. The remaining coins. Random things I'd found during The Long War.

I threw the strap of my bag around my shoulder, and the three of us—me, Deedee and Truckie—headed for one of Truckie's secret tunnels to the city down below. Bulldog-Jeff had left earlier, to get a head start, maybe. He didn't explain, and I didn't ask.

We would all return to the world below. The children there needed me, and I very much needed them, which was something I'd known long before I held Dreck's memories—his pain, his shame. I worried that I would let them down, that I could hurt them, but they'd been looking for me (for Dreck) for so long. And I was finally here for them. A pang of guilt hit me because while I hadn't intended to, I'd abandoned all my children. Truckie's words about my not being his father had stung. They'd broken my heart, but it was what it was.

I was ready to start over. Again. And I did not fear who or what I would become.

CHAPTER 49

gent Aggie sat at Frankie Attanasio's desk, leafing through documents, sourcing them so he could write up a final report on what had happened. The rest of the ReCo team was boxing up Frankie's things, labeling, and categorizing.

An old man walked in. He wore thick, round ebony spectacles; on his head was perched a black knit cap, wild gray-black-white strands sticking out from under it. He was dressed in a wrinkly, ratty old double-breasted suit.

Aggie spoke in surprise. "Mr. Monzram, sir. I didn't expect that you'd be visiting the site yourself."

"I wasn't sure that I'd be coming down, Aggie. But after the door closed in the Levant, I thought this case merited special attention."

"Yessir. Understood, sir."

The Monzram (as he was referred to) smiled and sat on the milk crates stacked next to Frankie's desk. Aggie deferentially began to sit up to offer him the proper desk chair, but with a vigorous wave, the old man let Aggie know that he should remain seated.

"Relax. Relax, Aggie. I'm just here to tell you something. I'm not here to micromanage or examine your conduct. Try, best as you can, to talk to me like we're just two peers speaking with one another."

Aggie nodded in acquiescence.

"I just wanted to tell you, Aggie, that I think you did a very nice job. Things are shaky now; the world is just calming down enough for us to have a place. Civil servants we are: that's a phrase we weren't thinking about at all during the War. Either way, I think you did nicely. Your first time as the point-man, and I think you did just fine."

"But I didn't do anything," Aggie protested. "I held back until the last possible moment, and by then, they'd saved themselves."

The Monzram could only smile. "Then you've learned one of the most important lessons you can learn: that control is an illusion; that subsidiarity has its value; that beings with capacities beyond your own are better suited to battle against demonolatry. You learned to hit the brake and not the accelerator. And you managed to resist yourself. I'd say that's a job well done. Does that make sense?"

Aggie spent a moment thinking on it. "Yes, I think so."

"Good."

The Monzram patted Aggie on his knee in approval, then stood slowly and moved effortfully from the milk crates. As he neared the exit, he turned back to Aggie. "I'll see you at the office?"

"Yessir."

"Good, good, good. You did a good job, Aggie. A good job."

EPILOGUE

Elizabeth, aka Miss Runny, looked out over the golden fields. Today, they were filled with children, some of whom had been born in this place. Since she had last seen Frankie in that faraway moment of time or timelessness, she had kept up with her younger manifestation. Not that she didn't enjoy being the elderly sagess—she very much did. But she found that when she visited this place, with its golden mountains and ever-blue sky, its sun-kissed denizens happily lolling through fields and streams, she wanted to look a touch more welcoming.

No one knew what Elizabeth Runny had done before The Long War. Not even the select few who glimpsed some of her secret knowledge. A young boy with side curls ran past Elizabeth but then stopped to look at her. The young boy's gaze beamed into Elizabeth's own eyes, and for a moment, he looked like he was trying to remember something. Then, the kid spoke.

"Vos ken vern fun di shof az der volf iz der rikhter."

"Good memory," replied Elizabeth, smiling.

She then pulled a hard candy from her jacket pocket and handed it to him, just as The Monzram appeared on the horizon, and began slowly approaching her.

"Tending to your flock?" the old man asked.

"You look old, Monzram," she replied, still smiling.

He placed his hand over his back as he creakily lowered himself to sit on the hillock beside her. "I *am* old, Miss Runny. But not half so old as I feel. I heard what the boy said to you."

"*Sprach Sie Yiddische?*"

"I do," he said without pride, as though he was telling a joke.

"*What happens to the sheep when the wolf judges them?*" he translated. "Is that why you made this place?"

Elizabeth looked out at the hills. There was peace, serenity, joy, tranquility. In this place she had constructed, there were millions of such hills, and millions of people populating the golden lands that the hills dotted. All of them—and all the people, the topographies, the metaphysical stasis she bottled them up in—were frozen outside of temporality, linearity, and the confines of commonly understood space-time.

"I made this place because when there's a war that involves the whole world, it rarely bodes well for the *yidden*."

"Yes. Yes, that's true," The Monzram said as he pulled out a pipe and packed it full of tobacco. He took his time, knowing that Elizabeth was in no hurry. He struck a match against his thumb, slowly lit the tobacco, inhaled in bursts to get the tobacco burning, and then took in a satisfactory pull. Still in slow motion, he blew the smoke out—it formed the shape of balloons and drifted off past some of the children, who laughed and chased after the wisps.

Finally, The Monzram sighed. "You can't keep them here forever."

"Says *you*," Miss Runny shot back.

"Elizabeth…"

"*Monzram*," she retorted, if a bit mockingly, then added, "I know what I'm doing."

The old man said nothing, only looked at his smoke-balloons.

Then he replied, "*Di eyer viln zayn kliger fun di hiner.* You know that one?

"The eggs think they're smarter than the chickens. Fine, I'm a dumb egg."

"That's not what I mean to say," The Monzram replied before taking another pull from his pipe. "I'm just saying, it can't last forever. They won't let you keep them here."

"Well, then maybe *they* should make the world a little kinder than it is."

At that, The Monzram nodded in a friendly titter of agreement. He shook the ash from his pipe and tucked it into his cloak.

"They're not half so bad as you think them to be," The Monzram said after he was already a few steps away from Elizabeth.

She didn't answer.

Before he vanished over the horizon, The Monzram added a final epitaph.

"Der tayvl iz nit azoy shvarts vi men molt im."

He then faded into a spot of night that appeared in the glistening twilight of the Elysium that Miss Runny had created.

Despite the incredible victories that had been won, despite her deeds of guardianship, Elizabeth still had her doubts. It wasn't always (or *ever*) so easy to know what was right. She sat alone, on that hillock, looking out at the people she had hidden from the world, reflecting on those last, lingering words from The Monzram.

The devil is not as black as we paint him.

ACKNOWLEDGMENTS

This is a book about fathers and sons. It became clear to me while writing *Dreck* that the tragedy, triumph, comedy, sorrow and sweetness of life all come pouring forth from the bloodline. So, what I've written belongs as much to my father, Roger Grass, as it does to me.

And then there are the others who have wrestled, too—whether with their own G-d or His celestial proxies here on Earth. In my heart—a vessel of faith, an organ and instrument of the spirit—I know that my family is familiar with the shadows, wherein lurks the Black Dog, as much as the light.

Thank you to the Grass Clan. Granny, Uncle Marty, Aunt Liz —*everyone* (you too, Grass Bears), including those who have passed, those who remain, and those for whom some version of this story is already well familiar, being written in their very souls.

Thank you to Ed Moran, a Scranton boy, just like my Grandfather (whose name I share).

Thank you to Mom. I hope I honor her parents in writing this.

Thank you to Maria Meador, who taught me a world of kindness and demonstrated the infinite world of love waiting to be birthed in every human soul.

Thank you to Uncle Burt and Aunt Marian.

Thank you to Eric Ogg and Melissa Carmean of Not in Vain Editing LLC. They knocked this sucker out of the park.

This book is for all those people—and, when the time comes that they might understand it, for my sons Joseph and Louis.

Finally, this book is for every Pennsylvanian who's loved their home, even after deciding that they had to leave it to find that love.

P.S. My wife Gina got into med school. She's smart, we're proud of her, and her boobs are really, really *great*. What a rockin' bod. I'm bonin' a doctor-lady. *Noice*. Or, as William Shakespeare said: "Bro, dost thou tappeth thine betrothed's booty?" Yes, Bill. Yes, I dost.

Made in United States
North Haven, CT
29 November 2021

11707787R00189